COOL IN TUCSON

Elizabeth Gunn titles available from Severn House Large Print

McCafferty's Nine

COOL IN TUCSON

Elizabeth Gunn

Severn House Large Print
London & New York

This first large print edition published 2008
in Great Britain and the USA by
SEVERN HOUSE PUBLISHERS of
9-15 High Street, Sutton, Surrey, SM1 1DF.
First world regular print edition published 2007 by
Severn House Publishers, London and New York.

British Library Cataloguing in Publication Data

Gunn, Elizabeth, 1927-
Cool in Tucson. - Large print ed. - (The Sarah Burke series)
1. Women detectives - Arizona - Tucson - Fiction
2. Detective and mystery stories 3. Large type books
I. Title
813.6[F]

ISBN-13: 978-0-7278-7732-1

Printed and bound in Great Britain by
MPG Books Ltd, Bodmin, Cornwall

Acknowledgements

This book could never have taken shape without the generous help of many people in Tucson law enforcement. In particular, I want to thank Sgt. Mark Fuller, who was chief of homicide investigations while I was researching this story, and Detective Lorraine Thompson; in street patrol, Sgt. Kerin Fuller and Officer Nathan Tullgren; in the Tucson crime lab, criminalist Andrea Gemson and crime scene specialist Karen S. Wilken; and in the Tucson branch of the federal Drug Enforcement Agency, Special Agent Steve McGuigan. They kindly took time from their busy lives to help me get it right. Any mistakes are entirely my own.

One

Didn't even plan it or nothin', Hector thought happily, heading east on I-10, *and look how good it turned out. Just showed you should go with the flow and not sweat the details so much. I mean, look at me now.* Rolling out of town in a top-dollar SUV, thick wad of money in the bag at his feet. Hadn't even stopped to count the money yet, but he knew it was plenty.

He really wanted to go home, but he had to get the car out of sight so he could pop the plates and replace them, and there was no shelter in his mother's yard. Best thing to do, even if he didn't feel like it, was drive to Aunt Lucia's house in Benson, make up a reason why he needed to put the car in her shed. He knew she'd fix him some food, let him take a snooze in her house.

Late afternoon, he'd call the guy at the feed store in Benson. Dude had a little side business going in replacement plates. Julio, that was his name. And while he waited for Julio he could call Bernie Estes back in Tucson. 'Estes the Bestes' he called himself, a counterfeiter working out of his house up on Princeton Road. Big phony in a lot of ways, but Hector had seen some of his work and knew it was good. So he'd paid a big deposit on a fake passport and visa, car registration and driver's license. Gave Estes his picture and told him the name would come later.

He'd intended to boost the car of his choice when the time came, but now that he had Ace's SUV he'd tell Estes to make the records read Adolph Alvin Perkins, read him the numbers from the records he had right here in the car. How cool was that?

He had Ace's wallet and credit cards, too. Next thing he needed was a money belt, or maybe one of them armpit bags, for all the cash he'd be carrying. He chuckled a little, thinking about the cash. Damn, this was more like it, y'know?

Soon as he had everything lined up, tomorrow sometime, he'd come back to Tucson. Pick up his new papers and the roll of bills he had stashed under his bed, pack a few clothes and be on his way.

He couldn't get over how quick and easy it had been. Wasn't quite five hours ago, Ace had still been ordering him around like he always did – go here, pull up right over there, not so damn close. Walking up to the houses and back like he owned the ground he walked on, confident and easy, moving like a big cat and hardly making a sound. He'd walked back from that last delivery on Cinnamon Street, tapped once on the smoked glass of the passenger-side window, just that one little tap and you better be ready. Hector flipped the lock, Ace got in and closed the door quietly in the dark, the dome light off like it always was when they made deliveries. Said, 'OK, that's it for tonight.'

'Still got a couple of eightballs,' Hector said.

'Too late now.' One of Ace's many rules for staying inconspicuous was that they get off the street before the bars closed at two, so there were still other cars around. Lot of old farts in Tucson went to bed with the chickens, Ace said, you had to think about these things. He fastened his seat belt in the finicky way he had, checking that it was straight and lay flat across his shoulders.

Hector put the Ford Excursion in gear and rolled south on Shannon and then east on River, staying two miles under the speed limit although the wide street was almost empty as far as he could see in both directions.

'Drive like your grandmother,' Ace had said, the first time he handed Hector the keys, and it turned out he meant absolutely *como su abuela*, every time with no exceptions. A few days later when Hector executed what he thought was a slick-as-snot little lane-jump to make the light on Speedway, Ace said, in a perfectly friendly way, 'Pull into that strip mall up ahead there.'

As soon as the car stopped rolling he jumped out on his side, leaned over and pulled Hector across the seat by his ears. Stood him upright beside the car, Hector grunting with surprise and pain. Slapped his face, forehand, backhand, twice on each side. Dropped him on the asphalt then and stood over him saying softly, 'Now walk home, asshole. Tomorrow you come and see me in the afternoon, ask me real nice, I might give you your job back.'

Hector could still taste blood on the inside of his cheeks the next day when he walked into the coffee shop at the Congress Hotel and stood beside Ace's table, waiting quietly. When Ace looked up from his New York steak, rare the way he always took it, mashed potatoes and green beans on the side, Hector said, 'Ace, I'm sorry—'

'Hector.' Ace shook his head, a scant inch back and forth. 'Don't waste my time with sorry.' He took the keys to the Excursion out of his pocket and held them up. 'Just do as you're told. Get the car out of the lot back there on Toole Street and bring it around here to the hotel parking lot. Park as close as you can get to the door and wait.'

The man always knew what he wanted, give him that. He was over six feet tall and strong, no signs of age on him except his eyes, which looked like they'd been dead for several years. Hector never got in the car with him again without wishing he was someplace else. But he hid his fear and anger and hopped whenever Ace said hop because where else in Tucson was he going to make four hundred a week tax-free for a couple of nights' work?

Tonight when Ace came back from that last delivery and buckled himself in, he put an old disc in the player, that band with the weird name, Creedence Clearwater Revival. Singer with a gravelly voice yelling something about a bad moon rising, trouble on the way. Didn't make much sense really but it stuck in Hector's mind because it described how he always felt on that job. Every moon he ever saw while he was riding with Ace Perkins was a bad one.

Hector thought it was lousy music but at least it filled that heavy brooding silence that always followed Ace into the car. He watched the lights as they approached First Avenue, thinking that in a few minutes he could get out of the car and put another night's work behind him. Got a big jolt of surprise when Ace said, 'Turn south here. Pull into that Rillito Park there and park up next to the bike path. I need to piss.'

Hector's chest tightened up and he felt the blood surge in his head. Ace's routines were, like, set in cement, he never changed anything. He always emptied his bladder just before they started the run and never stopped again, wouldn't let Hector stop either, till they were done.

So Hector wondered, had Ace hired his replacement? He'd heard rumors about a boy named Ernesto who'd worked for Ace before and now seemed to be gone from the neighborhood. Was this going to be the night Hector's name joined Ernesto's on the list of the disappeared? His mind ran in circles, hunting for clues. Everything had been going so well, why would Ace off him now?

But with a guy like Ace you never knew.

Ride with him ten years, all you'd be sure of was he didn't give a shit for nobody.

It was a hot night, Hector had been guzzling water out of a liter bottle clamped in the carrier between them, and Ace as usual had the big bottle of orange Gatorade open on his side. They'd had plenty of liquid since they left the rusty mobile home where they packaged the product, but didn't they always drink a lot on these runs? So, as he parked the car he dropped his left hand on to the seat, ready to reach under the loose leg of his cargo pants for the knife he kept sheathed there, a boot knife with a sturdy grip, slender in the blade and razor sharp on both sides.

Ace got out of the car as soon as it stopped, walked up on the crunchy gravel toward the mesquite tree, carrying his bag as always, unzipping as he went. He set the bag down and had his pecker in his hands, watering the base of the tree, in about two seconds. *Guess he really did need to go*, Hector thought, and began to relax.

But then, maybe because he got so wired there for a few seconds, his brain seemed to keep running along by itself, *ticka ticka tick.* And what it said was, *Maybe this is opportunity knocking, ticka ticka tick.*

He had been getting ready to leave for some time. He had the fake passport ordered from Estes and enough money to pay for it, had a friend of a friend across the border in Santa Ana who had said yes, always jobs on the supply side if you weren't afraid to work. He had been waiting to save more money but now he thought, *What the fuck, there's over seven thousand dollars in that sack.*

And then the thought of never having to sit in that car with Ace Perkins again blew over him like a fresh breeze right out of heaven, so sweet that without any more hesitation he pulled the knife out of its sheath and opened his door.

He walked up toward Ace, who was just zipping up and turning around. Hector held the knife in his right fist, pressed against his leg out of sight.

He smiled the silly fawning smile he used on Mama when he wanted a favor, and said with an apologetic chuckle, 'Just realized I gotta do that too.'

Ace frowned and started toward the car with his mouth turned down at the corners saying, 'Well, hurry up.' Hector walked right on as if to pass him but turned as they drew even, pointed across the front of Ace's chest with his left hand and said, 'Look out!' As Ace turned to look where he pointed Hector lifted the knife and plunged it into the base of Ace's neck, inside the collarbone, below his ear.

He knew how to do it because he'd done it once before during his stretch in Catalina Mountain, when Ray Muñoz demanded he kill Boo Hirtz as the price of admission to the gang that ran Building Nine. Ray had showed him how, explaining where the artery was, so deep under the collarbone and such a gusher you were toast as soon as it was cut, nobody could save you. He had only had a shank then and was shaking with fear, but even so Boo Hirtz fell over backwards like a stupefied buffalo, never said a word and was dead by the time he hit the ground.

Three years later under the mesquite tree in the dark, with distant city noises coming faint across the dry riverbed, Hector swiveled the handle once to make sure the artery was cut, and stepped back so he wouldn't get blood on himself. In the two seconds before the light went out in Ace's eyes, Hector watched him trying to reach his gun. Not smiling now, he leaned toward the dying face and said softly, 'Shoulda been more careful who you pulled around by the ears, asshole.'

Two

North of the river, Delaney had said, a new office complex. 'Big sign, Rillito Business Park, you can't miss it.'

You want to bet? I don't see any sign. Halfway across the bridge, Sarah spotted it. *Oh hell, he meant* just *north of the river.* She hit the brakes and turned hard right on to a gleaming expanse of fresh asphalt.

The Catalinas towered over the top of the street, a shadowed mass against a sky full of fading stars. The cloudless eastern horizon had turned the color of pewter. In the gray light she could see the outlines of Delaney's Chevy and two patrol cars huddled together in the empty lot. She parked next to the sergeant's car and got out, moving deliberately to stay cool.

In the last week of September, the summer rains had ended but the heat was hanging on – downtown Tucson would be sizzling by noon. It felt good to be outside in the predawn hush, the thermometer at sixty-five and small birds making optimistic noises in the dusty bushes.

Delaney's silhouette was a darker gray shape among the trees, up by the bike path. Sarah walked toward him at the street cop's steady pace, confident and unhurried. Seasoned and slender at thirty-five, she had replaced her youthful bloom with burnished fitness and a put-together look that said, to her peers, 'Trust me,' and to malefactors, 'Don't even think about it.'

Occasionally some fool thought about it anyway, and for those times she wore a Glock nine in a paddle holster on her belt. Thirteen-plus years in the department, five in investigations, had fixed her attitude, wary and seldom surprised.

A narrow cement sidewalk slanted up through gravel beds filled with desert plants to an asphalt bike path along the river. Two uniformed officers were stringing crime scene tape around an area between the mesquite trees. Beyond the path, an iron railing kept people from sliding into the sandy pit of the riverbed.

Delaney was standing just outside the tape, staring into the circle of light his flashlight made on the ground, talking quietly to the patrolmen beyond him. 'Soon as you're done with that, you better go on down the path a couple of hundred feet and set up a barrier, OK? You got signs with you?'

'Yeah, I got some,' one of the men said. 'You know we're both due off in half an hour?'

'Oh, right ... you called for replacements yet? We'll be a couple of hours here at least.' One of the uniforms muttered something. 'Good. Will you hang some of those signs on this side too? And then just ... keep people away from here till you're relieved.' The patrolmen disappeared beyond the trees.

Sarah stepped up on to the bike path and said, 'Hey, boss.'

Delaney, without looking up, said, 'Morning, Sarah.' He had the pale skin of a redhead, blotchy from the punishing desert sun. His very pale blue eyes were rimmed with white lashes that blinked rapidly when he was concentrating. He stood cocooned inside himself like that for a few more seconds before he turned and said, 'You'll be the primary on this one.'

'You said, on the phone.' Did he think she was going to argue? His crew took turns leading investigations, in strict rotation with adjustments for vacations and illness and court dates. Sarah already had a heavy caseload and she knew very well what the department remedy was for that: suck it up.

She had transferred into Homicide a little over a year ago, because Auto Theft had begun to feel like a revolving door and she was ready for bigger challenges. Her other incentive for making the move was the chance to work for Delaney, who had a reputation in the department for rigorous investigation and a good clearance rate. More ambitious than ever now that she was single again, Sarah wanted to work with the best people, hone her skills, keep moving up.

The first six months in Delaney's section had been all she hoped, and she had congratulated herself for making the move at exactly the right time. Learning fast and feeling at the top of her game, she was certain she was gaining the good opinion of her peers and her boss.

But sometime in early spring, by almost imperceptible degrees she had felt Delaney begin to turn against her. At first she told herself she was imagining things, because he never complained about her work. But as she redoubled her efforts to please him, it appeared that the harder she worked, the more he turned away. He was polite and fair, but his face closed up when she approached and he talked to her only as much as necessary to get the work done, never more. She watched his easy way with the other detectives, who were all men, and decided she must be looking at a case of male chauvinism.

Why the delay, though? He had been friendly and helpful at first.

By July she had made up her mind to talk to a counselor. But then she lay awake all one night composing the first few sentences: *I can't exactly put my finger on it, but something is wrong. My boss just doesn't seem to like me any more*. Even to herself, it sounded like a high school girl getting dumped. She imagined her statement on a sheet in her service jacket, and decided to keep her grievances to herself.

A couple of times she almost blurted, 'Please tell me what you're mad about.' But he didn't seem angry, exactly. Cold and distant. Detached, but not punitive. In her mind she could hear her own voice begging for an explanation, see the contempt in his pale, blinking eyes as he said, 'I don't know what you're talking about.'

So this morning in September she stepped up on the knoll beside him steady as a rock, wearing the demeanor she had decided on, all spit and polish. Whatever happened, the fault would not be hers; she was going to deliver one perfect day's work after another while she waited for the axe to fall. *Damned if I'll beg. If he busts me he busts me. At least then he'll have to say why.*

They turned together toward the dead man on the ground. Number five male, Delaney had said on the phone, using the HIBOW code they all used: Hispanic, Indian, Black, Oriental, White. A correct call if ever there was one, Sarah thought; the victim was so white he was almost blue. Probably because most of his blood was in the ground around him. Blood had saturated his shirt, too, and the back of his pants, and caked in his hair. The air was heavy with the sickly sweet smell of it, and the salty stench of urine.

Nobody I've ever arrested. She remembered people she'd put the cuffs on. *Late thirties, maybe early forties. Buffed up. Looks like he worked out.*

The victim was not sprawled exactly but crumpled, as if he'd fallen straight down in a heap. He had been neatly dressed before he bled out, in good walking shorts and a white golf shirt. Odd, in view of the catastrophic bleeding, that she could see no wound.

'Here comes the crime scene van,' Delaney said. 'Let's get her going here, and then we can start.'

Gloria Jackson parked beside Sarah's car, hopped out and waved before she hurried to the rear door of the van, her taffy-colored curls bouncing above her gleaming amber cheeks. At that moment a blazing sun rose above the mountains east of town, lit the tops of the buildings and trees around them, and turned Gloria's hair to glowing brass.

Six feet tall and moving like the high school basketball star she had been in LA, Gloria was building a reputation in the Tucson Police Department as a mood-enhancing presence at a crime scene. 'Soon's I found out I wasn't getting no scholarship to UCLA,' she had told Sarah, 'I said, "Let's get out of these baggy pants then, and have some fun!"'

'That when you dyed your hair?'

'Bleached it to match my skin,' she said, nodding happily, 'and bought the tightest jeans I could squeeze my ass into. Whoo! Believe me, girlfriend, it made all the difference!'

Sarah believed her. When the men were around, Gloria never had any trouble getting help with her equipment.

Radiating energy now, she came chattering up the path. 'Wow, am I holding you guys up? Jeez, and I hurried like *mad*. How'd you get here so *fast*?'

'I don't have to comb out my curls,' Delaney said, lifting his baseball cap to show his receding hairline. Gloria brought out the jokey side even in Delaney, who was usually about as amusing as a quarter pound of tofu.

That one quick pleasantry was all he had in him, though; he looked at his watch, shuffled his feet and said, 'Ready to get to work?'

Gloria gave him a radiant smile, said, 'Mos' def,' and followed him to the tape.

'Looks like everything's within this perimeter, right here.' His flashlight didn't work very well as a pointer now that sunlight was filtering down through the sparse foliage of the acacias. 'See here? The body and the area right around it. Blood all seems to be pooled right here. I haven't seen any spattering at all.' He led her around the body, pointing. As soon as her camera began to flash, he came back and stood beside Sarah, who had to stay outside the taped-off crime scene till Gloria finished.

The victim's features were thrown into high relief by the slanting rays of the rising sun. His handsome face and the grace of his strong, supple-looking body made a striking contrast with the reeking, blood-soaked clothing, alive now with crawling insects. *Why is he so white?* Even newcomers, after a few days in Tucson, usually picked up a little color. This man's face looked as if he'd been working underground – or maybe at night?

The rising sun warmed them up fast. Sarah unbuttoned her shirt at the neck; Delaney rolled up his sleeves. Gloria and the two patrolmen soldiered on in stolid discomfort in their dark blue uniforms. Sarah saw Jimmy Ibarra, down in the parking lot, take off his jacket and toss it in his car.

'Here comes your back-up,' Delaney said. Ibarra saw them and started toward the trees, a round, rosy-cheeked man with an extra chin that bounced a little as he walked. 'Hispanic in name only,' was how she thought of him; his family went back a couple of generations farther than hers did in this valley and he used the same southern Arizona argot they all did, a blend of accents from all over. Historically a waypoint on the shifting border with Mexico, long an oasis for armies, evangelicals and fortune hunters, and now a magnet for retirees, Tucson was the quintessential melting pot.

'Sure I speak Spanish,' Jimmy Ibarra said of

himself. *'Arroz con pollo. Pan dulce.'* He got the broad vowels right but flunked rolling his r's. Cheerful and pragmatic, a veteran homicide investigator who knew all the short cuts, he was Sarah's favorite partner. Happily married, he never laid any moves on her, and was always willing to trade favors, information and inside jokes.

'Who else is coming?' she asked Delaney.

'You two are it, so far. We had a shooting at a drive-in out on the east end of Speedway around midnight and the rest of the crew is still out there. The two of you can manage this, can't you? Eisenstaat can give you a boost with the paperwork. There aren't any witnesses to interview and I don't see much physical evidence.'

'I guess,' Sarah said. 'If I need more help I can ask for it, huh?'

'Right,' Delaney said dryly, 'you can ask.'

You bet. But she knew that shorting her crew on this job was no sign of malice on Delaney's part. He was doing the best he could with what he had. Tucson had logged forty-odd homicides so far this year, and he and his six detectives were investigating all of them. Keeping pace with last year. *Which we said at the time was above average, but hey.* Given the area's growth rate, they were not likely to return to the body count of the year before last.

Ibarra walked up to them, panting a little. He planted his feet wide on the path, patted his belly and said, 'Hey,' smiling, showing his dimples and gold tooth. He looked at his watch, smiled again in his self-satisfied way and said, 'Fifteen minutes from the Tangerine Road turn-off, pretty good.' Making a big macho deal out of tucking in his shirt, ignoring Delaney's little snorts of impatience, he rolled his large dark eyes casually toward the body on the ground and asked, 'What we got here?'

Delaney flipped immediately to the page of notes he had bookmarked. 'Here's all we know: jogger called it in. Here's his name and phone numbers.' He handed Sarah a slip of paper. 'Said he had to go to work, he'll be available to interview by four this afternoon. He's working now at University Medical Center if you feel you need to talk to him sooner. Soames and Daly answered the 911 call.' He gestured toward the uniforms, who were finishing their barriers. 'They secured the scene and called the paramedics. The paras called in his vitals and the ER doc pronounced death. Soames and Daly are both working, what, eight to oh-six hundred?' Both men looked up and nodded, Soames pulling a pitiful face and pointing to his wristwatch. He liked to get back to the station and take his sweet time logging out. 'Right, so their back-up's coming, and we need to get 'em downloaded and out of here as fast as we can.'

Sarah looked at her watch. 'We got an ME coming?'

'Yeah, whoever's on call, he'll be here any

minute. It's warming up fast,' Delaney pointed out, unnecessarily. Sweat had begun to pool under his eyes and run down his pale, freckled cheeks. He had the wrong metabolism and pigmentation for summer in the Tucson valley. But his parents and all his siblings lived here and he had never thought of moving. 'I already called for the van, we don't have a whole lot of time.'

'Yeah, and the driver'll be yelling to transport about two minutes after he gets here,' Sarah said.

'Man, yeah, somebody at County's lit a fire under those guys,' Ibarra said. 'They don't even say "Hello" anymore, just "I gotta go".' He looked at Sarah and said, 'So shall we get a move on?' As if he hadn't been the last one on the scene.

'Well, we can't start till Gloria's done,' Sarah said.

'Listen,' Delaney said, 'just do what you gotta do, they can all wait if they have to. Here's all your initial crime report forms, the case number's on 'em.' He handed her a manila folder. 'Assignments aren't a tough call since there's just the two of you. Sarah, you'll take the body, of course, here and at the autopsy, I'll help with that if I can. Jimmy, you'll be the scene detective, whatever Sarah shows you, bag it and tag it. And be sure you get all the stats, times and temp and so on, and measure and sketch the scene, of course. And the follow-on will be whatever she says it is, hard to say right now with so little to go on.' Delaney cleared his throat and looked around in that absent-minded way he had. Sometimes he stared right through you when he was thinking. 'Only witness you've got is that jogger who found the body. He almost stepped on it, he said. Yelled out loud and fell over. After that I think he was too shocked to see much for a while. So ... up to you to find everything else, guys.'

Behind his back, Ibarra's mouth formed the silent words, *No shit?* Sometimes the sergeant let his mouth run on while his mind went off to other cases. Sarah looked at her watch again to keep from snickering, and kept her voice neutral. 'Fine. And here come the replacements for Soames and Daly, so, Jimmy, will you get their information and turn 'em loose before Soames has a worm over there? And then get the new guys walking the area, OK?'

'You got it,' Jimmy said. He pulled out his pocket recorder as he walked toward the parking lot, where the night shift uniforms were briefing the day shift.

Gloria ducked out from under the yellow tape and said, 'OK, that part's done. Sarah, you the primary on this?'

'Right,' Sarah said. 'I'm leading this great big crew.' They walked back inside the ring together and began surveying the body and the ground around it, looking for evidence items to mark with flagged pins so Gloria could photograph them.

'Yo, pretty scarce, huh?' Gloria said.

'For sure. No weapons, not even a bloody rock. Is that a scrape mark? Let's call it one. This could be a footprint – too dry to be sure. Let's mark it and take a picture, sometimes things show up better on film. Isn't this strange? Such a violent death with no signs of a struggle. All we've got is the body. And the blood.'

'But plenty of that. *Shee...*' Gloria made a face. 'Sure ain't your daddy's cologne, is it?'

'You need some Vicks?'

'Nah, I got some gum.' Gloria was from South Central LA – she had her pride. She liked to point out that 'compared to the place I grew up in, Tucson's just a peaceful little village'.

Delaney was standing a few feet down the path, fielding one message after another on his cell phone, already multi-tasking although his official workday wouldn't start for another hour. Sarah thought he micro-managed a little too much and made himself more accessible than he needed to, though she had taken advantage of his availability gladly enough when she first came into the section. *Back when we were still talking.*

Last winter she had made something of a game of identifying grunt work she thought she could offload when, as she firmly intended, she eventually got his job. Now it didn't look as if she could expect a recommendation from Delaney. But then he'd be gone by the time she was ready. He'd been top dog in Homicide for four years already, and the powers that be in the department seemed to think five years in his pressure-cooker job was long enough. Sarah disagreed with that policy too, and knew her chances to change it totaled zero.

'OK,' Delaney said, snapping the phone shut. 'Sarah, I'm going to have to leave in a minute. Ready to talk?'

'Sure.' They stood together by the victim.

'What do you see so far?' he asked her.

'Good-looking man. Took care of himself. Nice clothes.'

'Uh-huh. Those shoes cost one-fifty easy.'

'They did? I guess you're right, Doc Martins. Calvin Klein walking shorts. His hair has a nice trim, too, doesn't it? And his nails are clean.'

'Do a scrape anyway.'

'Oh, we will. Not a homeless guy, is all I meant to say.' She looked around. 'Where's his car, though?'

'Not in the lot, obviously. Soames and Daly looked around before I got here, they didn't find anything nearby.'

'Well, he wasn't jogging in those shoes. Not really dressed for biking either, and there's no bike lying around, is there? So, how'd he get here? Walking in the dark?'

'Good question. Also, why no watch or jewelry? This look like a mugging to you?'

'Maybe. Big strong guy though, I wouldn't pick him to jump unless I had plenty of help. And the thing is, there's no sign of a struggle.'

'I know. You think he got those muscles

lifting weights? He sure doesn't look like a laborer. Although his hands –' he pointed to a couple of fingers without touching them – 'they look a little crooked, don't they? Maybe he's a fighter.' Delaney looked at his watch. 'Well, I'll call in, tell 'em what we got here, and then I have to go – I'll see you back at the station.' He walked away punching numbers into his cell. *So much for his help with the body. Well, I never counted on it anyway*. It was a rare day when you finished one whole conversation with Sergeant Delaney without his phone ringing several times.

Sarah finished her walk with Gloria and turned her loose to start her blood samples and fingernail scrapings. The two patrolmen were walking toward their cars. Ibarra came back punching his recorder off, and Sarah said, 'OK, Jimmy, you ready to take a look?'

They both gloved up. Ibarra's round face took on the clenched look he wore at messy crime scenes. He enjoyed the intelligence-gathering part of his job, the piling up of evidence, the endless phone calls and interviews that nailed a case down solid. But he still, after years in Homicide, had to grit his teeth and focus hard to tolerate the stench of death and the appearance of bodies that had been abused.

For Sarah, it was just what she did at work. She had decided on police work in her first semester at Pima College and could no longer remember any of her earlier ambitions. The bad behavior of live people still bothered her sometimes, but she had no problem with the dead. Sometimes they took on a dignity they had lacked in life. And the bystanders you encountered at crime scenes, in extreme states of fear and grief, were often more truly themselves than at any other time.

'OK, let's do it,' Ibarra said. They squatted on either side of the dead man on the ground, and began going over his body like pick-pockets, looking for money, wallet, jewelry, dog tags, all the closely-held artifacts of life whose only use to the victim now would be his own identification.

But this victim had nothing. 'Not even lint,' Ibarra said, with an inside-out pocket in his hand.

'I got ninety cents over here. Otherwise, squeaky clean.' Sarah sat back on her heels and looked around. 'A robbery, then? But I don't read this as a gang hit, do you?'

'Nah,' Ibarra said, 'in this part of town? And where's all the bullet holes?' He looked at the few flags stuck in the ground. 'You and Gloria didn't find much, did you?'

'No.' Sarah slapped her neck. 'The body, a possible footprint, a scrape mark and a million insects, some of which are biting me right now.'

'Damn, it's already getting hot, too, isn't it?' Ibarra wiped his face with the back of his sleeve, holding his gloved hand carefully away. 'Here comes the ME. Hoo boy, we got Animal today.'

'Morning, group,' Dr Moses Greenberg

said, walking up with his bag. 'What do we have here?' A taut type A at work and radically over-trained athlete in his free time, he had run marathons and done white-water kayaking ever since medical school and was now, in his late thirties, escalating to triathlons and Iron Man competitions. Coupled with the demands of forensic medicine and a couple of shifts a week at a volunteer clinic in Sells, his insane schedule and the physical demands he placed on himself made him so tense he seemed to vibrate slightly when you stood next to him.

'We have a well-dressed victim who's lost most of his blood,' Sarah said, 'as well as his car and ID.'

'Well, no use letting him lie around here while you search.' Greenberg opened his bag. 'Feel that sun? We need to get this body to the cooler before it turns to *mush*.' He opened his bag, shone a light in the victim's eyes, took his temperature, and looked at his fingertips. As Sarah watched, he held the two hands up together and looked at them thoughtfully. *Noticed them right away, I knew he would.*

Sarah tolerated Dr Greenberg's shoot-the-moon persona better than most of the detectives. He was arrogant and impatient, but she liked his results. He was quick and precise and he never bluffed. His knowledge of forensic science was awesomely comprehensive, and if he didn't know something he had no trouble saying so. One benefit of a towering ego, Sarah thought; Greenberg didn't need approval from the likes of them.

He did seem to be wrapped a little tighter every year. TPD Homicide Division had a pool going for the expected date of his collapse/implosion/freakout. In the meantime, working around him felt like trying to deal cards in a tornado. All around the department, people had learned to beware of Dr Greenberg's short fuse.

'The wagon's on its way,' Sarah said. 'OK if we roll him? I'd like to find out where all this blood came from.'

'What, this much blood and you haven't found his wounds? Christ, looks like he was shot by a cannon. OK, let's do it. You two got him?'

The stench was stronger for a few seconds. The blood-soaked shirt was almost black on the back and turning stiff. Intact, though.

'I don't see any holes back here either,' Ibarra said.

'Wait, I see it. Base of the neck,' Greenberg said. 'Put him back.' He pulled aside the collar of the shirt.

'That's just a little cut, isn't it? Doesn't look like much,' Sarah said.

'Made by a sharp narrow blade, *very* sharp on both sides and long enough to cut the subclavian artery. I *think*. And if I'm right you're not looking for any ordinary mugger, kiddies.' There was something uncommonly condescending about the way Greenberg said 'kiddies'.

'What're you saying? Mack the Knife?'

'Somebody with street smarts, anyway. You've got to be *bold* to cut a man this way. What's this?' He pulled the collar farther aside.

'Now those look like jailhouse tats,' Ibarra said.

'Sure do,' Sarah said. 'No color, and kind of crude. They don't match the rest of him, do they?'

'Jesus,' the doctor said, 'cops know such weird stuff.'

'Oh, and doctors don't? Subclavian artery, hoo-ah.'

'That's Anatomy 101, don't be impressed by that.'

'OK, I'm not impressed,' Ibarra said. 'You gonna do your wise-ass forensic doctor thing and tell us how long he's been dead?'

'Sure. Let's see. Body temperature ... oh ... by the book, maybe a couple of hours. Of course we live in a warm climate.' Ibarra made a derisive sound. Greenberg cocked an eyebrow at him but didn't pause. 'Lividity –' he lifted the victim's left leg and peered at the underside of the buttocks – 'looks like three to twelve hours. Also –' he lifted an arm and looked some more – 'doesn't look like he's been moved since he died, you glad to know that? Let's show a little gratitude then!' He put the arm back down. 'Let's see. Beginning rigor mortis –' he touched the jaw, neck and shoulders, extended his long-fingered right hand and rocked it – 'maybe two to six hours. Or more. Or possibly less.' He divided an ironic smile equally between the two detectives. 'Take your best shot, kiddies.'

'So sometime last night,' Sarah said.

'I should think so,' Dr Greenberg said.

'Call me crazy,' Ibarra said, 'but I think I could have guessed that.'

'Why are you wasting my time with it then? Let's go, guys.' Muscles twitched in Greenburg's cheek as he packed his kit.

Sarah said, 'You picked a time for the autopsy yet?'

'Uh ... is today Tuesday?' His life a blur of over-reaching, he had trouble keeping track of days.

'Yes.'

'So ... sometime tomorrow. I think. Probably morning but I'll let you know. Depends on ... you know. Today.'

'Right. OK then, I want to ask you for a favor. This body's got no ID on it at all and now it looks like there'll be no ballistics. How about letting us do the fingerprints at the lab, before you put him away?' She looked at Ibarra. 'You agree with me this guy's probably done time, right?'

'The tattoos look right. And the fingers.'

'So, what, you're looking to ID him off a record?' The doctor had pulled off his gloves and was looking around for the trash.

'Yes. Here.' She held up a bag and he dropped the gloves in. 'And you know, if he hasn't been out here more than three hours...' She looked around and said, 'Gloria?'

'Yeah?'

'You got your fuming gear along?'

'Uh-huh.'

'Then I'd like to do that, too. This body was stripped of all ID, money, wallet – somebody had to touch him. We might lift a print before we put him in the cooler. How about it?' Sarah asked the doctor. 'You can delay storage for an hour, can't you?'

'Oh, yeah, once I get him inside out of this heat, one more hour ... but what's your hurry? He'll still be dead tomorrow.'

'He will, but fuming works better if we do it before he's cold.'

'Ah. OK, if you want to. Seems kind of overzealous, to me, for a John Doe in a park.'

'Ah, well, a little zeal...' Sarah imitated his hand-rocking motion. 'I can hide that in the paperwork.'

Greenberg rolled his eyes to the sky and muttered, *'Oy vey*, a comedian.'

'Oh, damn,' Ibarra said, 'here's the wagon and I haven't diagrammed the crime scene.'

'Do it now,' Sarah said. 'You got a tape on you? Gloria, come and help us.' She called out the distances she wanted and the other two did the measuring, from the body to the trees, to the bike path, to the railing – Ibarra taking a gleeful pleasure in watching Gloria Jackson out on the far end of the tape, running around.

'Damn,' he said, his gold tooth flashing in the sunlight, 'just like an antelope, ain't she?' Even Jimmy Ibarra, whose devotion to his wife was legendary, could not resist the pleasure of watching Gloria Jackson run.

He called out the last of the numbers as a county driver parked and got his rear doors open. Sarah closed her long notebook and stuck it in the back of her pants, gloved up again and helped the driver get the body on to the gurney. Watching it slide into place in the transport vehicle, she told Jimmy, 'OK, Gloria and I have to follow the body. You be OK here alone with the rest of the site work?'

'I have a choice?'

'No.' They exchanged jaded smiles. 'Listen, when you're taking ground samples? Don't just get dirt from under the body, take some from out at the edges of the circle, will you? Always a chance the killer shed something.'

'So?'

'So Delaney tells me we've got a forensic geologist at the university now that we can use if we don't get any other leads to the killer. He can analyze dirt and pebbles, tell us if any of it came from someplace else.'

'Oh, my. Way cool.'

'Uh-huh. And this case is going to need all the cool we can scare up before it's ready to go to court, wouldn't you say?'

'About as close to *nada* as I've ever seen,' Ibarra said.

'Right. So ... first I'm going to try to expedite his prints, see if we can get an ID.' She watched as another department vehicle turned into the lot. 'Oh, hey, here comes Cunningham. I forgot—'

'Go ahead,' Ibarra said, '*I'll* take care of *her*.'

He did a Groucho Marx thing with his eyebrows. He wouldn't really make any moves on the new public information officer, but she was young and attractive and he was a Tucson cop with a Hispanic name; he had to show some *cojones*.

'Good. Tell her a John Doe for now, but say we hope to have an ID by tomorrow. Try to make us sound like we know what's going on.'

'Uh-*huh*. The old knowledgeable ploy, that could work.'

Sarah pulled her car into line behind Gloria and the county van. Waiting for the break in traffic that would let them all on to First Avenue, she glanced at the clock on the dashboard and thought, as she usually did now on school mornings, *Hope Denny's getting off to school OK*. In her mind, she reached out and gave her favorite niece a little pat. *You get a good breakfast, babe?*

Denny had stayed with her for a couple of months last fall, while they got her clothes ready, got her registered and started in school. The rest of the family thought she should stay in the country till ... they didn't say till when. But Sarah argued that Denny's best shot at a successful year was to get started in her own school, get to know her teachers and have that much going for her when her mother got out of detox.

Janine came out of the hospital radiant with hope and saying, 'I can't wait to get my baby back.' So Sarah helped her find a rental and reluctantly took Denny back to her mother.

She didn't see she had any alternative, but letting the child go set up a jangling conflict in her mind that ate at her nerves. She'd always been fond of Janine's child, but now that they'd been alone together for several weeks she felt responsible for her in a new way. Besides, they were friends, understood each other, got along. And she knew Janine's resolve was fragile.

A little girl wanted her mother, of course. Everybody knew that. But what if Janine ... Every day now, underneath her unease about Delaney and her job, Sarah's worries about Denny ran like a slow-moving dark river.

Three

When the alarm rang, Denny shut the noise off quickly and lay still a minute, thinking about the day ahead. She had clean clothes ready and some money stashed, so she figured she had a fair shot at making this Tuesday an OK day.

OK days didn't just happen; they took planning, hard work and attention to details. Well, and maybe some lying and stealing.

She was ten years old, so she had to take the days as they came along. Grown-ups ran the world, and they didn't run it to suit kids. But they didn't always have as much control as they thought, either, so if you kept your eyes open you could do yourself some good around the edges. She was beginning to be quite proud of the ways she had learned to do some good for herself.

It was important not to expect too much, so you didn't get disappointed. She knew better now than to look for really ring-a-ding days like the first half of last year, when Mom was just back from rehab and had a good job doing accounting in an office. Mom was a whiz at her job, she said so every day. She kept saying other things like, 'Knowledge is power' and 'Today is the first day of the rest of our lives'. Denny thought that was all pretty obvious but she wasn't going to argue as long as Mom stayed sober and happy and there was food in the house.

All last fall until almost Christmas, they'd had buffed-up extra-credit days together. That's how it had felt, like they were reporting in to some invisible school counselor, showing off clean clothes and brushed hair and good grades in social studies, so they could get to the head of whatever class Mom was enrolled in. They'd start with cheery breakfasts, Denny with a dishtowel over the front of her clean school clothes and Mom making her face beautiful for work. As Denny walked away toward the school bus stop, Mom would be waving from the doorway of their house. Smiling back through the bus window, Denny knew she could count on a good dinner and help with homework later if she needed it.

Something about Christmas made Mom moody and sad, though, and in January she started keeping beer in the refrigerator again. By the end of February she was calling in sick about one day a week, and when the company announced layoffs at the end of March she was one of the first to be let go. Unemployment benefits lasted for several weeks, so although they ate a lot of beans and macaroni they had a roof over their heads, as Mom said, while she looked for something new. She would make Denny laugh after school, describing the appointments she went to, imitating the really stupid people who luckily hadn't offered her a job.

She told Denny not to worry. Everybody knew she was a whiz at anything to do with a computer. But everybody wasn't calling. In fact, nobody called about anything, and the longer she stayed home the less housework she seemed to get done.

By May they began to have some really bad days, when there was hardly anything in the house to eat, Mom was sleeping like a stone when she left for school, and Denny couldn't find any clean socks or lunch money.

Sometimes the house was empty when Denny got home, and Mom came in late and made a lot of noise getting into bed. When Denny was hungry she woke up easily and had trouble going back to sleep, so the bad day was followed by a rotten night and a worse tomorrow.

In June Mom had to borrow money from Aunt Sarah to pay the rent.

'Janine, now, don't start this,' Aunt Sarah said. 'I'm just getting back on my feet myself after the divorce.'

'Well, Jesus, Sarah, I'm not doing it for the fun of it,' Mom said. 'I got laid off, remember? I mean, I'm doing my best, I've got applications in all over town and I'm living in a duplex on Lurlene Street, for God's sake. A block from Kolb Road where half the traffic in Tucson goes by every day.'

Kolb Road seemed to feature in all their fights now. Mom had seemed grateful while Aunt Sarah was helping her get settled in a place she could afford. But since she lost her job and couldn't afford much of anything, she brooded about the fact that Sarah's house was in a nicer neighborhood than hers. Their brother Howard had the family ranch and Grandma had moved to a new development with a swimming pool in a suburb west of town. 'But Denny and I drew the slum. If this block gets any noisier we'll have to wear earplugs. Is this really what you want for your niece?'

'What I really want for my niece,' Aunt Sarah said, 'is a mother who can get her ass in gear and find another *job*. And clean up this house, for God's sake!' They yelled at each other like that for a while and then cried and hugged and made up and Aunt Sarah gave Mom some money. That was about standard for how it went between them when Mom was off the wagon and trying to hide it. She picked more fights with Aunt Sarah then because she was trying to keep her on the defensive.

Aunt Sarah was edgy lately too, probably because she could see her sister was in trouble again and dreaded talking to their mother about it. Denny had a bigger worry than that: if her mother went to rehab, she'd probably get sent out to the ranch to live with Uncle Howard and Aunt Jane like the last time. The ranch was OK and Uncle Howard tried to be nice, but Aunt Jane and the two girls hated her guts and wanted her *gone*. So when the fights started between Aunt Sarah and her mother, Denny stayed out of sight till the hugging started. Lately she even skipped the hugging part if she could manage it.

The next day after the rent-money fight, Mom got a Mondays-only job in a second-hand clothing store called 'Twice As Nice' that said its merchandise was 'gently used'. Just a fun gig till the world got serious again, Mom said. Then she found a waitress job in a bar on Speedway, Friday and Saturday nights only, so she took that too. After that she countered any criticism of her housekeeping by saying, 'OK, *you* try being a single mother with two jobs.'

At least she made good tips at the bar, she told Denny, so they'd be fine till she could find a real job. She told many funny stories to illustrate how unreal her present jobs were. Without knowing how to say it, exactly,

Denny saw that her mother was using humor as a shield, to fend off questions about her drinking. One of her lines was, 'Go easy on me, I'm still in recovery from rehab.'

Besides tips, though, the other thing Mom made at the bar was a lot of new boyfriends. They called on the phone and came home with her sometimes, bringing plenty of beer and sometimes pot. More and more afternoons now she got that hazy look, the little smile and the 'hmm' that meant you could forget about supper unless you fixed your own.

Summer was like drifting in a risky swamp, long hours of nothing and then scary times with loud music and new boyfriends in the house. Mom stayed in bed a lot on her days off, but Denny got her to drive to the library once a week or so. It took a lot of nagging but was worth it, because with enough books she could stay in her room almost forever and pretend the boyfriends weren't there.

Aunt Sarah called often and took her out to dinner and a movie for her birthday. Mom was supposed to go too, but at the last minute she got a terrible headache. Denny enjoyed being alone with Aunt Sarah till she started asking over dinner if everything was OK with Janine. Denny wasn't going to get caught in the middle of that. She said, 'Sure' and changed the subject, and for the rest of the evening they kind of looked past each other and talked about books a lot.

Getting Mom to help her register for school

in mid-August was like herding cats. Mom never said no, but somehow she was never ready to do it either. Finally Denny threatened to call Aunt Sarah, and then Mom brushed her hair and got in the car. Her lipstick was on crooked and the teachers kept giving her long looks. She was very angry by the time they came home, but Denny didn't care because she had a piece of paper that said Denice Lynch was in fifth grade at Erickson Elementary.

Luckily Mom didn't know the threat to call Aunt Sarah was mostly bluff. Denny was determined never to ask Aunt Sarah for anything again if she could possibly avoid it, because of what happened when Mom got out of detox.

A few months before Mom came home, Aunt Sarah came out to the ranch and said, 'Denny should come to town now, and stay with me till school starts, she needs to get her clothes and books.' Denny was so glad to get away from the aunt who couldn't stand her and the cousins who whispered behind their hands and never included her in games, that at first she just enjoyed shopping and asked no questions. But when it was time to register she asked, shouldn't she transfer to a school closer to Aunt Sarah's house? She had begun to believe that was the plan, that she would stay at Aunt Sarah's house and Mom would come to visit her there. She couldn't tell for sure from Aunt Sarah's answer, which was, 'I guess we shouldn't change anything till your

Mom gets home and we see how that goes.'

She was sure Aunt Sarah liked having her around. Denny always did her chores and homework on time and made sure she was no trouble. And they got along great, did projects together like trimming the hedge and refinishing an old Morris chair they found at a yard sale. Aunt Sarah noticed everything, she knew without being told that Denny wasn't welcome at the ranch. And she certainly knew by now that Mom couldn't be trusted to take care of anybody, even herself, so didn't that settle where Denny should live?

Mom came home on a Sunday in the middle of October. While they were changing the bed where Mom was going to be sleeping with her that night Aunt Sarah said, 'I know your Mom's anxious to move into her own place as soon as possible, and Grandma and I'll help her as much as we can.'

Denny took a deep breath and tried to get the courage to ask, But I'll stay with you, right?

Aunt Sarah went right on talking, though, in that fake-cheery way grown-ups use when they know they're telling a whopper. 'I'm going to miss you around here something awful, Denny, you know that? I've really enjoyed this time we've had together. But your Mom is just living for the day she gets you back, it's all she talks about when I go to see her.'

Denny barely kept herself from saying, Doesn't anybody ever wonder what I want?

She finished making her side of the bed with arms that felt heavy and hot with shame. She had been so sure Sarah enjoyed the things they did together as much as she did, walks and homework, talking about books and movies and laughing at the same things.

Aunt Sarah had found her a site on the internet called 'Fanfiction', where kids posted stories they made up about their favorite characters in TV shows and books. When Denny wrote a story about SpongeBob Squarepants on the Nick channel, Aunt Sarah helped her create a user name for herself and post her story on the site. Denny got good reviews for her story, and she thought Aunt Sarah was just as proud and excited about them as she was.

But that Sunday, making the bed, she realized Aunt Sarah had just been humoring her, and was probably counting the days till she got this kid off her hands. Of all the days Denny could remember in her life, that one was the worst. Mom had done some bad things – she forgot about Denny sometimes, left her hungry or cold with no idea when she might be back. But Denny had always known Mom wasn't reliable, so she got mad at her sometimes but not disappointed.

Aunt Sarah was different, though. She had always told Denny the truth, asked her opinion and remembered things that mattered. Denny thought they were friends. She got the worst hurt of her life when Sarah took her back to Mom. From then on, she made up her mind not to pin her hopes on anybody that way again.

Mom brightened up for a while after she finally got Denny registered in school. She convinced herself it was all her own idea, and while she was still feeling proud of herself, she asked at the bar for a couple of extra shifts and got them. Denny had to do a lot of reminding to get her there on time, but Mom used the money to buy shoes and a couple of almost-new outfits for Denny at Twice As Nice before school started. The day they did that shopping, Mom was smiling and humming coming home from the store, and Denny almost (but not seriously, she told herself later) let herself believe Mom was going to save herself and they could have a life like other people.

And school made everything better. It gave her someplace to go every day where people, some people anyway, made sense. She made an effort to please a couple of the best teachers, ignoring her classmates' muttered comments about sucking up. Mrs Thorpe helped her get into some accelerated classes, so homework got more interesting. And that was good, because Mom's reform period didn't last. She went back to having company a lot, and the guys she brought home were getting rougher.

Denny spent more and more time in her room. She almost always fixed her own food now, and sometimes, depending on how gross the company was, she had to be quick about it. On the other hand, she had found a laundromat only four blocks away, and the woman who ran it was good about showing her how to work the machines. One good thing about this neighborhood, a lot of people had problems, so you didn't have to explain why your Mom wasn't around.

Money was her biggest problem, she couldn't earn money yet. She took to stealing small amounts from her mother, and larger amounts from the boyfriends. They were always drinking and usually high besides, so they weren't careful. She went through their clothes while they were sleeping, and stashed what she took in small amounts around the house, under the laundry hamper and in the broom closet, never in her own drawers. Even if Mom found some of it by accident she never found it all, and Denny never got caught.

Evenings and weekends were tricky, and she couldn't ever have a friend come home, but once school started she felt like she could keep most of her days somewhere between a C-minus and a C-plus. And she could live with that average.

This Tuesday morning, as usual she spent the first few minutes after she woke up figuring out how to get through the day. Checking on Mom came first. If Mom was awake and alone Denny ate breakfast, asked for lunch money and went to school like a normal kid. There was no man in bed with Mom this morning, but she was snoring hard and out of it. Denny got dressed fast, put money from one of her stashes in her clothing and books, and bought breakfast at the Donut Wheel. Then she had to run to make the school bus.

Once on the bus she could relax a little. The school system was in charge of the day now till three o'clock, and then she had her room, and homework, and a book to read until bedtime. And three more days of school before she had to negotiate a weekend.

She managed her life like that, a few hours at a time till she'd made it through one more whole day. She almost never let herself look down the long corridor of days and wonder how she was going to get to the relative safety of, say, age fifteen.

But at least she knew what she was going to do when she got there: talk to Aunt Sarah, sign up for all the right courses, get great grades and pass the tests as soon as they'd let her take them. By the time she was twenty-one, maybe sooner if they still made exceptions, she'd be a Tucson Police Officer, sworn in. And then for the rest of her life she was going to keep everything under control.

Four

Why can't I control this stupid AC? Hot and frustrated, Sarah pulled her car into line behind Gloria and the county van. The fan was still blowing hot air. She rolled down the windows to vent some heat, and heard the thunk of the cooler kicking in as they turned south on First Avenue and crossed the Rillito.

'The Ree-yee-toe,' Sarah always had to explain to visitors. 'Spanish for Little River.'

'So little I can't see it,' a friend had said recently, peering down.

'Well, it's dry right now. Actually it's dry most of the time now, the water's all gone to the cotton fields and suburbs. It was running full a couple of times this summer, though, after those big rains we had.'

'Hard to believe. You like living where it's so dry?'

'I guess. It's home.' Like Delaney and Ibarra, Sarah belonged to the small percentage of natives in this city crowded with transients. They clustered in the municipal jobs: police, fire department, courthouse.

The three vehicles traveled in caravan from the north edge of town to the south, sticking to major streets with lights because the cross streets were filled curb-to-curb now with work-bound vehicles roaring in from the suburbs at daredevil speeds. They all treated amber lights as if they were green and then blasted through the last half of the intersection on the red. Sarah dodged around a fender-bender at the Grant Road intersection, and waited through three light changes to cross Speedway.

'Well, that was an adventure,' Gloria said as she unloaded her gear at the Forensic Center. 'How about that jam-up on Speedway?'

'If somebody doesn't do something about the streets in this town,' the county driver said, 'pretty soon we'll all have to get up at three o'clock in the morning to get to work.'

'Not me,' Sarah said. 'I live in the Campbell-Grant neighborhood, right in the middle of town.'

'How can you stand to live downtown? I got me a double-wide out in a wildcat settlement on the other side of Oro Valley. Man, it's nice out there.'

'So whoever does something about the streets in this town,' Sarah said, 'I guess it won't be you, will it?'

'What're you,' he asked her, scowling, 'some kinda activist?' He wheeled the body into the building on its gurney and they followed, Gloria loaded with nylon bags of fingerprint gear and Sarah carrying the clanking bag that held the disassembled fuming tent.

'You don't need a table, do you?' Greenberg asked. He looked as if he was already sorry he'd yielded to Sarah's request.

'No, the gurney's fine,' Gloria said. Greenberg led her to a small examining room, where she went to work with inkpad and high-gloss paper. She was quick and skillful with the simple tools of manual fingerprinting, which everybody in the department agreed were still better than the electronically scanned ones they made at the jail. When she finished with the victim's fingers, she began putting the tent-frame together.

'C'mon, you're not going to need a tent in here,' Greenberg said, frowning.

'Well, the AC makes quite a breeze. Only takes a minute,' Gloria said, leaning gracefully over his taut little body like some exotic giraffe over a grumpy gazelle. Her dazzling white smile, shining out of her round taffy-colored cheeks, seemed to promise him better days than this one in the antiseptic cold of the lab.

Greenberg backed away from her Supergirl sexiness, shaking his head ironically. 'OK, Einstein. Don't take all day with this experiment, please.' He walked away punching numbers into his Blackberry.

'Yo, have no fear,' she called after him, in her funkiest ghetto accent. Shaking her head, chuckling, she set the frame in place on the gurney. 'That Animal, ain't he something?' She fastened the tent around the frame and squirted something out of a plastic bottle on to the little hot plate built into one corner.

Sarah looked at the bottle. 'Cyanoacrylate.

This is what you use now?'

'It's the same thing,' Gloria said. 'Somebody just figured out what was in the SuperGlue, so we can leave those stupid little tubes for the hobby train set.' She plugged in the plate and stood by, watching it bubble.

While they waited, Sarah speed-dialed the fingerprint lab and listened to five rings before a deep voice boomed, 'Ganz.'

Sarah said, 'Oh, Bud, good, I'm glad you're working today.'

'You are, huh? I'm not, I'd rather be shooting pool. Who is this?'

'Oh, sorry, Sarah Burke. I was just thinking—'

'Thinking? On the police force? What're you, some kind of a troublemaker?' He laughed and then coughed explosively, hurting her ear. When he could talk again he yelled, 'You were thinking about asking for a favor, weren't you? Huh?'

'Bud, are you too busy to talk?'

'Hell, no,' he said, subsiding into a normal tone of voice, 'It's been kind of a slow day for laughs around here, so I'm giving you a bad time. Whaddya want, sweetheart?'

'I've got a body with no ID on it except a couple of nice big tats, look like they might be jailhouse specials. I thought if you could run his prints against AZAFIS database...'

'I might get a match and you could start to look very smart, huh? You want this miracle today or yesterday?'

'Well, I could have them up there in a few

minutes, if—'

'And you think I'm so easy you can just run up here and pinch my butt and I'll put your stuff right at the head of the queue, do you?'

'I didn't mean...'

The terrible laughing and coughing rattled her eardrums again. Bud Ganz really needed to quit smoking. But when he recovered he said, 'Sure, bring them up whenever they're ready, Sarah, I'm just ragging on you.'

'Gloria's going to bring them. In just a few minutes.'

'That big tall girl from the lab? Tell her to call me when she checks them in, I'll find a stepladder and we'll make love.'

'I'll tell her that and I'm sure she'll be looking forward to it.'

'Uh-huh. No matter how much you stroke me, Snookums, I might not be able to get to your prints till tomorrow. But I guess he'll still be dead tomorrow, won't he?'

Must be the new mantra.

'All *right*,' Sarah said, folding up the phone.

She repeated Ganz's instructions to Gloria, who shook her head and said, 'So bad,' absent-mindedly, intent on the view through the little window in the tent.

When Sarah couldn't stand the suspense any longer she said, 'You got something?'

'I think so,' Gloria said as the bell rang on her timer. 'One good one, coming up on the inside of the right leg, see?'

'Oh?' Sarah looked. 'Oh. Oh, my.' She watched Gloria peel off the tent, thinking this one print could make all the difference if ... They looked at it together. Sarah realized she was holding her breath. 'Couldn't hardly be the victim's print, could it? On the inside of the leg like that?'

'Well, we'll check that first, but no, not likely. Looks like one quick touch from a pickpocket, on that little smooth place with no hair.'

'Now when you take this to Ganz,' Sarah said, 'be sure he knows we think this one print might be the killer's.'

'Gotcha. Hey, wouldn't it be *estupendo* if we matched this up with some thug in the system? Whee, I could call my mother and tell her I solved a murder case all by myself. No, maybe I won't.' Gloria drew herself up and launched into an imitation of her mother saying indignantly, 'Girl, you get back here to LA this minute!' She rolled her eyes up. 'Mama wants me to go to beauty school and learn how to paste on those acrylic fingernails.'

'Well, the smell is different,' Sarah said.

'But no better. And the conversations are even worse.' She was frowning over the body. 'Anything else I see here is less than a partial, Sarah – just fragments. But this one's a winner, I think – looks like it might be an index finger.' She got out her camera and took a picture, dusted it with magnetic powder and took another picture before she lifted it on to a strip of gummed paper.

'OK, let's bag him up,' Sarah said, pulling

on gloves again. When the victim was zipped inside the bag she signed the department sealing tape and spread it carefully over the pull tab. From now until the autopsy, nobody could get access to this body without leaving a record. 'I'll stop at Greenberg's office and tell him he can put his body away.'

'Fine. You know, Sarah,' Gloria said, pressing the last fingerprint into her spiral book and noting the location, 'this guy...'

'The dead guy? What?'

Gloria brooded. 'He's not your average John Doe, is he? Looks like ... I don't know ... somebody.'

'I thought so too. Seems like we should be getting some inquiries.'

'If he belonged to me I'd sure be asking by now. Hoo! Hunky dude like this in a park all alone? Why?'

'I guess I don't think much about the *why*.'

'You don't? Motive doesn't matter any more?'

'Well ... it does to a jury. But to tell you the truth, the reasons people give for killing somebody usually don't make any sense.'

'People don't know why they kill other people?'

'I think by definition killing's an irrational act.'

'Oh, now, hold on, I know *some* people – you take my Uncle Budge—'

'But you haven't killed him yet, have you? Because all your constraints are in place and working.'

'And besides I don't have to see him any more. If I did—'

'Uncle Budge would be toast, huh?' Sarah hung her purse and briefcase on her shoulders, smiling. 'We all *say* that. "One of these days I'm going to strangle her with my bare hands." My mother says that about my sister almost every week. But very few of us do it.'

'I wonder what would pop my cork?' Gloria straightened up from the table and rubbed her back with a little groan. 'Rage, I guess. Sex, of course. What else do people kill for?'

'Oh, in Tucson, these days,' Sarah said, 'we usually just look for the drugs.'

Five

Rudy Ortiz woke before dawn Tuesday, as he did most days. He lay still a few minutes listening to his wife's gentle snoring, thinking about the day ahead of him. When his plans were complete he got up and dressed silently in the half-light, down to his socks. He carried his boots out through the kitchen and into the garage, where he sat on the cement step to put them on. The garage door lifted discreetly on silicon rollers and the motor on his Buick Century, always kept in perfect tune, purred quietly to life. He backed into Thirty-Second Street at sunrise without even waking the neighbor's dog.

His wife kept plenty of food in the house and would have fixed his breakfast if he asked. But it had been some time since they wanted to talk to each other first thing in the morning. Besides she usually had the house full of grandkids and down-and-out nephews and nieces, and rather than risk waking any of them and hearing what they had to say he got in his car and drove around aimlessly, smoking and looking at the weather. When he got hungry he drove to the WhataBurger on Sixth Avenue, ordered a taquito with cheese and sausage at the drive-in window, and ate alone with the radio tuned to KZLZ, the Spanish-language station. His Spanish was sketchy so he got only the vaguest notion of the news, which suited him fine.

Any other day but Tuesday he would have driven randomly, then from one to another of his businesses, arriving at a different time each day so his managers never knew when to expect him. Keeping his employees a little on edge was a feature of his management style. He would walk in without greeting anyone and stand or sit somewhere, in a spot that was inconspicuous until he chose to occupy it. While he was there, all his employees watched it covertly. He always wore a Black Stetson and dark sunglasses, so it was impossible to tell where he was looking as he slowly scanned the room. Sometimes he left after a few minutes without saying a word. Other days, he might start a conversation with a customer or one of his employees that would last an hour and include a stroll around the store.

If anything displeased him he took the manager aside, described the problem and told him how to fix it. It was a short conversation because there was never any discussion. He was polite and quiet but had a reputation for widely spaced violent rages during which somebody usually got hurt. You never knew what might set him off, which was, of course, the point.

But this was Tuesday so he went to the tire store as soon as it opened, at eight o'clock. It was the oldest of all his properties, a shabby place crowded with new and used tires stacked on wheeled platforms. Many hand-lettered signs, in English and Spanish, advertised bargains. There was one hoist in a greasy work bay at the side of the building where the tires were changed. On the counter that faced the door, an ancient mechanical cash register covered with scrollwork had a bell that rang when the drawer was opened. Rudy liked the cheerful sound of it. He kept it and all the other vintage tools in the place in good repair, but did nothing to upgrade the building. For his purposes, it was perfect just as it was.

Tilly Stubbs was waiting for him, sitting behind the wheel of his Escalade in the small side parking lot. Rudy walked past him without a word and went into the store. As usual Tilly followed him to the tiny office at the back, where Rudy sat down behind the scarred oak desk. Tilly closed the door, found the armless chrome kitchen chair that was always there somewhere, moved it to the wall behind Rudy, and sat on it, facing the door. They would stay in that crowded space, smelling petroleum products and sweat, most of the morning, counting money and watching the people who brought it.

Rudy supplied his dealers on short credit. They sold cocaine in both powder and crack form, some heroin and a little marijuana as a convenience to customers. Fronting the money like that, Rudy took a higher risk than the suppliers who insisted on cash on delivery, so he charged a higher price. He was the supplier of choice for poor young men getting started. Rudy's risk was manageable because he had lived in this neighborhood all his life and had watched most of his dealers grow up. Besides, he had a reputation as a bad man to get on the wrong side of. He kept his pushers on a very short leash, made them pay in full within a week.

He changed the locations of both his supply depot and payment office frequently, and switched pick-up and payment times on short notice. But they all paid him on a mid-week morning at one of his businesses, at a precise time and place assigned by Rudy when they picked up the product. Weekly pay-offs avoided confusion, he said, but the morning meetings served another purpose for him. His drug salesmen, normally night creatures, had to get up early one day a week and face him in a brightly lighted office, close to the clatter of a busy kitchen, or the hiss of a pneumatic lift or the punishing clamor of tools dropped on cement.

Rudy watched them open the door to his office, kept his eyes on them as they walked or sidled or staggered to his desk. He judged how easily or painfully they sat down on the hard straight chair, listened to their voices and noticed whether their hands shook. From these signals he could judge accurately when they began to use their own product, how fast their use escalated and how much alcohol they were pouring in alongside the other poison. He had seen many men go to hell in the drug business. By now he could judge accurately when to start looking for a replacement pusher.

He assigned his morning pay-off times in the order of his dealers' importance: the newest men had the earliest appointments. As they built up a client base and brought in more money, they worked up to slightly later times. It was one of those small favors he doled out sparingly, to keep people hopeful but wary.

This Tuesday, every one of them was right on time with the correct change, bam bam, like robots. Tilly had nothing to do but watch, and the money piled up in the drawer.

Ace Perkins was the last one, due at ten-forty-five. Ace was an anomaly, not a local but recommended five months ago by a reliable source. And he had proved to be the kind, damn, you'd like to clone him, you know? Biggest producer for the last three months, had a string of solid clients that he took care of like a mother. If he had any self-destructive habits Rudy hadn't been able to spot them. Sometimes Rudy worried that maybe Ace was too good to be true.

But his arrest record said otherwise. Rudy paid a stipend every month to an inside man at Tucson Police Department, so when he needed to know something he got it toot sweet, no arguments and no dealing. Before he hired Ace he got a copy of his Arizona prison history, three-plus years served of a three-to-ten for cocaine trafficking. Not extensive but not pussy either. He had served his time in Florence where he got those dragon tattoos and, Rudy guessed, the crooked fingers that didn't match the rest of his handsome appearance.

He'd shown a lot of street savvy right from the start, had no trouble finding good corners for his crack business and quickly established a great roster of high-end clients for the snow. He knew how to find the lawyers and real estate brokers, restaurateurs and high-end trophy wives who could come up with the cash, none of this whining around about credit that some dealers listened to. Rudy had never seen anybody put together a client base from the low and high ends of the Tucson coke trade any faster than Ace had.

The other thing he liked, Ace was as big a stickler for precision as he was himself. Set your clock by the guy, almost. So when his watch read five to eleven, Rudy began tapping his fingers on the desk. At fifteen past he turned a puzzled face to Tilly Stubbs and said, unnecessarily, 'Ace is half an hour late.'

Tilly nodded, his shaved head reflecting the dim light in the tire store. His hair had been strawberry blonde when he had any, and he'd kept the high coloring that went with it, pink cheeks and bright blue eyes. An abused childhood had left him with an off-center nose and one oddly dented cheek, and the gang warfare of his youth in the rancid slums of Detroit had cost him several teeth and a piece of one ear. So instead of the jolly appearance nature had designed for him, Tilly had a face that looked almost as dangerous as he actually was.

He stood up, his white T-shirt straining to cover his massive chest and biceps, and said, ' 'M on it.' Because his larynx had been damaged in a fight during his first prison term, his voice had the dry rasp of gravel sliding over rock. Graceful for a big man, he moved without making any noise.

He walked out on to the cracked asphalt parking lot in front of the tire shop with his cell phone at his ear, calling Sanchez and Brody, Rudy's other two street thugs. Rudy's operation wasn't big enough to need three goons full-time, so the other two men ran errands too and moved a little coke on the side. Sanchez was Rudy's main snoop, too, and Brody doubled as chauffeur and gofer.

Brody had once explained to Tilly why the boss loved to call at weird hours and get you to do these stupid chores that shouldn't be your job at all.

'That way he feels like you're loyal, you'll do anything he asks. It's nothing personal,' he added, resting a gritty callused fingertip briefly on Tilly's huge forearm. 'Ol' Rudy, he's a equal-opportunity ball-buster.'

After Tilly left, Rudy stayed where he was, sorting the money into piles by denominations. He banded it, entered the total in a tiny spiral notebook that he carried in his shirt pocket. Just the total, everything else was in his head. He packed the cash in the bottom of a yellow plastic toolbox he'd bought on special at Sears twelve years ago, and covered it with a set of socket wrenches glued to a false plastic bottom cannibalized from an identical box. He replaced the cantilevered upper shelf full of screwdrivers and pliers, snapped the lid shut and carried his toolbox out to his three-year-old Buick. The dowdy older car worked for him just as the tire shop did, hid him in plain sight. For the rest of the day he worked his carefully crafted magic, transforming drug money into payments for car repairs, groceries, booze, and the price of two used Toyotas.

But under the stoic busyness of his day, the nagging worry ran like water under rock, *Where's Ace?* He knew very well what he controlled and what he could not control, had lived a long time with the fear that must never be mentioned but never went away. *It will be some little thing that gets you if you stay in this too long,* he had told himself many times, s*ome stupid little thing you never saw coming.* He was not a fool, he knew nobody beat the system forever. He only needed two more years, three at the most. As careful as he had been, he thought, three more years was not expecting too much. But all day Tuesday he asked himself, *Is this the day of the stupid little thing?*

Six

Always some stupid little thing. Damn. Sarah folded up her phone, grousing to herself, as she stepped out of the lab into the dazzle of a hot morning. An attorney trying one of her cases, yielding to an anxiety fit, wanted her to review the testimony of a witness – *how many times have we been over this?* – and call him back before noon. She promised matter-of-factly to do it. 'Sure, no sweat.' Because you could never have too many friends around the courthouse, could you? But as she walked to her car she grumbled to herself. She wanted to go back to her desk right now and type up this morning's notes before they got cold. Damn! Never enough time in a day.

Back at the station she caught a little break,

though; Jimmy was still out and all the other detectives in her section were up on third floor, checking in evidence from the shooting out on Speedway. Nobody wanted to talk to her. She grabbed an orange out of the snack bar in the break room, peeled it quickly and ate it a section at a time while she pushed herself through the drudgery of reading through case notes from last spring. When she finished the call-back to the attorney, she laid her notes from today's crime scene by her keyboard and typed them up quickly with no interruptions.

Pleased with herself, wanting somebody to brag to, she looked around for Ibarra. He was at his desk. She walked back to tell him that Animal had set the time for tomorrow's autopsy.

'Two o'clock, and that's pretty firm, there's only one case ahead of us.'

'Damn!' Ibarra said, and smacked his desk.

'What?'

'Something's gotta give around here,' he said. 'How can I be at the lab with you tomorrow while I'm talking to all these family members that want to give me information in the Grayling shooting?' He held up a fistful of phone messages. 'And Delaney's on my tail to finish the interviews from that stabbing over on Miracle Mile. What the hell?' He threw his pencil down on the desk. It flew off across the room, narrowly missing the detective at the next desk, who sent him a black frown but went on with his phone conversation. 'Shit, the faster I work the deeper I dig the hole!' He slammed some papers around on his desk for a few seconds, then calmed down and looked sheepishly at Sarah. 'Sorry.'

'You need some Tums?'

'I'm not having gas, I'm having a hissy fit.'

'We don't both have to go to the autopsy,' Sarah said. 'I'll take good notes and you can read them. Or are you really having a hissy fit about something else?'

He rubbed his face hard with both hands, got up and picked up his pencil, came back and sat down. 'Good call. Two of my kids have got sinus infections. Sandy and I haven't had a decent night's sleep since last week some time. You're talking to the walking dead.' He did a zombie imitation, eyes rolled back and tongue hanging out.

'Jimmy, why don't you put in for some family leave?'

'I'm saving it up for when I get my vasectomy,' he said, and they both laughed. Jimmy's family planning negotiations with his devoutly Catholic wife had regaled the section for years.

'Forget the autopsy,' Sarah said. 'I'll handle it.' She was secretly pleased. She always thought she learned more at the investigations she did alone. But she went back to her desk reflecting that Jimmy's family situation was going to damage his career if he didn't find some way to get it under control. She wished she knew how to help; she had been to the edge of that cliff herself.

She was answering emails when her phone rang. A man's voice yelled, 'One thing I hate it's a smartass.'

A little buzz of satisfaction raced along her nerves. 'This wouldn't be Bud Ganz, by any chance?'

'Not if he could help it but yes, this is "Ganz by any chance".'

'And are you calling to tell me that you've already found a match?'

'I sure as hell am, lady.'

'Well now, ain't that a hole in the boat? How come so fast?'

'My next work order after I talked to you, there was a mistake in the request so I had to send it back. So I said to myself, "Self," I said, "let's show that uppity Sarah Burke she may look good in pants but she isn't any smarter than the rest of us."' He coughed again, terrible whoops that made her hold the phone away from her ear. She put it back fast when she heard him say, 'But now instead of that, goddammit, I gotta call and tell the uppity woman she was right.' Actually he was bursting with pride, she thought – over the moon in love with himself.

'Where'd you find him?'

'Florence. Your victim is Adolph Alvin Perkins, aka Ace. Cute, huh? Ace.' He made a rude noise. 'Served three years and three months of a three-to-ten for trafficking cocaine, released early this year. I'll copy this to your email.'

'Good. Just that one conviction, huh?'

'Well, in Arizona. I'll do the nationwide search some day soon, but you seemed like you wanted this before the body got cold, so—'

'Yes. Has anybody mentioned to you lately that you do very superior work?'

'Go ahead, flatter me shamelessly.'

'I mean it. I owe you a big one.'

'You want to pay up? Sex is always good.'

Ganz always made verbal passes at her, but in a routine way that made it easy not to take offense. In a workplace that was still mostly male, Sarah picked her fights carefully, but tried hard to win the ones she couldn't dodge. She traded a few more giddy jokes with Ganz before she thanked him again and hung up. As soon as his email arrived she charged out of her cubicle, crowing, 'Hey, Jimmy, we got an ID on our victim already! Bud found him for us!'

'No kidding? Lemmee see. Oh, this is great, Sarah.' When he'd read the record she laid in front of him he said, 'Why don't you get somebody on the support staff to do a search for his address and phone number?'

'I will. And if they find it, you and I better take a look before we let the tech staff in there. Oh, but you're too busy today, aren't you?'

'Hey, I'll make time for that.' He looked at his watch and did a jittery little sitting-down dance of conflicting impulses. 'But listen, I've got a carload of Graylings waiting to talk to me right now...'

'No problem, I have to get a warrant anyway. How long will you be?'

'An hour. Two at the most.'

'Go.' He grabbed his recorder and headed out the door. Sarah sent her information requests to the support staff and called Delaney.

'Good job, Sarah.' Delaney was too fair not to give her the praise she had earned. 'Good call. You found an address yet?'

'We're searching – should have it any minute.'

'Good. Next step is a warrant, right?'

'You bet.'

'Good. Don't forget closets, storage sheds, garage.'

'Right.' Did he think she'd never asked for a warrant before?

'Computers, files, books, what else? Get everything! Wish I could come with you, but I've got a meeting. Keep me up to date, though – oh, and pass it along to the PI, will you?'

'For sure.'

She was making her list for the warrant when the jittery kid from the support staff, the one with the coke-bottle glasses and bad acne, appeared in her doorway. What was his name? *Scott. I think.* Lately he had taken to covering his insecurities by giving himself titles that grew more presumptuous every week.

'Genius Geek has done it again,' he said, handing her a memo, snapping the rubber bands on his braces as he bowed to imaginary applause. Was it Scott Tracy, or Tracy Scott? Anyway he knew how to get maximum drama out of a routine search. 'Perkins, Adolph. Address and one cell phone number.'

'No land line?'

'No.'

'OK. Paseo Redondo, that's the little street off Granada, right?'

'Correct. Just a few blocks from here, actually.'

'An apartment, right?'

'In a big building full of many apartments. Genius Geek looked up the manager. It's that second name and number there.' He pointed to the paper she was holding.

'Well, hey, Genius Geek, go to the head of the class! Thank you very much.' *Never fail to praise extra effort. People remember praise.* If he needed to invent a ridiculous name for himself, what harm? The least she could do was play along and please him. She could never remember his name because this kid annoyed her almost out of her mind sometimes – he always seemed to be in antic mode when she was grim, and lethargic when she was in a hurry. But today she needed him so she slathered on flattery. 'Now I can get my search warrant right away, and call this manager and get him to meet me there, see how you expedited? Could you go after the phone records next, have you got time?'

'Genius Geek can do that with ease.' He responded to praise by growing taller and rosier. Swaying above her, gleaming, he asked, 'How far back you want to go?'

'He's only been out of prison since early this year – if you just get everything for this year, that'll do it.'

She called Judge Garrity's office first because she was tight with his clerk, Phyllis, who said the judge was in chambers, and yes, she had time to type a warrant and sure, they'd put a rush on it. Phyllis was another of the good-to-know people Sarah was constantly collecting inside the system – they made all the difference when you needed to move a case along.

She tried to hold on to the warm feeling from Phyllis's favors while she passed the victim's ID to Jenny Cunningham in Public Information. Something about Jenny's perkier-than-thou persona ticked her off. She didn't know why, and she didn't want to think about it today, so she focused on the ceiling light while she reeled off the facts and got off the phone.

Still waiting for Ibarra, she read over the dead man's prison record again, and dialed an outside line.

'Dietz.' Good voice today, steady, no tremor.

'Will, it's Sarah.'

'Hey.' The voice warmed up half a notch. 'What's shakin'?'

'Quite a bit. I went to work before sun-up this morning.'

'Oh? What'd you draw?'

'A jogger found a body in Rillito Park.'

'Ah. Le Fever said he saw a scene getting taped up there. Up near the racetrack, right?'

'Yes. Almost on the bike path, actually. Started out as a John Doe, no ID on him at all, but we got lucky and matched his prints. So I thought I might tap your vast store of information.'

'My vast store, *ach du lieber*.' A tiny chuckle, almost soundless. 'My store's pretty empty these days, but you're welcome to what I've got.' The new Will Dietz. Before he got shot, he'd been undercover in Narcotics and not inclined to tell her much more than the date and time.

Sarah had greatly admired the old Will Dietz. Before the bullets found him, he had seemed like an unshakeable iron man, capable and smart, a tower of strength. But she was beginning to like the new, vulnerable Will Dietz so much she wasn't sure she wanted to see his rehab succeed all the way. *Where was I?* 'Our victim was a guy named Adolph Alvin Perkins. Any chance you'd know him?'

'Uh ... don't think so. Should I?'

'Well, he was released early this year from Florence. Three-to-ten for trafficking. I thought he might be your collar.'

'The name doesn't ring any bells. Tell you what, though, I haven't gone to work yet, I'm in my car a couple of blocks from you. Why don't I come up and look at what you've got?'

'Oh?' She had intended to fax it to him if he showed any interest. 'Well, if you have time...'

'Won't be ten minutes.' He hung up before she could argue.

Eight minutes later he stood in her doorway, a medium-sized nondescript man with plenty of mileage on his face. Working undercover had augmented his natural tendency to disappear into the woodwork; he was usually the last person in the room people noticed.

A seasoned Homicide detective when she transferred in from Auto Theft, he had helped her plenty during her first months in the section. Impressed by his skills and savvy, she maneuvered to get put on his cases. He was thorough and shrewd, had a wry sense of humor that helped on rough cases and an instinct for organizing information so the hard kernel of truth dropped out of the chaff of conflicting testimony.

'Everybody tries to put lipstick on the pig,' he told her. 'Even when they mean to tell you the truth, they'll still do their best to make their part of the story look better. Watch their eyes and hands when they tell you the parts where they come in.' He was totally professional, so they had been colleagues rather than friends. But she came to rely on his judgement and missed him when he transferred to Narcotics a few months later.

Six months ago, after sirens had wailed around town for an hour, the detectives at Stone Avenue began hearing the terrible story of how Will Dietz and his partner, on what should have been a routine interview, happened into a shoot-out between dealers.

Dietz took five shots, two of them life-threatening, and lay a week in Intensive Care. Sarah learned they had the same blood type when she, like everybody in the department, volunteered a donation. He sent a note from the recovery ward thanking them all for that 'good tough cops' blood that pulled me through'.

Hard months of therapy and counseling followed before he was pronounced fit even for light duty. When he turned up at her elbow at a department party in mid-summer, for a second Sarah wasn't sure who he was. He was thinner and gray-faced, walked with a slight limp and had a new part in his hair in addition to the old one. His eyes were like a TV screen when the power's off, and his hand shook when he picked up his glass.

Because she'd worked with him and knew how able he'd been, Sarah couldn't get his predicament out of her mind. She began to find excuses to email him with a bit of gossip, a copy of a clipping or a question. Afraid a one-woman campaign of friendliness might get too obvious, she got Jimmy to phone him with a question, maneuvered Eisenstaat into passing along a news item. She was gratified when he began to initiate a few emails himself.

It was odd, how fast she became invested in his recovery. A couple of weeks ago she had caught a glimpse of him chatting easily in a restaurant with some other people in the department, and felt her throat grow tight with pleasure at the sight. She told herself wryly that she had better be careful who she donated blood to if she was going to get this involved in the outcome.

Now he stood in front of her desk with his eyes crinkling a little at the corners and said, 'My God, Homicide finally got new chairs.'

'You haven't seen them? Well, please.' She waved him to a seat.

He sat. 'Oh, excellent. My tush endorses the choice.' They both laughed. The awful chairs in Homicide division when she came on board had introduced Sarah to the reality that the bitching in Homicide was every bit as colorful as any she had ever heard in Auto Theft.

His color was good again, his voice had regained the quiet crackle she remembered. He even smiled. He had not been much given to smiles while she worked with him – another improvement, she thought. *Maybe we should all get shot now and then.* She beamed back at him, delighted to see he was most of the way back.

He looked around, nodded to Eisenstaat, turned back and smiled some more. 'Well ... is the arrest record here, or...'

'Oh, here.' She passed it to him and he sat in front of her, reading. There was a deep line between his eyebrows now, but his hands, holding the paper, were perfectly steady. Square and capable looking ... Had somebody turned up the heat?

He looked up and shook his head. 'On my

way up here I tried to remember his name and couldn't. And now that I see his picture I'm sure – I don't know him.' He thought, scratching his chin. 'You know a lot of people in Narcotics?'

'No. Except for you, hardly anybody.'

'And now I'm not there.' He didn't say if he wanted to go back. 'But ... I think who you ought to talk to is Tony Delarosa. He's been there for years and he works on everything, he'll know if your victim's been a player here. You're after personal habits, friends, stuff like that?'

'Yeah, anything that gives me a place to start.'

'Tony's your man, he'll know. You want me to call him?'

'Would you?'

'Sure. Glad to.' He made notes in tiny, neat handwriting. 'Have you had time to run him through NCIC yet? I'll probably have time to run some searches tonight, would that help? See if he turns up in other parts of the country?'

'That would be great. Thanks.'

He stood up. She scanned the notes on her desk but found nothing more she could possibly ask him.

He squinted down at her humorously and said, 'Well, what other occasions for merry-making are coming up, hmm?'

'Actually, second floor's thinking of working up a bash for Hallowe'en,' she said. 'You mind wearing a mask?'

'Aren't they kind of hard to drink through?'

'Oh, we'll have straws for the booze.'

'That sounds good. You mean I'm invited?'

'Absolutely.'

'Terrific! I'll get my broom ready.'

She stood up while they were both still smiling, reached across the desk and shook his hand. It felt just the way she'd expected, firm and dry. She let the touch last one extra second before she said, 'Thank you so much for coming in.'

It occurred to her as he walked away that he had not needed to come up here to exchange this little bit of information, they could easily have handled it by phone and fax. So when he turned at her doorway and nodded, she sent him a smile that said plainly, *I wanted to see you too*.

Sitting down when he was gone, unreasonably aglow, she began reviewing a shortlist of her best friends in the department. Who could she get to stir up a Hallowe'en party? *What came over me?* She had no time to sort it out because her phone was ringing.

Phyllis said her warrant was ready, and she wanted to know, was Sarah working the Speedway hold-up or the body by the Rillito? Phyllis, like everybody in the system, got her jollies by being in the know about the stories behind the headlines. Sarah fed her a few details, as much as she could within the bounds of discretion, because Phyllis had made a big difference by getting out this warrant so fast.

As soon as she was off the phone she stepped over to the half-wall that separated her cubicle from Eisenstaat's. 'Am I talking,' she asked across the wall, 'to that dashing Harry Eisenstaat who's way past due for a breath of fresh air and would not mind driving to the courthouse to pick up a warrant at Judge Garrity's office?'

'Fresh air can wait.' Eisenstaat, the graying, cynical, self-appointed time-server of the section looked up from his keyboard, wearing the trademark sneer with which he fended off work while he waited for retirement. 'But dashing Harry would sure like to dash over to Starbuck's for a chocolate frappuccino. Hurry up with it, will you?'

'It's ready now. Get your frappo in a go-cup, will you? I need that warrant back here ASAP.'

'Sure, sure, sure.' He took his sweet time getting up, straightening his stiff knees. 'Relentless Ruthie's in a hurry, what else is new?' Somehow he'd learned that her middle name was Ruth, and begun using it to characterize her as a driven workaholic. Sarah smiled as if she thought he'd paid her a compliment as she grabbed her once-again ringing phone and said, 'Burke.'

A voice she didn't know said, 'This is Tony Delarosa. I'm downstairs. You got a dead man you think is Ace Perkins?'

'Yes. Wow, that was quick.'

'Dietz caught me in my car, a block away. This a good time to talk?' It wasn't, but he was here now, ready to do a favor. She told him how to find her.

In two minutes he was standing in the door of her cubicle, a square-jawed, ruddy man with dark eyes and black hair curled tight against his skull, his shoulders bulging against his shirt. *Weightlifter. Showboat. What else?* He said, 'You pretty sure about this?'

'We made him off his prints.' She showed him the records.

'Son of a gun.' He sat down and crossed his legs, put his blunt-fingered right hand on her desk and began tapping some brisk rhythm he seemed to hear in his head. All his movements had the heft and energy of over-abundant muscle. 'Where'd you find him?'

Sarah described the scene in Rillito Park, and asked him, 'Are you the one who sent him to Florence?'

'No. I busted him three months after he got out. Bought half an ounce of coke off him, slapped on the cuffs and asked him if he wanted to help himself. Had him on my team in half an hour. Ace was a pro, he knew the drill.' He had a way of nodding to himself between sentences, as if to endorse something he had just said.

'Ace was your snitch? Oh, well, then.' She smiled and he smiled back, a flashy, assertive man who appeared to get his share of the groceries, maybe a bit over, every day. The extra muscle must come from his efforts to work off some of the food, she thought. He seemed pleased about his bulk, though; he wore his clothes snug. 'So,' Sarah said, watching his face, 'you want to tell me who killed him?'

When he laughed, the dark eyes almost disappeared into the round pillows of his ruddy cheeks. 'Wouldn't it be wonderful if Narcs knew as much as people think? The truth is I'm really surprised to hear about this.'

'You are? I thought Narcs never got surprised.'

'Be nice, now.' A smaller smile this time, one quick gleam in his deeply tanned face. 'As far as I could tell, Ace was being very careful and playing strictly by the rules. I mean, you know ... street rules.'

'Uh-huh. Was he, um, an important player in the Tucson drug trade, reports of which we all agree are greatly exaggerated?' Sarah thought the way drug interdiction worked, or mostly didn't work, was crazy. But it wasn't on her worksheet and she had never been one to fight the system; she just threw a jab at it now and then to show she wasn't intimidated. *Which, when you come right down to it of course I am.* You didn't get ahead in the Tucson PD by dissing the drug war.

He gave her the standard heavy-lidded look she always got from Narcs when her question had been indiscreet. 'We're going to bust it wide open one day soon and then I'll answer all your questions.'

'I'll look forward to that. How was Ace doing for himself?'

'Very well.'

'And for you? Were you satisfied with the quality of his information?'

'Well, like the song says I was making a list and checking it twice. But it looked very good. I thought...' He sat up straighter and the tapping stopped. 'Now it looks like I better check my list again.'

'I see.' She watched him carefully while she asked the next question. 'You check off anything I might be able to use, will you be able to share?'

He looked friendly and candid as he said, 'Oh, if I get a lead on Ace's killer you can have it, Sarah, of course. Could I ask, is the body at the Forensic Sciences Center?'

'Yes. Why?'

'You mind if I take a look?'

'My pleasure – I'll set it up for you. An eyeball ID would be great right now. If you see anything that doesn't match with your memories, you'll call me?'

'Of course. The autopsy hasn't been done yet, has it?'

'Two o'clock tomorrow. You want to come?'

'I can't, I've got a – another thing. But I'll run by there and take a look right now, if that's OK.'

'I'll tell them to expect you.'

He started out, turned in the door and said, 'Sarah, can I just – say something? You could be looking for a very dangerous guy.'

'You think?'

'Well ... Ace Perkins was experienced and tough, he wouldn't go down easy.'

'I suppose that's true.'

'You want to be pretty careful how you—'

'Tony, I'm always careful.'

'I'm sure. Don't take offense. I just mean ... Ace Perkins was no pushover.'

'Understood.' She got up and walked around her desk to shake his square, meaty hand. 'I do thank you for taking the time to come by,' she said, and smiled up at him graciously, because you could never have too many friends in Narcotics. But now, why was he holding on to her hand? She met his eyes and realized that he was coming on to her, using a slightly more ham-handed version of the same move she had just used on Will Dietz. She squinted at him humorously while she pulled her hand away and said, 'Then again, you know, we could be looking for a mugger who doesn't even know he just killed a guy with connections.'

Tony Delarosa didn't like being turned off. His eyes turned flat and cold above a small, condescending smile. 'Oh, I seriously doubt that, Sarah,' he said. He put both hands in his pockets and stood there jingling his coins, considered a few seconds and gave another of his little self-endorsing nods. 'But if you do catch a guy like that, you know what you'll have?'

'What?'

'The luckiest dumb sonofabitch in the world.'

Seven

First thing to do after I get the car put away, Hector decided as he neared Exit 303, *is call Mama.* Tell her I got this chance to make a few dollars doing clean-up in a pecan grove in Benson, and I'll be home tomorrow, sometime late.

Hector was nineteen, still lived at home, paid his mother a little every week. Called her *Mamacita,* hugged her a lot and showed her his dimply smile – that shit-eating grin she called it, pretending she didn't like it, saying, Don't you come around me with that shit-eating grin – but it always worked. She was happy to cook all his favorite things, keep his room nice and give him his space.

He paid his two sisters in middle school a little something too, to do his laundry every Saturday like Mama showed them. Besides that he had two aunts in the neighborhood who doted on him, were glad to warm up a plate of beans and rice any time. Hector had things pretty much the way he wanted in his life except when the women started in on him about school, saying you should go back while you're still young, at least get your GED. School, shit. Equivalency degree, for what? Hector had a plan.

He had been working for Ace for almost four months, had a little over two thousand dollars saved, in fifties and hundreds in a tight roll saran-wrapped and taped to the bottom of a loose floor tile under his bed. Owned an '87 Subaru Brat with a dented hood, no air but it was paid for, had papers for it so he didn't have to worry like before when he was boosting cars. It looked about a hundred years old but the brakes were good and he kept it tuned. It took care of business for him now and would make the trip to Mexico when the time came if he couldn't trade up by then.

He still kept his stupid part-time job at the car wash that paid a couple bucks over minimum wage and they took out payroll taxes besides, *shee-it*. But it was good cover, kept his parole officer happy. He even bagged groceries sometimes at the Food City down the road, his mama and aunts saying, Good boy, works so hard. Since he did that stretch in juvie, his mama and aunts would do just about anything to help him stay straight. Funny how things worked out sometimes, ever since he served time they treated him sweeter than ever and with more respect – like he was a man now.

He understood of course that Ace had arranged to have him take most of the risks and do all the worst drudgery for a small cut of the money. That was what you had to put up with in the beginning, to get started.

Hector and his friend Miguel, when they talked about getting started, agreed they were lucky to live in Tucson.

'Always plenty of action here,' Miguel said. 'Been working a safe house for a *coyote* lately, you wouldn't believe how many people he's got crammed in there. All's I do is stand around with a gun under my jacket, three or four days whenever he needs me, and I make me some damn good money.'

'There you go. And any time crossers and dope get slow,' Hector said, 'you boost a car, it's only sixty miles to the border.'

'Fact. Anybody says he can't get started in Tucson gotta be a real *menso*.'

Privately Hector thought Miguel was welcome to those crazy *coyotes*, always ready to cut your throat any time they got spooked by the border patrol. Ace was scary but not crazy, and this fat deal they had going wasn't even hard work.

Some time on a weekday, ten a.m. Monday this week, Hector picked up the product, that's what Ace called it, at the auto repair shop or the back door of one of Rudy's bars. Went where he was told to go, stood in a corner with his mouth shut till Rudy or one of his goons put a package in his hands.

He tucked the package in the wheel well of his old red Subaru Brat and drove six miles or so northwest across town to the rancid single-wide Ace rented in a mobile home park in the Flowing Wells area. It was a last outpost for people who were not quite homeless yet, free-lancing whores without pimps who worked the corners on Euclid, and long-standing addicts who managed their habits well enough to work a few shifts a week. The small spaces between the plastic cribs were drifts of beer cans, dog shit, condoms and cigarette butts. Ace and Hector paid no attention to the filthy garbage underfoot or to the pleas and fights going on in the squats around them. They walked inside silently, Hector carrying the brown paper package, and locked the door.

Ace spread a clean sheet over the wobbly table, pulled the bag of white powder out of Hector's parcel, and divided the cocaine into two parts. Hector washed his enamel pot, mixed the coke Ace measured out for him with water and baking soda, and started it heating slowly on the stove. While the crack was cooking, Ace would tear off short lengths of waxed paper all over the table and divide the rest of the snow into precise little piles in the middle of each piece. Hector wrapped the little piles into twists of waxed paper, put the twists in gallon baggies and tucked the baggies in a Trader Joe's grocery sack, the sturdy paper model with handles. Ace liked everything neat.

As soon as the crack had floated to the top and the soda settled to the bottom, they would skim off the crack and lay it out on the table under a heat lamp. It didn't take long to finish off in Tucson, where the bone-dry air sucked the moisture out of everything. They would eat a snack, nap for an hour in plastic chaises under the rattling air conditioner, and then portion and wrap the crack.

By the time the shit was ready to go the sun had set, and thanks to Tucson's dark sky policy, which kept street lights scarce to accommodate the astronomers up on Kitt Peak, much of the city was as dark as the inside of a boot. It was a little unhandy for taxpayers trying to get home from a movie or the symphony, but a nice convenience for pushers.

They usually started in Mansfield Park, where the children of hard-up parents played on swings and softball diamonds in the day-time, and whores and pushers started work around sundown. If there was nobody there or too many dealers were there ahead of them, they'd try a corner up on Castro or go on to the motel strip out on Miracle Mile near the highway. Hector persuaded Ace to buy a little weed for the johns because some of them liked to loosen up with a toke first, save the hard stuff for later. Ace would say, Hell, weed's for sale in every other house south of Twenty-second Street, why fool with it? But Hector showed him he could get steady crack customers who'd come to him because he could be trusted to carry a little hemp along, and what did it hurt?

Ace would park in deep shadows nearby and protect his investment while Hector, his pockets full of waxy twists and change, sold the crack. Whenever he ran low he returned to the SUV for more, paying for it like a bar waitress dealing drinks as Ace counted out the packets. Ace kept his money in a plain white business-size envelope inside the Trader Joe's bag, all the bills turned the same way neat as a bank teller, never made a mistake making change.

If the corner they chose didn't produce in a few minutes he would hop back in the Ford and they'd move on; they didn't fool around. Hector trolled; Ace idled along behind. At eleven o'clock, or when the crack was gone, whichever came first, Hector walked back to the SUV and Ace moved once again to the passenger side. With Hector driving, Ace quietly speaking the next address each time he got back in the car, in a couple of hours they could deliver their snow orders to thirty to fifty regular customers scattered around the north and east side, some in very impressive houses.

Ace carried the money and the cocaine packets in the grocery sack, kept a Ruger 9mm tucked in the belted waistband of his walking shorts, under a loose shirt. He was a good-looking man, always neatly dressed in high-end sports clothes. Fussy about details; he kept a waterproof jacket in the bag in case of rain, carried along a bottle of Gatorade for if he got tired. To replace his electrolytes he said, whatever the fuck that meant. Hector thought it was a hoot to see this big badass drug dealer drinking Gatorade. But he had to admit, if you saw Ace get out of the big shiny car and walk toward the well-tended houses carrying his Trader Joe's bag, you would think he was a friend coming to visit with a couple of bottles of wine.

Much as he hated Ace, Hector knew they made a good team and it had been damn smart of Ace to figure it out. Hector fit into the twenty-buck crack peddling scene along Grant and Oracle, and Ace looked at home in the sleek cul-de-sacs up north and east. That was where he moved the orders that really put money in the sack, Ace coming back with fistfuls of hundreds for the orders he had pre-sold by phone during the day. Tucson wasn't the big city yet, offered nothing like the market up in Phoenix and Scottsdale, but then it didn't have the competition you had up there either. By being consistent and reliable Ace had just about doubled his business since Hector had worked for him. Hector knew stuff like that, he paid attention because he intended to get ahead.

When they finished the run Ace would slide a CD into the player, set the volume on low, ease his seat back a couple of notches and relax while Hector drove back to the motor home park. He liked seventies music, Rolling Stones and Beatles. Shit like that all sounded alike to Hector. When they got to the single-wide Ace would hand him two hundred-dollar bills and get out and walk around to the driver's side. Hector would get out without a word and walk through the drift of clanking beer cans underfoot to his own old

Brat, and drive back to his mother's house on Ohio Street.

He was no later getting home than many of his friends who had just been riding around picking fights and chasing pussy, and unlike them he kept quiet coming in and usually got to bed without waking anybody up. He slept late. His mama fed him breakfast when he got up, sighing over him as she had been doing since he was in seventh grade, already two years behind and a handful. She'd eased off on the sighing lately because she thought he was settling down. Which he was, in a way; he drank a few beers on his nights off, enjoyed a little Mexican Gold with his friends sometimes, but he kept his life quiet now, he didn't want anything to mess up his plan.

So, as he turned into his Aunt Lucia's driveway and saw her plump figure under the acacia tree, hanging out a load of laundry in her purple printed housedress, he fixed the shit-eating grin on his face and got his head set to do the standard Hector snow job. *Couple more days of this shit,* he promised himself, feeling satisfaction spread in his chest, *I'll be down in Mexico actin' as bad as I really am.*

Eight

'OK, I've got the warrant,' Sarah said when Jimmy walked back into his workspace. 'Ready to go? I'll call that apartment manager.'

'It's lunchtime,' Jimmy said. 'Aren't you hungry?'

'No,' she said, but when Jimmy raised his hands in prayer mode, she relented. 'OK, I could eat. Let's find a drive-in on the way and call the manager from there.' She was in her doorway, clipping the paddle holster for her sidearm on to the belt of her slacks. She disliked carrying openly but it was too hot to wear a jacket. 'You checked out? Where's your weapon?'

'Oh, good gracious, you think I need a firearm?' Clowning to cover his embarrassment about forgetting it, he laid the back of one hand over his upturned forehead. 'Great Scott, Holmes, you mean our lives will be in danger?'

'Quite possibly, Watson.' She watched him find his recorder, clip his Glock on his belt, find his little notebook in a pile of papers. *If I ever do get Delaney's job, I'm going to teach a class called Housekeeping for Hogs, and make all these bozos sit through it.* Nobody in Homicide was neat enough to suit her.

'I asked for back-up when we go in,' she told him. 'Chase said he'd try to have somebody meet us up there but they're very busy right now.'

'Ain't that a shocker? They're Tucson police, for chrissake, of course they're busy.' He was pulling on a jacket.

'You'll be hot,' Sarah said.

'You're right.' He took it off. 'Hell with it, let the gun hang out.'

Without any discussion, they took Sarah's car. Sarah always drove when she was the primary investigator on a case. It was one of several small moves an older woman on the force had steered her toward when she first earned the rating. 'Street patrol, you're on your own a lot,' she said, 'but in here you're working mostly with men and you have to hold up your end.'

'How do you keep your car so neat?' Ibarra said, getting in. 'Mine's got files and junk all over it.'

'It's just the way I am,' Sarah said. 'I can be in a room all day, and walk out and you'd never know I was there.'

'And you think that's good?' They stared at each other for a couple of seconds before they burst out laughing.

The Lumina was almost cool by the time they got to the drive-in. Jimmy Ibarra ordered a double bacon cheeseburger, curly fries and the biggest sloshing tubful of coke and ice they sold. Sarah watched him anxiously as he brought it all aboard, making small chuckling sounds, and began spreading salt with a lavish hand. 'What's junk about it?' he often asked defensively about his favorite menu. 'Fast food tastes great to me.'

Sarah got a fish sandwich, hold the mayo and tomatoes. It tasted like fried cardboard, but it didn't drip.

The apartment manager was waiting nervously outside the door of the three-story building off Granada. 'Stan Clark,' he said, shaking hands. He rolled his eyes downward toward their weapons. 'Are you expecting a fight?'

'You tell us,' Sarah said. 'What kind of a tenant was Adolph Perkins?'

'The kind you hope and pray for,' Clark said. 'Paid his rent on time, never made noise, kept his place clean.'

'How long's he been a tenant?'

'Since the first of April.'

'He live here alone?'

'Yes. Never had any company I saw. You saying somebody killed him? I can't *believe* it.' The neighbors were always astounded when there was violence. 'Such a nice quiet person,' they said. Sarah sometimes longed to point out that nobody lives near a guy who keeps making them think, I bet that sucker's a mass murderer.

'Honestly,' Stan Clark said, rolling his eyes up, 'Tucson's just getting awful, isn't it?'

'True,' Ibarra said. He had often told Sarah

how lucky he felt to live in this beautiful valley, how much he loved the way the desert smelled after rain and the way the light slanted across the mountains on winter afternoons. 'The reason the contractors can't build houses fast enough,' he told Clark now, 'is that we've ruined this place.'

'Ha ha, never thought of it that way.' Clark was looking at him anxiously, probably wondering why a detective, of all people, would be defensive about the crime rate in Tucson.

A squad car slid in beside the curb and a tall young officer got out and said, 'Hey, Sarah.'

'Hey, Fritz. This is probably nothing. We're just checking out a victim's apartment.' To Clark she said, 'Here's the search warrant. You want to open it or...?'

'No, you can do it,' Clark said quickly, holding out the key. 'Top of the stairs on your left there.' He dithered behind the three of them as they went up the stairs. Jimmy and Fritz drew their weapons as Sarah knocked on the door and called, 'Police!' She waited twenty seconds, knocked and called again, waited again, opened the door.

They all peered in at an immaculate empty hall. After a few seconds of silence the two men with guns sidled through the door with their backs to the wall, took two minutes to determine that all the rooms were empty, and came back out.

'OK, you can be on your way, Fritz,' Sarah said. 'Thanks.'

'Sure you don't want me to stick around? I

could check under the beds.'

'Tough shift, huh? How much time you got left?'

He shrugged. 'Two hours. Another ten or twenty calls. Then I gotta take my three-year-old for his shots. Now *that's* gonna be frightening.' He holstered his weapon and went back to his car to drive away.

'Let's see what we've got here. Don't touch anything,' Sarah said sharply, as Clark started toward the drapes with his hand out.

'All *right.*' He jerked his arm back, offended. 'I have to be here, though.'

'Fine. Good idea, watch everything we do. Did Perkins have a cleaning service?'

'It's not included with the rent but everybody in this building uses Spick and Span, they got a group rate. I'll give you their card before you go.'

'Fine. Utilities included?'

'No. All metered.'

'Good, a paper trail on everything,' she told Ibarra. Then she said to Clark, 'We'll give you a list of the items we remove.'

'Let's start in the bathroom,' Ibarra said. As they walked down the hall together he asked her, 'Does this place look like it was lived in by a drug dealer?'

'Hardly looks like it was lived in at all.'

The bedroom was sparsely furnished. There was a good light by one side of the bed, though, and two books stacked under the light: a thriller and a non-fiction book about Iraq, both from the Pima County Library.

The pusher read books? Maybe a habit picked up in prison. In the closet, shoes were lined up in a precise row along one wall, pants and shirts and a couple of jackets ranged above. It looked like an ad for closets.

In two hours they were loading Perkins' laptop and the contents of his desk into Sarah's back seat. Sarah gave her card to the manager as she fastened a crime scene lockbox on the door. 'I keep the key. This apartment's impounded till further notice.'

'How long...?'

'I can't say. It takes as long as it takes. You'll see various forensic scientists here, dusting for prints and collecting DNA and so on. They'll take some articles of clothing – they'll leave you a list of anything they take. They'll have the key and they won't need any help.'

'I really have to know—'

'Mr Clark, I know it's disturbing. We only do what we have to do. You have a deposit, don't you? Use that if you have to. By the way, did Perkins list his next of kin?'

'No. I said to him, "You must have somebody you'd want notified in case of emergency?" but he insisted, no, there wasn't anybody.'

'That's pretty unusual, isn't it?'

'Unheard of. Everybody's got somebody.'

'Well ... if you hear from anybody will you call me at this number, please?'

In the car headed back downtown, she asked Ibarra, 'Did you notice the man in the Escalade parked in the turnaround?'

'The one we passed on the way out, you mean? Uh ... not particularly. He wasn't parked, was he? I thought he was just leaving. What about him?'

'I don't know. His face didn't quite match the car, did it? Big beat-up looking guy, looked like a brawler. Elegant car.'

'Jesus, do we have to match our cars now? You can be very demanding, Sarah.'

'OK, forget it. What grabbed you about the apartment?'

'Just what we said at the beginning, too neat and clean. Not enough *stuff*. No pictures but those three stupid prints – I asked the manager and he said they came with the place. A few paperbacks, no music. The cheap TV goes with the rental. Three fishing magazines in a little row, like a dentist's office. Even the closet has too few clothes.'

'Yeah. Good clothes only – like what you'd take on a trip.'

'The refrigerator – six bottles of Gatorade and two of Bolla Soave.'

'Uh-huh.' Sarah squinted into the punishing afternoon sun, remembering. 'Trader Joe's wine, did you see the sacks in the cupboard?'

'Neatly folded and stacked just so. Must have got his Gouda there too, and his ship's biscuits. Nothing on hand for a real meal, though. Peanut butter and two apples.'

'Granola bars in the cupboard and a jar of instant coffee. I looked under the sink, it was as clean as the living room.'

'Unreal.' Ibarra was flipping through his notes. 'Either he's the most extreme neat freak I ever saw or he really lived somewhere else. How much do you bet there isn't a fingerprint in the place that isn't his or the cleaning crew's?' Sarah gave him an 'oops' look and he said, 'I'll do it,' and added 'cleaning crew prints' to their wants list.

'His bill file looks neat and complete, though,' Sarah said.

'Uh-huh. Like it's all ready for the auditors.'

'So where does a pusher go to turn in his scrupulous records?'

'Wouldn't we like to know that?' Ibarra scratched the side of his nose thoughtfully, staring west at the purpling slopes of the Tucson mountains. 'A systems obsessive pushing drugs on the street? The man's personality is all *mixed up*.'

Ibarra was fun to work with at the beginning of an investigation, when all the balls were up in the air. So long as alternative tales could be spun out of the early facts at hand he stayed fully engaged and happy. Wrap-up time, when the likely suspect had to be caged inside the available evidence, Ibarra's inner worry-wart surfaced and he went nuts re-checking his lists.

'We'll understand him better after we've been into his computer,' Sarah said. 'He never had a chance to delete anything.'

'How do you know?'

'Think about the crime scene – he wasn't expecting an attack, was he? Looks to me like he was taking care of business when some bozo jumped him with a knife.'

Ibarra rolled his large brown eyes toward the roof of the car and said, 'Nobody much stands around and lets it happen, do they?'

'I'm just saying we probably have a virgin computer here.'

'Oh sure, *now* you talk dirty, when we're almost back at work – what a tease.' He watched her maneuver into a cramped space beside the Stone Avenue station.

'Come on, you know what I'm saying, he never got a chance—'

'To dump any files. I know. But you have the autopsy tomorrow, right? And I have that goddamn report. Why don't you get Harry Eisenstaat to have a look at the computer?'

'That's what I'm thinking. Harry's fast and he notices all the whad-ya-call-it – anomalies and stuff.'

'And Delaney told him to lend us a hand if we needed it. Not that he gives a fiddler's fart what Delaney says.' He yawned. 'Man, it's a long day when you start before sun-up, huh?'

'Maybe your kids will let you sleep tonight.'

'Maybe I won't give 'em a choice.' He yawned three more times while they unloaded the car, which started Sarah doing it.

'Come on, cut it out,' she said, 'you're making me sleepy, and we've still got all this stuff to take in.'

'I'm gonna phone upstairs and get Harry to come down,' he said. 'Why should he sit on his ass while we sweat?' The thought of passing some of the pain around perked him up a little. But even though it was only two loads, he was wilted again, drenched with sweat by the time their boxes were piled by the freight elevator.

Eisenstaat stepped off when the doors opened, grumbling, 'My God, what did you do, bring the whole apartment? Don't we have work crews for this?' A lean, irascible man nearing retirement, he hated physical exertion of any kind. His long face grew mournful over the weight of his box; he began talking at once about suing the department if this donkey labor gave him a hernia.

'It's just one stinking box,' Sarah said, 'quit bitching, Harry. Any progress on Perkins' car?' She had asked him to call DMV.

'Of course. Where Eisenstaat goes there's always progress.' Eisenstaat preened over the top of his box. 'I already put out an APB. But can you believe it, Adult Probation can't locate his parole officer?'

'What are you saying, they've lost a parole officer?'

'Probably not, but they've lost the record. In their vast and no doubt scrupulously correct filing system, there is no record of a parole officer for Adolph Alvin, aka Ace.'

'Devastatingly weird. Well, it'll surface soon.' They reached their floor and began sliding cartons down the hall. 'Meantime, will you take that computer you're carrying into your workspace and pick its brains?'

'I suppose I can crowd it in. You want bank

accounts, customer lists, what else?'

'Well, let's see now,' Sarah said, pausing to wipe salty sweat out of her eyes. 'A pusher and a murder victim, I probably don't need his recipe for chicken soup.'

'Oh, my. You get mean after you've been out in the weather, don't you?'

'Hundred and three degrees on that asphalt, Harry. Don't mess with me.'

Sarah had once presented Eisenstaat with a T-shirt that read: 'I kvetch, therefore I am.' Burned out long ago by the explosive growth and relentless flow of illegal immigration always threatening to swamp the resources at Stone station, Harry Eisenstaat was just waiting to get his ticket punched. He actually complained at least fifty per cent more than the rest of them, which was really saying something, endless rants being the default response to their heavy workload.

Sarah was worried right now about what Delaney might be going to do to her career, but she had no complaints about the city she worked in. She saw Tucson as a revolving door filled with opportunity, a constant flow of needy people clawing their way up from the south, well-off seniors moving optimistically down from the north, and greedy hyenas waiting to pounce on any opportunities that surfaced in the dysfunctional interface between the two societies. A smart cop's dream city, in fact. And the door turned a little faster every year, pushed along by the drug trade, the engine with no off switch.

Nine

Rudy's tire store was a perfect place to hide an illegal business in plain sight. It had stood on the same block on Fourth Avenue for so long it had become part of the street, like the curbs and the bushes. People hardly saw it any more unless they were hunting cut-price tires.

Rudy's grandfather Raymundo started it with two partners in 1949, three Mexican–American vets using GI loans, all of them married and so poor it took everything they could scrape together to buy a few tires and rent the space. For the next dozen years, Raymundo busted his hump in the tire shop, his wife cleaned houses for the Anglos and raised a houseful of kids. Somehow they managed to save a little something every month, so when their oldest son Alberto turned sixteen they bought out the other two partners and put up the sign, *Ortiz and Son*, that still hung out front.

Alberto was not the great tire salesman his father was, but he followed orders and worked hard, so when he got a girl pregnant a few years later the family was able to set him up in the tiny house on Eighth Avenue where Rudy grew up. The store and both houses were in South Tucson, the square-mile city-within-a-city that was swallowed by urban growth during Rudy's childhood. It was almost downtown now and much smaller than the sprawl of houses below I-10 that the locals called south Tucson without the capital S.

Vanloads of illegal immigrants arrived in South Tucson every week. The ones that didn't get caught and sent back stayed till they got established and then usually moved on. But Rudy's family stayed in the barrio. In fact there had been Ortizes living in that part of the Tucson valley since the days of the first missionaries, his grandfather once told him proudly.

'How come we ain't big shots, then, like Ronstadts and them?' Rudy was young then and said whatever came into his head. His own grandchildren did the same thing now and he could hardly bear to listen to them. They made him realize how foolish he had been once, never considering the wonderful possibilities of silence.

That day when Rudy blabbed his first thought, Raymundo had been deeply offended. Turning to Alberto he said, 'Perhaps you could take the time to explain to your son how discouraging it is to work hard all these years, starting from nothing, and become the owner of a thriving business only to hear disrespect from one's own grandson.' He had never liked Rudy, who resembled his mother, the woman Raymundo still considered a slut for her moment of weakness in Alberto's arms. Raymundo didn't speak to Rudy again until the middle of the following year, when Alberto lay dying of cancer.

That day he sent Rudy's uncle Manuel to the house on Eighth Avenue, so crammed with Ortizes now that Rudy and his sisters never came home except to sleep. Standing in the doorway, looking guiltily out the window because he could not bear to see how Alberto lay suffering, Manuel told Rudy, 'He wants to talk to you.' Manuel was too cowed by his father to call him by name.

Rudy followed him back to Raymundo's house. Manuel stopped on the sidewalk by the front door, said, 'He's in the parlor,' and went on around to the kitchen door in the back to let himself in.

'*Bueno*,' Raymundo said when Rudy stood in front of him, 'Alberto has always been my right arm, my other sons are worthless. Now it must be you. I have never seen any sign of intelligence in you, but your mother and sisters have no one else, and your father insists that you can learn. So you will come to my shop tomorrow morning.'

Aside from the impossibility of arguing with his grandfather at such a time, Rudy was glad enough to drop out of tenth grade. Like most of the men in his family he could read and write adequately, and add and subtract rapidly in his head, and considered all other formal education a mysterious nuisance. He hated the thought of working for his overbearing grandfather, but promised himself it would not be for long.

Raymundo was astounded by how good Rudy turned out to be at the job. Rudy wasn't surprised at all; he had always known he was a born entrepreneur, quick to learn, tireless and shrewd in the pursuit of profit. His sisters and classmates were not surprised either. Rudy had always grabbed the extra dish of flan and hogged the ball.

By the end of the year, standing beside his grandfather at his father's funeral, Rudy had already figured out how to make a fortune in the tire business.

The first move was the hardest because Raymundo was a cautious man, and even Rudy's mother, whose resentment of the old man matched his contempt for her, would not listen to her son's plan to stage an open revolt.

'Your father loved him and made me promise to look after him,' she said. 'I would go to hell.' She crossed herself and added thoughtfully, 'But talk to the old bastard again, flatter him if you have to. It's a good idea.'

His grandfather did not dispute his suggestion that an auto repair shop would help the tire store and vice versa. But it was still too risky, he said, Rudy was too young. His attitude changed when Rudy said, of the man whose shop he wanted to buy, 'Cisneros says if you're not up to working full time any more maybe he'll buy you out and make me a partner, would you like that?' That was a lie; Cisneros had a bad heart and was only hanging on till he could sell, but Raymundo didn't find that out until later. When he did, he began to watch his grandson more carefully, pleased that his acquisitiveness had been passed along but wary of the extra edge of ruthlessness Rudy had shown him. He told his wife, 'Who would ever have expected Alberto to nurture a viper?'

Raymundo had great credit at the bank, so Rudy made the deal easily for less than the asking price. He might have haggled it lower but the purchase price, he knew, was almost irrelevant, because as soon as he was out from under his grandfather's eye in a separate store he began to set up the part of the deal he never told his mother about.

He started with small orders of marijuana that he could receive and dispense himself to a growing circle of friends. At first he sold only to people he knew well, but as soon as he saw the potential he began accepting referrals. He ran all the cash through the till, ringing it up as brake linings, motor tune-ups, lube jobs. That made it all taxable but he compensated with some very creative paid-outs, so that most of the extra cash ended up being just that, extra. By the time his grandfather was ready to retire, Rudy had paid off the second shop and was able to arrange a nice pension for the old man.

'*Mire*,' Raymundo said when they concluded the deal, 'for the record I am not such a fool as you think, I know you have not made all this money fixing old cars. You had better watch your back from now on, Señor Smart Pants, I will not be here to turn away questions.' They regarded each other coldly for a moment before Rudy nodded. Raymundo walked out of the store where he had spent his whole working life and never came near it again.

With access to both cash registers Rudy could handle more dope, so he hired a pusher named Brody, an outcast and bully from just outside the barrio who also helped fend off would-be competitors. Later the same year he hired Emilio Sanchez, an unassuming distant cousin who was happy to sell tires in the afternoon and dope in the evening. Emilio enjoyed both trades because they fed his real vocation, which was gossip. Gradually he sold less and less as he became, in effect, the company spy. Rudy loved getting these little extras from the two of them, but he tired of the constant arguments their odd working arrangements generated, so from then on he set up his drug traffickers as franchisees, who bought from him and sold on their own.

By the time his fourth child was born, Rudy was looking around for another business. And it had to be something bigger, because he was getting into the cocaine trade. He had hesitated a long time because it felt like roller-skating at the edge of a cliff; cocaine suppliers were stony-eyed killers who would cut off your head if they got angry. Some of them would do it for fun on the days they'd been using the product themselves. But weed was becoming so common that the price was coming down, there was less money in it every year. Profits in the cocaine business, on the other hand, were extraordinary; the prices people would pay for this crazy white powder were freaking unbelievable compared to what they'd give for something they really needed like a wheel alignment. As soon as he started dealing coke he saw that the biggest problem was going to be hiding the money.

He bought a restaurant and bar where he could launder a large volume of cash, and thought hard about the problems of dealing with cocaine suppliers. An important component of his success had always been his ability to accept the truth about himself, like the fact that although he was ruthless enough about manipulating people and cheating the government, he knew next to nothing about killing and was probably too old to learn. That was a problem because the men he was dealing with now were like jungle cats, they would pounce if they sensed any weakness.

He made inquiries and hired Tilly Stubbs, who had been in and out of the prison systems of several states since the age of fourteen. He was new to Tucson; Sanchez found him by following a rumor about a monstrous-looking thug who threw two men out of a bar on East Speedway. 'Two at once into the middle of the street during heavy traffic,'

Sanchez told Rudy. 'One of them with a broken jaw.'

'I don't need no crazy guys,' Rudy said.

'He ain't crazy. He was gone by the time the cops got there.'

'What was he fighting about?'

'They were making fun of his looks.'

'Oh? What about his looks?'

'Somebody beat him up a lot when he was a kid, I guess. His head's kinda funny-looking.'

Rudy met him in front of the Sears Store in the Tucson Mall. They walked through the aisles of jeans and bras, talking softly. For the job Rudy had in mind, Tilly's looks were perfect: a deeply dented forehead, a cauliflower ear and a nose that angled noticeably to the left. He had hands like anvils, too, and slabs of muscle across his chest and shoulders. He was ugly and thuggish but not stupid. Rudy offered a thousand a month more than he had intended, gave him cash in advance and a cell phone.

He was very glad to have Tilly along the day, a month later, when two hard-eyed couriers tried to take Rudy's money and skip the delivery. When he saw that Tilly had arranged to have the other two enforcers in port-a-potties near the park table where the delivery took place, he congratulated himself on hiring a planner. Brody knew a spot in the desert where a couple of bodies could be quickly buried, and Tilly brought back the heads of the hard-eyed men as Rudy had asked.

Rudy stuffed the correct payment in their open mouths, wrapped them in plastic so they wouldn't leak and Fed-Exed them to their employer with a note saying, 'Next time send the honest ones.' The note was in bad Spanish because Rudy couldn't ask his elders for help, but the dealer in Hermosillo got the message and Rudy had no more trouble with his shipments.

The day after he mailed the heads, Tilly asked for a sizeable raise in pay. Usually Rudy haggled tirelessly over raises, inserting so many new demands on the employee that he ended up almost even or sometimes a little ahead. But he was so pleased with Tilly's skill sets that he gave him his raise without argument.

Sanchez and Brody gained status from that day's work, too; Rudy began to treat them less like gofers and more like the full-fledged goons they were turning into. Each of the four had knowledge, now, that was worth a death sentence for the others, from either the government or the drug trade, depending. Bound together in a new, edgy equilibrium, they watched each other carefully, and before long Sanchez and Brody got raises, too.

But in spite of the added expenses, the money kept piling up; Rudy spent most of his time now moving cash around. Outwardly he remained a small dealer in car parts and food, but over the next couple of years he bought silent partnerships in another bar, two fast-food restaurants and a liquor store.

He made occasional mistakes, like buying a shop called Fancy Wheels, which he off-loaded again quickly when he found out it really did gross as much as the previous owner had claimed. The male youth of Tucson, it turned out, would scrimp on new clothes and even beer and weed in order to put useless flashy extras on their rides. Rudy couldn't insert much drug money into the remarkable cash flow at Fancy Wheels, nor at Candy, the lap-dancing bar downtown that was his other mistake.

Cash flow wasn't all he underestimated at Candy. Having been absorbed in the pursuit of money since puberty, he had no idea, until they were right under his nose, what an impact all those bare backsides would have on his libido.

'Might as well have some today,' his new partner said, seeing him looking. 'You ain't gonna be no younger tomorrow.'

Soon he had a girlfriend named Steffi and more expenses, but even so he was running out of places to hide the money till he found Pappy Grimes.

Actually Sanchez found him, following Rudy's precise instructions. 'I need me a big-time Anglo,' Rudy told him, 'somebody from downtown that's got a problem. I ain't too fussy what problem, except gambling or pussy'd be better than drugs or liquor. That way he's got his brain working when it ain't on that one stupid habit, you see what I'm saying?'

Sanchez passed a happy week sitting around bars downtown, trading obscene jokes and sordid conjecture with a parade of envious louts who had bar gossip instead of a life. He came back with the name of Sean 'Pappy' Grimes, an auto dealer with two big, glossy dealerships, one new and one used, on Auto Mall Road. An entrepreneur with plenty of public persona, who featured himself in his constant advertising, he was also a showy philanthropist whose name appeared often attached to innovative charities like dogs for blind kids and dream trips for terminal cancer patients.

What the advertising and self-promotion didn't say was that he had gambled his way to the brink of bankruptcy. He bet on all pro sports worldwide, played high-stakes poker locally at the Indian casinos and flew to Vegas once a month for long weekends. Shrewd in business, he was in deep denial about his lack of skill as a gambler, and the word on the street, frequently doubted but still persistent among barflies, was that his losses were threatening to destroy his prosperous and comfortable lifestyle.

'Beautiful,' Rudy said, when Sanchez came back with the story. He slid a couple of large bills into Sanchez's shirt pocket. 'Take the day off and get drunk, you did good.'

Grimes was such a perfect fit that Rudy suspected he must be a trap. He hired a private detective, who confirmed Sanchez's report that Pappy was mortgaged to the hilt and living on the float from his huge cash flow. 'But he's in trouble now,' the detective said, 'because electronic money transfers are making float go away.'

Rudy didn't want to talk in Pappy's office, so he made an appointment to discuss the purchase of a fleet of used cars for his crew and three of his nephews. He told Pappy's secretary, 'Tell your boss Mr Ortiz will only deal with the owner.'

Grimes had the usual cluster of short-term loans coming due. He had spent the last two days reviewing inventory on his used lot, marking cars that hadn't moved in sixty days, getting ready to send them to the auction block. But he was afraid the money wouldn't arrive soon enough to keep the banks off his back.

Grimes rarely did his own selling any more, but Rudy had made the deal sound fairly large, and Pappy's cash crunch was approaching the point of pain. So he chuckled and said, 'Well, criminy, I guess if the fella wants a little extra attention – what the hay, we can do that.' That was his style, folksy. He ran with high rollers but he had made a fortune by staying, as he often said, just as plain as an old shoe.

He peeked out into his waiting room when his secretary said Mr Ortiz was here, and saw Rudy out there in his black cowboy hat and dark glasses, black pants tucked into his gaudy boots. Grimes thought he was kind of a hoot, and that this transaction would make a good story for the golf course later. He came out of his office with his arms spread wide and his smile at full gleam, saying, 'Well, hey there, neighbor, how are things in South Tucson, by golly?'

They started their tour of the used car lot with Grimes' long left arm draped over Rudy's shoulder, his seersucker-jacketed right arm making generous sweeps around the glittering acre of rolling stock at his disposal. Rudy, watching behind his reflective lenses, decided this was the phony of his dreams, and went to work. They strolled and talked in the sunshine for an hour, paying less and less attention to the cars. By the time they came back inside, the checked sleeve of Rudy's western shirt was draped possessively around Pappy's neck. Pappy's shoulders had rounded somewhat, sweat was rolling off his chin on to his clean white shirtfront, and his condescending smile had faded. His freckled left ear was tucked under Rudy's big black Stetson, listening with rapt attention to every word of the shorter man's proposition.

Grimes had two huge lots that sold thousands of cars a year. Rudy's money-laundering capabilities took a quantum leap. For a while, he had much more capacity than he could use. Then he hired a couple of go-getters, pushers with previous experience in larger markets who for one reason or another wanted to live in Tucson now. Soon Pappy was transferring funds to offshore accounts in the Caymans, and Rudy, on one of his trips to the islands, found a vacation home Steffi agreed was just precious.

By the time he found Ace Perkins, he was set up to make the most of an enterprising dealer, and Ace did not disappoint. Sitting in the old tire store on Fourth Avenue, Rudy watched his wealth begin to grow like prickly pear cactus in a wet year.

He still didn't let it show. His family lived comfortably but quietly in a solid home in South Tucson and drove ordinary cars; his children went to trade school or Pima College and became plumbers and medical technicians. But the money was piling up in the Caymans and one of these days he was going to disappear like a Mexican ex-president, tucked away safe in a country that couldn't afford to turn him down. All he had to do was hold everything together for a couple more years and he'd be set for the fat life forever.

Tilly called late Tuesday afternoon. He never identified himself on the phone, just said, 'I'm down by Food City,' and hung up without waiting for an answer. They met in the parking lot and sat in Tilly's car because his air worked better.

'Ace wasn't at the Congress Hotel for lunch,' Tilly said. 'I checked the gym where he usually works out, he hasn't been there today. Sent Brody to his apartment, he called and said there's cops in there. I went up there and watched for a while.' Tilly rubbed his cheeks, which were hot and irritated from too much time in the sun. 'They were detectives, a good-looking woman and a man. I still can't believe women cops, can you? I mean, what a crazy idea.'

'Fix the police department some other day. What else?'

'Just what you'd expect. About an hour ago they started carrying stuff out of there. They made several trips, took boxes of records and so on, and a laptop. The broad carried her share, I'll give her that.' What he didn't tell Rudy was that she had looked straight at him as she drove away, in a way no woman had ever looked at him before – not provocative, more like she was measuring him for a suit. 'Now there's a lockbox on the door and a sign says it's a crime scene.'

'OK. I called my *boca*.' That was the name he used – mouth – for his man inside the police station. Only Rudy knew who he was. The deal was, call from a pay phone, and never say his name any other time. 'I left a message two hours ago. Haven't heard back yet. He has to get to an outside phone alone. What about that kid Ace's been working with, what's his name?'

'Hector. Sanchez went to his house. His mother hasn't seen him. I'm asking around.'

'Gotta find him.' Rudy frowned thoughtfully at the grackles strutting around the crumbs in the parking lot. 'I got till next Monday with suppliers. But dealers, I'll have to start warning them tomorrow if there's something...' He tapped his upper lip a couple of times with his right index finger. After he thought a while he put his hand back on the dashboard and nodded. 'If the cops are in Ace's apartment it means they got him, in jail or in the morgue. I need to know which it is. If he's dead they might not know what they got.'

Ten

'All that fancy work you did with the fingerprints,' Greenberg asked, getting ready to start the autopsy, 'you prove anything with that?' In his voluminous plastic robe and cap, with his shiny lab tools around him, he looked more like a doctor and less like an action figure that's been wound too tight.

'Yeah, we ID'd him off his prints like I was hoping. He just got out of Florence last winter, three-to-ten for trafficking.'

'That so? Well hey, mark up extra points for Sarah, huh? Anybody keeping track of those?'

'What, my extra points? Not likely. Right now I'd be happy just to see a match to that fingerprint Gloria lifted off this victim's leg.'

'That would really turn you on, huh?'

'Well yes, it would be way beyond cool to have the high-tech stuff work the way it's supposed to, for once.'

'You know what would be cooler than that?' He treated her to an evil, sneaky smile. 'If you just left the guy who killed this pusher alone.'

Sarah laughed. 'You want me to let a murderer go?'

'Why not? Stall for time till he gets away. He did us all a favor.'

'Ssss.' Sarah hissed through her teeth. 'Rotten attitude.'

'Just common sense. These outlaws want to kill each other off, I say hand 'em the weapons and get out of the way.'

'Uh-huh.' Sarah pulled on gloves. 'You're the one was telling me yesterday this killer was such a dangerous man, right? You said, "You've got to be bold to cut a man this way."'

'Oh, you got me now, girl, I love being quoted.'

'Bet you do. Delarosa agrees with you, by the way. He said I should be careful because I'm looking for a dangerous man.'

'Who's Delarosa?'

'Didn't he have to ask you to view the body?'

'Oh, that curly-haired Narc that was here yesterday?'

'Uh-huh. This victim was his snitch.'

'Now, see, a pusher *and* a snitch. Good riddance, I say.'

'Nevertheless...' Sarah was brooding over the con with the improbably noble face. 'I'd sure like to get his killer off the street.'

'There'll just be another one to take his

place. You don't expect to make a difference, do you? Come *on* – I haven't puked since my first year in medical school.'

'You're feeling extra hard-nosed today, aren't you?'

'Just about average. You ready to start?' He stepped up to the table, carrying scissors. She hurried to grab an evidence bag and help him cut off the blood-soaked garments.

'Well, you called it about the artery,' she said, three hours later. 'That's what killed him, right?'

'In about a New York minute. He was in excellent health till it happened, too. I rarely see a heart and liver this good.'

'All buffed up on the outside, too. A hunk, really, except for the tats and some scars. Well, and broken fingers.'

'But no needle marks. His arms say he wasn't shooting anything and his nose says he wasn't snorting anything. And I can't prove it till the tox screens come back, but looking at his liver and kidneys I'll bet you twenty right now he wasn't ingesting anything much stronger than an occasional beer.'

'Why would I bet against you?' Sarah flexed her back, which hurt from standing so long. 'A clean-living drug dealer, go figure. A neat freak, too, by the way. Those scars on his chest, though, you think they're burns?'

'From a cigarette, probably.'

'And his hands ... what did we see on the X-rays, three fingers broken?'

'Four.'

'Plus marks on his back that could be from a whipping. Or more than one?'

'Probably two. Some of the scars don't quite match.'

'So, torture.'

'I'd sure call it that if it was happening to me.'

'And all the marks are old?'

'Old enough so they're completely healed over.'

'But are we talking years or decades?'

Greenberg shrugged. 'Two or three years to whenever. It could date back to adolescence, but I'm betting not childhood. He's a big strong man, all his muscles well developed. Abused children don't usually grow the way they should.'

'So this could have happened in prison?'

'Anywhere. In a police station, for instance.' He cocked an ironic eye at her. 'You using much torture in interrogations these days?'

'No, and I don't know anybody who does if that's your next question. OK if I send Detective Ibarra over to look at these scars?'

'Sure, fine. That other guy you sent over, what's his problem?'

She cleared her throat. 'Delarosa? Why do you ask?'

'Got a mean streak, if you ask me. You think maybe he's dipping his nose in that white stuff himself?'

Sarah laughed. 'He's nobody's huggy-bear, but no, he's not a user, he's a Narc.'

'Who says you can't be both? Never mind,' Greenberg said, holding up one long-fingered hand in a peace gesture, 'I mostly see cadavers, what do I know?'

'Too much, is my guess.' She looked around, thinking. 'Let's see, what else?'

'Well, if you've got your ID on this victim, you're not in any hurry on the DNA, right?'

'No, DNA can take its own sweet time, I guess.'

'And boy will it ever. Be a couple of weeks for my reports, too – I'm snowed right now.'

'Everybody is. I'll try not to harass you.'

'That'll be a switch.' He was already looking at his watch.

'Pleasure to work with you, Doctor,' Sarah said, zipping her briefcase, 'when I can stand the pace.'

'Likewise,' Greenberg said, absent-mindedly. Sarah thought he was already calculating the time to his next task.

One thing about working with Animal, she reflected as she walked out, it makes everybody else seem easy-going for a while. *I wonder what Delarosa did to make him think … probably that tapping thing. Narcotics must be a bitch.*

She hadn't known how stiff she was till she started the long walk along the cold tiled hallway. At the door she took a deep breath before she stepped out on to the asphalt parking lot. The change to the oven temperature of afternoon felt shocking, even dangerous for the first minute. Heat waves rising from the desert floor turned into dust devils that whirled across the horizon, throwing off stinging pellets of sand. She left her car door open while she started the motor, to let the fan blow some of the hot air out. Heading home, she kept all the vents aimed at her face, blowing her hair back. The intense hours of concentration, standing in a cold room by a tall steel table, had tired her, and now the sudden heat drained the little energy she had left. She longed to take her shoes off in her small, orderly house, eat a quiet meal and go early to bed.

Mid-town was filled curb-to-curb with rush-hour traffic. Sarah, fretting through two rotations at a light on Oracle, looked north to where the late afternoon sun slanted across Mount Lemmon, making it glow like some improbable pink jewel. She took a deep breath and told herself to relax. *The first day of autumn light. Beautiful.* The mountain turned lavender as she headed home on Grant. By the time she walked into her house, it was purple with slate shadows in the canyons.

Getting out the lettuce for a salad, pouring a glass of wine, she hummed a contented scrap of an old song. The phone rang. She looked at the number calling, picked it up and said, 'Hi, Mom.'

'You always spook me when you do that,' her mother said. 'Why do you want to know who's calling before you even answer the phone? I don't get that.'

You don't get why a police detective in a major city might want to know who's calling before she answers the phone? Or maybe you just feel like arguing tonight. Her mother had about as many anxieties as the average widow in her seventies, and there was no use letting her wine get warm while they bickered over any of them. She kicked the refrigerator door closed, sat down on the stool and said, 'It's just handy sometimes. How are you tonight?'

'I'm fine. I just got back from bocce and I've got to hurry up with supper because it's my bridge night.' Retired from ranching, Aggie Decker had moved to a senior citizens' community west of town and discovered games. 'But I thought I'd just check up on you first – are you behaving yourself?' The wink-wink question betrayed growing anxiety about what she saw as her elder daughter's monkish existence since her divorce. Aggie wanted to hear about a little hell-raising so she'd know the wounds inflicted by 'that cheating wretch', Andy Burke, had begun to heal.

Sarah had several times resolved to make up a few credible lies about high times in the Old Pueblo, but her imagination boggled when she thought about it so she put it off. Maybe she'd have verifiable dates to report on soon; she had been ready to start for a while but all the men who had laid the moves on her since her divorce had been married. To change her mother's drift she said, 'How's Sam?'

'He's fine. He went "geocaching" all morning and played five games of Spider this afternoon. I believe he's beginning to see life as one big puzzle.'

'Well, you know what? Tell him I think he may be right.'

'I won't. Don't encourage him. I want him to get away from that computer and take me ballroom dancing.'

'Are you serious?'

'Absolutely. There's a great group here and I could join it if I had a partner.'

'I don't remember ever seeing you dance with Dad.'

'We never did. We worked too hard all day to dance at night. So I should do it now.'

'What does Sam say?'

'Oh, you know Stonewall Sam. He says, "Better still, why don't you get me some toe slippers and a tutu, and we'll take ballet lessons?" '

'Oh, I love it! Let's make it pink!' Sarah seized delightedly on the image of her mother's boyfriend, thick-fingered, wattled and grizzled, in a tutu. Aggie's third boyfriend since she moved to town, he seemed to be lasting better than the first two, who dumped her after she turned down their proposals. 'I don't need the sex anymore,' she said, 'so why do the laundry?'

Now she had finished with the dancing jokes and was ready to get down to the real business of her call, the Big Worry. 'Honey, have you talked to Janine lately?'

'Um ... not for a couple of days.' *Not for two*

weeks, actually. Since the last time she threw dishes at my head. That answer would delay dinner for everybody, and she was too tired for family drama tonight. So she said quickly, 'I was thinking I'd call tonight, maybe ask Denny over for the weekend. Have you seen her lately?' She passed the ball back to her mother's court.

'For a minute last week. She was doing her homework.'

'Good. How's she doing in school, did she say?'

'Denny's fine. She was born fine, luckily. The question is, how's her mother?'

Sarah got up with the phone cupped in her shoulder and began pulling salad dressing, onions, peppers and shredded cheese out of the refrigerator. She was not that hungry but she wanted a distraction from the anger she felt bubbling up. *All I want is a little peace and quiet, do we have to talk about this every time?*

'I'm sure Janine's drinking again,' her mother said, 'and I think she's using too.'

'What makes you think that?' Stalling.

'I was over there on Friday and she acted really odd. The most infuriating thing is that she always imagines she can hide it from me. She strikes these elaborate poses about being terribly busy – getting ready to go to work in that bar with her lipstick on crooked. "Gotta go, Mom," so she won't have to talk to me. It's so demeaning to be lied to that way...'

Sarah set food down on the counter and closed her eyes. How many times had they said these things?

'So I always go along, like a fool, pretending I don't notice as long as I can stand it. Why do I do that?'

'Because she scares you.'

'And because I never know what I *could* say that might get her stopped. Is there any right thing to say?'

'Probably not. Where was Denny?'

'In her room, surrounded by books. I tried to get her to come out with me for a while but she said she had homework. On a Friday? That's the other thing that's giving me a rash, is that now Denny doesn't want to talk to me either. What's that all about, do you know?'

'She's stand-offish with me, too. I think she's afraid if we blow the whistle on Janine she'll have to go back out to the ranch and live with Howard and Jane again.'

'So? What's so bad about that? A nice house in the country and good meals.'

'Come on, Mom. You know very well Jane and the kids treat her like dirt.'

'They don't. What a thing to say. Howard's girls aren't bright and clever like Denny and maybe Jane doesn't enjoy the contrast too much—'

'Maybe if you didn't rub their noses in it quite so often.'

'Oh, now it's all my fault. You're on a rampage this afternoon, aren't you? What's the matter, did you have a bad day?'

'Long. Started with a homicide at five in the morning.'

'That job of yours, how do you stand it? Oh, well, I mustn't start that again. Sam said if I don't stop agonizing over your job and Janine's lifestyle he's going to find a new birding partner.'

'That's just a bluff. Where would he find another lady who can spell phainopepla and pyrrhuloxia?'

Aggie giggled. 'You're right, he's lucky to have me. Listen...' Sarah heard her mother take a deep breath. 'Can we just agree on what kind of a ... benchmark we're looking for here? When are we going to say that's it, we can't wait any longer?'

Why don't you ask your son, the rancher? Or Janine's counselor? Why do I have to decide? But Sarah knew how adroitly the paid professionals who counseled addicts for the county passed the buck back to the family. *You're the best judge of that, of course* ... Decisions about Janine always came back to Sarah and her mother, with maybe a furtive boost from brother Howard when his wife would let him open his mouth.

There now, I guess I insulted everybody enough for one day. Aloud she said,

'Mom, you know we can't get ahead of it. Something will happen – she'll disappear for two days or smash up the car – and then we'll decide something.' She made a face at the refrigerator. 'I've been hoping she'd put it off a while.'

'God, you make us all sound crazy.'

'Well, we're not exactly sane, are we?

Addicts' families never are.'

'Sarah, you don't think Janine would hurt Denny, do you?'

'No, she dotes on Denny like we all do. It's just ... when she gets into the beer and the pot she neglects her sometimes. I'll try to get Denny over here for a weekend, give her some help with her clothes. She's looking kind of tacky.'

'That sounds good. And she knows your number, right? She can call if—'

'Absolutely. While she was staying with me last fall, I typed my phone numbers and my email address on a card and framed it for her desk. I gave it to her that last day, just before I took her to Janine's house, and I made her promise she'd call me if she ever needed anything.'

'And you think she'd do it?'

'Of course she would, why not? Denny knows how much I love her.'

Eleven

When Denny got home from school Wednesday afternoon there was a loud-talking man with yellow teeth in the kitchen with Mom. Denny wanted a glass of milk to go with the cookie she'd brought from school, but the man gave her a funny crooked smile and said to Mom, 'Well, hey, you got yourself a real little honey here, haven't you?' He reached for her, saying, 'How about a hug, Honey?' but he was kind of sprawled in his chair, and his hand–eye co-ordination wasn't all it might have been after several hits on the bong. Denny slipped past him and got into her room, closed the door quickly and wedged a chair under the handle.

She could hear him through the door, growling, 'Well, shit, what's she being so snotty for? I's just being friendly.'

Mom said, 'Oh, she's just shy. Forget it! Let's have another beer.' The flip-tops popped, the lighter wheel grated against the flint. In a minute a fresh haze of cannabis wafted under the door, and they were laughing again.

Denny did the first half of her social studies workbook, all but the essay questions. She liked to take her time with them and get the sentences just right, and the increasingly giddy laughter in the next room made it hard to concentrate. She decided to save the essay questions for last. Maybe the man would leave.

She started on math, and stuck with it as their talk got quieter, turning gradually into whispers and giggling. They made a couple of groaning noises, a chair scraped back, and they moved into Mom's bedroom. Denny turned her radio on, turned it up as the sounds of their pleasure grew louder, and finally found a rock station that all but drowned them out. Even so, she got so angry she stared at the same math problem for several minutes, unable to think about anything but how much she hated this rottenly stupid F-minus day.

Finally the noises ended in more giggling and then silence. She turned the radio down and went on to the next math problem, and the next. She was getting hungry, trying to decide if she wanted to risk going into the kitchen for some food, when she heard Mom say something softly about cigarettes, and ask for money. Denny heard padding footsteps and some throat-clearing and then a quiet tap on the door.

Mom said, 'Denny?' and the doorknob turned. She knocked again and said, 'Honey, are you all right?'

Denny got up, moved the chair two inches, put her face in the opening and said, 'I'm hungry.'

'Oh, well, I'm just going to run to the store. I'll get you some – what would you like? Hot dogs?'

'Is he gone?'

'Who? Oh – no, he's, um, he's sleeping.'

'I'm not staying here alone with that creep.'

'Oh, Honey, now – well, all right, come along.'

'I haven't finished my homework.'

'I'm just going over to Fry's, it'll only take a minute. Do you always have to argue? Come on.'

Denny followed her through the kitchen,

watching back over her shoulder for the big smelly man, and ran and jumped in the back seat where the belt was adjusted to fit her. She tried not to watch Mom's driving, but at the corner she couldn't resist looking and said, 'Look out for the pickup, it's turning—'

'I see it! Will you give me a break, Miss Busybody?' Mom gunned the motor to get ahead of the truck and Denny heard a screech of brakes, looked back and saw a man sitting in his pickup with his hands in the air in an attitude of angry disbelief.

After that she concentrated on the toes of her shoes and whispered one of the prayers Grandma Aggie had taught her years ago, 'Hail, Mary, full of grace...' Not that she expected any help from heaven. She figured if there'd been anybody up there assigned to her case he'd already had plenty of chances to show up and be useful. But the familiar words of the prayer brought back the comfort of Grandma Aggie's lap, years ago when she was little, and that helped her be quiet.

The big parking lot in front of Fry's was crowded. Mom started saying right away, 'Oh, now look at this mess, oh, there's one – no, there's a stupid motorcycle in there, why can't they park those things on the sidewalk?' She always got very sorry for herself in parking lots, taking it personally when she couldn't find a place near the store. Besides, Denny could see, she was anxious to get the beer and cigarettes and get back to the smelly man before he got angry. In a few minutes she said, 'Listen, I'm just going to pull into this handicapped space here, nobody'll know the difference.'

'You can't do that, you'll get another ticket.'

'I never got a ticket for parking in a handicapped zone, what are you talking about?'

'No, that's right, your tickets are all for speeding, aren't they?' Denny was hungry and mad and wanted to pass some of the pain around. 'Go *on*, Mom, you can't park here!'

'I'll only be gone two blinks, and look, I'll leave the motor on so you can have the AC. You stay in the car and I'll be right back, OK?' And she was gone.

Denny watched tired, hungry-looking people hurrying in and out of the store, pulling sullen children along, pushing others in strollers. Before long they all looked alike, and she was tired and beginning to be very hungry. The air conditioner was set too low, and being hungry made her colder. She found an old pillowcase behind the seat and wrapped it around her legs. Then she unbuckled her seat belt and lay down on the seat, pulled the neck of her T-shirt up over her head and slipped her arms inside too so her breath would warm her up.

Inside, in the gloomy half-light, she imagined she was a dog named Granite in a book she loved called *Child of the Wolves*. In the far north woods of Alaska, following a caribou herd, she ran with the wolf pack until she fell asleep.

Twelve

Driving back from Benson with the setting sun in his eyes, Hector smiled at the memory of the things Aunt Lucia said to his mother on the phone while he stood waiting to talk. 'Listen here, Carmencita, what you been feeding this boy of yours? Ooohh, my gosh, he's gettin' so tall and macho, I have to lock the door to keep the girls out now when he comes around.'

She kept on flirting around him like that while she fixed his *huevos rancheros* and beans. Of course he knew she was just trying to keep him there until she found out why he was out of Tucson and which way he was headed. All his aunts were helping Mama keep an eye on him, he knew that. So as soon as he got in the house he asked to use her phone to call home. Called Mama, said hi like there was no big deal, said he got a chance for some extra work over here and did she want to talk to Aunt Lucia now? No use getting Mama and the aunts all stirred up, plenty of noise in the world without that.

When he finished eating he asked Lucia if he could put the SUV in her shed out back. They had to move out a couple of old tables she was refinishing, and some strings of peppers. She didn't mind the bother but he thought she only half believed his story about doing a little detail work with a friend. He locked the Trader Joe's bag in the jack compartment of the Ford and asked his aunt could he sleep awhile.

'Ooohhh, you bad boy, you been out tom-cattin' all night, huh?' Giggling, she started up the old swamp cooler in the little room where her son stayed when he was in town, and the hum was perfect. Hector slept till she woke him, as he had asked, at three o'clock. He phoned Julio Mendoza, made a deal for him to bring over a set of plates after work. Drank a couple of beers and had a snack while he waited, called to check on his fake ID every half hour but Estes never answered. Julio brought a joint along to smoke while they changed the plates, so they took their time, didn't finish till after ten. By then Lucia was dozing in front of the late news, said sure he could stay over.

Estes finally answered around nine the next morning. Hector gave him the name and numbers he wanted and he said, 'OK, this won't take long, I'll have it ready tonight.'

'Can't I get it any sooner? Like to leave this afternoon.'

'Nah, it takes a while to dry. Late after-noon's the best I can do.'

Something in his voice made Hector think Estes probably hadn't done any work at all on his passport and visa, might be just starting on them now. But he had already paid eight hundred dollars, half the price, and this was no time to start looking for another guy who made counterfeit records. So he just said, 'Fine, then, five o'clock?'

'Gotta pick up my kid at five. Make it six, six thirty. Well, listen, I might have to stop for groceries, make it seven.'

Gritting his teeth against anger, Hector agreed to seven, but added, 'But I'm gonna be in a big hurry by then, so be sure you're ready, know what I'm sayin'?'

'Yeah, Hector,' Estes said sarcastically, 'that doesn't seem complicated, I believe I follow that all right.' He hung up before Hector could tell him where he could put that shit.

So then he was left to wonder, *Is that little prick gonna skip with my money and leave me with nothing?* It didn't figure, though. Estes had lived in that same house with a wife and two sons for four years that Hector knew about, done jobs for two of Hector's cousins. He had a part-time job as a graphic artist downtown somewhere and hung some freelance art in galleries around town. Why would he skip today? He was probably just feeling mean from the heat. Anglos got like that.

But the little stab of uncertainty came and went, making it all the harder to kid with Aunt Lucia as he helped her change the sheets on his bed, and replace the furniture and peppers in the shed after he got Ace's car out. They played some Hearts to pass the time, he managed a few lame jokes and hugged her hard the way she liked when he thanked her and said goodbye. She'd be on the phone with Mama as soon as he drove out of the yard, and he didn't want a lot of questions waiting when he got to his house. Get in, get the money and a few clothes and get out, that was his plan. He'd thought about telling Mama on the phone that he was going to drive down to Mexico for a week or two. Maybe he'd make up an invitation from a friend. But the thought of all her questions on top of everything else he had on his mind was just too exhausting. He decided to wait and spring it on her as he was leaving the house. Hop in the car quick and be gone before half those questions even got out of her mouth.

Sometimes lately he had begun to see that it wasn't all a plus, having all these devoted women in his life, talking sweet and cooking for him. Damn, you could send your laundry out, you know? And not be so obligated. Here he was trying to learn to be a tough guy, doing all right too, he'd just killed a man and got away with it, and still he had to worry about upsetting his mama? It was crazy, he'd be a lot better off when he was out on his own.

When he thought how close he was to that, to getting started in the drug business in Mexico and holding his own among other hard men, driving around like a big shot in Ace's flashy car, every mile he drove he felt better. *One of these days I'll come back to Tucson and be bigger than Rudy Ortiz.*

Signs for RV parks and casino gambling began to flash by and he was starting to see the big jets slanting in toward the airport up ahead, when in the rear-view mirror he noticed a Pima County sheriff's car behind him. He was staying two miles over the speed limit, no trouble there. The plates had been changed, there was no way anybody ... He watched for a couple of miles and the sheriff's car just hung back there. *What the fuck?* He broke a sweat and felt his heart knocking against his ribs.

He had intended to go home and pack before he went after his papers, but at Exit 270 he made a sudden decision and pulled off the highway on to Kolb Road. *Might as well find out right now if he's following me.* He drove north watching the rear-view mirror, but he never saw the sheriff's car again. The shock of feeling he was being watched had rocked him, though, so now he felt like a huge target in the big glossy SUV. He pulled into Fry's, drove through the swarm of cars in the lot till he got around in back by the delivery bays, and parked against the building out of sight of the street.

Sitting there with the air still blowing on him, he started to think about the fact that while the SUV was perfect for a trip to Mexico, in Tucson it was a risky vehicle for him to be driving. The new plates might keep the cops off his tail, but Ortiz and all the people who worked for him must be looking for Ace by now. And if one of them saw a dark blue Ford Excursion they weren't going to be looking at any license plates, they'd be looking at the driver. If Ortiz saw him in Ace's car ... He started to sweat again.

The thing to do, he decided quickly, was lock up this car and leave it here, up against the building where there was a good chance it would be overlooked for a couple of hours. Go out front, find an older car that would be easy to break into. He had his old ring of ignition keys with him, most of them would still work – he hadn't boosted a car in a while but he still knew how to do all but the newest models.

Sure. Didn't have to be anything fancy, just so it would run for a couple of hours. When he was done running his errands he'd come back and trade cars again and take off for Mexico. Whatever vehicle he grabbed, he could have it back here while the cops were still filling out the paperwork. Park it in a different part of the lot, they'd find it eventually and everybody would figure it was kids joyriding. OK, a plan! He grabbed the Trader Joe's bag out of the back and locked up.

He meant to start looking at the cars farthest from the store, where there were fewer people around. But as he passed the handicapped parking spaces up front, out of habit he scanned the door locks and saw this old Dodge Dart, sitting right there unlocked, with the keys dangling in the ignition.

He looked around quickly. It felt like a trap.

But there was nobody nearby, and nothing in the back seat but a pile of old clothes. He was in the driver's seat putting it in gear in two seconds.

He pulled on to Kolb road and headed south, going with the flow of traffic and looking for his first chance to make a U-turn and come back up to Princeton Road where Estes lived. But traffic was heavy and fast, and in a minute he decided it would be better to turn right on Stella and circle back to Golf Links where he could get the light and get back on Kolb going north. He put on his turn signal, sped up and tried to fake out the Camarro on his right to get into the turn lane. But the bastard leaned on his horn and shot past Hector's front bumper with inches to spare. Hector hit the brakes and cursed.

In the back seat, a small figure sat up suddenly and said, 'What happened?'

Hector's heart hit his ribs again. A person? He had only seen a pile of rags. Now a small scared face was watching him, cars were blowing their horns all around and he couldn't think. And the light was fading so he couldn't tell for sure if it was a boy or girl asking, 'Where's Mom?'

Thirteen

Janine came out of the store carrying two heavy bags, glad to know she'd left the car right next to the doors. The sun had gone down while she was in the store but heat was still buckling the asphalt in the parking lot. The contrast with the bone-chilling cold inside the store was disorienting; she felt like a time-traveler zapping between widely separated climates. Besides, she was still a little foggy from several beers and a number of long drags on a bong. So when her car wasn't right there where she knew it should be, she stopped and looked around, wondering, *What, did I come out the wrong door?*

She remembered Denny getting snippy about being left in the handicapped zone, and this was it, right here, wasn't it? With the painted white stripes, by the stacks of plastic lawn chairs? Maybe there were two stacks. She walked all the way around the front of the store, looking for another entrance with a handicapped zone and two stacks of lawn chairs with pukey green plastic strips.

Once she thought she saw her car just ahead, although there weren't any chairs near it, but maybe she remembered those from some other time. She almost ran toward the old brown car in spite of the heavy sacks, but when she got closer she saw it wasn't hers. Wasn't even a Dodge, just a tacky old Plymouth Valiant that was that same clunky shape, and brown like hers. Shit brindle, one of her boyfriends called it. Honestly, all those expensive designers in Detroit and between them they couldn't dream up any color in 1976 but dweeby fucking *brown*?

Her arms were very tired by then, the bags kept slipping and she had to stop and boost them up again, she should have brought a cart. But she was trying to hurry because the man who'd grudgingly given her the money for beer and cigs had said, 'Hurry up now, hear? I'll freak if I'm out of smokes very long.' And she certainly didn't want him freaked, she needed him nice and relaxed and still in bed so she could get the wieners and beans and milk unloaded for Denny before he saw the bags. Then she'd give him a big wet kiss with the change and maybe he wouldn't think about how much the beer cost.

By then she'd been all the way around the store twice in the heat, her clothes were sticking to her and sweat was running down her legs. She was just so frantic, running around this hateful store looking for a stupid old car that had somehow moved itself away from where it belonged, in about a minute she was going to cry. Then she was crying. God! Tears were running down her face into the corners of her mouth. They tasted salty and made her feel even more helpless and she couldn't even spare a hand to wipe them off, loaded down the way she was with these damn sacks.

A box boy named Roy, gathering up carts in the lot, found her trotting around out there in the hot carbon-smelling dusk, peering at cars and crying.

'Ma'am,' he said, 'somethin' I can do for you?' She kind of scared him but then again he thought he sensed an opportunity for growth here. He had just been born again and his pastor at New Life Fellowship had told him we grow toward God by giving help to those less fortunate than ourselves. Right now Janine looked less fortunate than anybody he'd seen all day.

'My car's gone,' she said. She dropped the sacks she was carrying into the bottom of one of the carts he was pushing and stood rubbing her arms. 'My car – my car – oh, my God,' she said, grabbing him suddenly by the upper arms, 'my daughter's in that car!' More tears ran down her cheeks and she clung to him frantically.

Roy had pulled a few shifts as an aide at Kino hospital last year as part of the Community Outreach program at school. He was looking for ways he might, as Pastor said, make a difference. They had taught him to keep his voice down, said it soothed the patients if you talked soft. He leaned close to Janine's tear-streaked face now and said quietly, 'We'll find it. You come with me and we'll find it.'

He had no idea where her car was or even if she had one, but he knew where the manager was and he led her there, talking softly and holding her by the hand. By the time they reached Mr Dowling's office Janine's weeping had grown louder, she had quit talking about her car and was concerned entirely with her child, and what she seemed to be wailing now was, 'Oh, my God, they've got my baby.'

When Roy entered Mr Dowling's office, leading a near-hysterical woman by the hand, he got an indignant look from the manager, who didn't care about making a difference but just wanted to see that the produce was iced down properly so he could go home to supper. At first he didn't even seem to quite believe in Janine's distress. He looked at the naked fingers of her left hand and asked her, 'Who's this you say's got your baby, missy?'

'The men who took my car!' Janine cried. She put her head back, closed her eyes, and let out a wail like a hungry coyote. Mr Dowling began dialing 911.

By the time the police car pulled up outside, Janine was telling the store manager about two dark men – Hispanic or African American, she wasn't sure which – who jumped in her car at the stop light in front of the store, pushed her out and drove off. She repeated the story for the patrolman, adding, 'And see, my poor baby's asleep in the back seat.' She was suddenly, mysteriously, sure about that. And every time she said, 'My baby,' she started to cry again.

On her way to the manager's office Janine had started to wonder if the box boy had noticed how much beer she had in those bags? If he had, he might start to think a woman who was careless enough to leave her child in a car in a busy parking lot while she went to buy beer deserved whatever she got. So in her mind she started to embroider her story a little bit.

By the time they got to Mr Dowling's office she realized her grocery bags were probably lost in that cart outside anyway. And by then she'd said several times, 'They've got my baby,' and though she had no clear idea who 'they' might be, she couldn't very well take it back now. Anyway it was true, basically, somebody had evidently driven off with her car and Denny was in it.

This nice-looking cop seemed to assume that by 'baby' she meant 'infant', and that part of the problem really got his attention. So Janine didn't correct him, because whatever got him excited about finding Denny was good, right? Wasn't that what cops were supposed to do, instead of harassing single mothers every time they accidentally drove a little over the speed limit? *Honestly.*

The patrolman took down the model and license number of her car, called the station and repeated it to someone there, and hung up and told her that every squad car in Tucson was now looking for her car. Janine dried her eyes and told the policeman how grateful she was for his help, and he kindly offered to drive her home if her car wasn't found soon. She went in the restroom and repaired her make-up a little so she wouldn't look like such a wreck, and by the time she came back out there was a reporter there who said he just wanted to ask her a few questions.

She knew things were getting a little out of hand when the reporter asked her to step out in front of the store where his cameraman was set up. But she still had to find her damn car and get Denny back, didn't she? So she licked her lips and went out and stood bravely in front of the lights telling her story for the third time, and now the two men who had pushed her out of her car were bigger and meaner and this time they had guns.

Fourteen

Sarah ate her salad while the dryer hummed. It was her usual dinner music in this small duplex, where the kitchen was also the dining room and laundry.

She had lived much larger during her marriage to Andy Burke; there had been plenty to like about those years besides the rampaging sex. While their love lasted, they had been an ambitious, cheerful couple, with two satisfying careers, many friends and lively parties, long contented days of hiking in the mountains.

The marriage soured when Andy's partner in his big, successful restaurant grew discontented and bailed out of the business unexpectedly. The longer work hours and financial pressure that came with the separation piled up stress that Andy dealt with, more and more, by drunken after-hours carousing. Guilt and the drag on his energy left him surly and apathetic at home, and Sarah, pushing to make it as a new detective and already worried about Janine, resented his lack of support and said so. Andy responded by blaming her unpredictable work schedule as a detective. Homeric battles began to rattle the walls of their stylish house in Oro Valley, followed by equally noisy interludes when sex settled the argument.

Andy had always been careless about time; his lateness grew egregious; soon there were nights when he never showed up. The final emotional train wreck occurred in the dawn hours after Andy's thirty-seventh birthday, when Sarah, seeing him pull into the driveway, began throwing his clothes out the door.

Scooping up dress shirts and boxer shorts as fast as his stupendous hangover would allow, Andy ran around the front yard accusing her of spousal abuse, yelling, 'How can you be so cruel?'

'This isn't cruel. This is angry.' She heaved another armload of suits on to the gravel in the yard. 'Cruel is when you spend the night with a waitress from your favorite bar while your spouse waits with twelve guests and the birthday dinner you knew she was cooking.' Silk ties landed in a bright pile on top of the suits; a few got caught in the cactus.

'All right, I misbehaved,' Andy said, as if holding your wife up to public ridicule were a boyish prank. 'Those are new shirts, Sarah, damn it, do not throw – I mean it now!' Festooned with clothing, he ran in through the door and slammed it shut. Birds flew up out of the tree in the yard, pans rattled in the kitchen. 'If I can admit I was wrong, why can't you be reasonable and accept my apology? It'll never happen again, Sarah, I swear.'

He had made these same apologies and promises several times before, and she had accepted them because, for lots of good reasons, she loved him. But this morning, even with rage putting a red halo around everything, Sarah saw the way his eyes gleamed as he faced her over the crusty remains of last night's ruined feast. And in that terrible instant, she understood: *Andy was getting off on this.* He had progressed from casual adulterer to emotional batterer. For him, now, her cries of outrage, his confessions of guilt and the mad lust of their reconciliations were the turn-ons he had come to need.

That epiphany gave her the strength to leave him, but the battles didn't end there, of course. During the demeaning fights over money and possessions that attended their toxic divorce, a friend reminded Sarah of the lyrics of a Paul Simon song from the seventies that suggested 'there must be fifty ways to leave your lover'.

'Not if your lover's got a lawyer and he's determined to punish you for leaving him,' Sarah said. 'You don't just get on the bus, Gus. You hire another attorney and spend most of the money you're fighting over, just to keep what you had when you married him.'

Embarrassment over her post-divorce impoverishment had kept Sarah from insisting Denny stay with her the whole time Janine was in detox, and from fighting to keep her after Janine got out. She knew her love for Denny was deep and real, that they enjoyed each other's company. And she was terribly afraid her sister was too frail to make a go of independent living. But she herself had so little to offer – a futon in the tiny study that had to be made up every night, half a toothbrush shelf in her crowded bathroom – how great a deal was that for a child?

And she could never tell, because Denny never complained, how much the little girl missed her mother. Some of the social workers she had talked to had told her there was nothing like the parental bond. 'Girls, especially, want their moms. We'll go an extra mile to keep families together.'

So when the time came, she took Denny back to Janine's house, with many admonitions about calling if she needed help. They'd still be in close touch, she promised herself, she'd know if Janine wasn't making it.

But staying in touch got more and more difficult as both Janine and Denny seemed to draw away. In the end, she admitted now as she put away her dinner dishes, she had grown tired of the pain and worry the phone calls gave her, and begun to put off calling.

Standing now by the kitchen counter folding towels out of the dryer, she picked up the remote from a nearby table and clicked on the TV but left the sound off. Yawning, she watched the opening credits of a sitcom, thinking maybe she'd watch one show before bed.

As she opened a drawer to put the dish-towels away, an amber alert interrupted the program and Denny's small, unsmiling face appeared on screen. A message scrolled below it, something about a missing child. Sarah grabbed the remote and turned the sound up in time to hear an announcer's voice say, '...Denice Lynch, age ten, weighing about sixty-five pounds, wearing a white T-shirt and dark blue shorts...' Sarah froze in place, staring in shock at the screen.

'...from Fry's food store on Kolb Road,' the reporter said. 'Janine Lynch, the girl's mother, has just reported a carjacking from the street in front of the store, and says that her child was in the back seat of the car.' He went on to report the appearance and license number of the car.

Silently, with the speed of long practice,

Sarah found shoes, clean shirt, weapon and shield. Keys. Purse. She set the lock on her door, backed into the street in one clean surge and was rolling forward while the statistics of Denny's weight and height still scrolled across her TV screen.

Grant Road was nearly empty. She put her flasher on, roaring east and then south on to Kolb Road. Pulling into the Fry's lot at Golf Links, she saw the TV crew packing equipment into the back of their van. Two squad cars were parked just beyond it. In one of them, Janine sat in the front passenger seat, twisting a handful of soggy tissue, talking to a patrolman in the seat beside her. A second uniformed officer stood a few feet away, talking to a teenage boy wearing a Fry's badge.

Sarah parked in the first space she found and walked to the blue-and-white where Janine sat. The officer behind the wheel was Arturo Mendoza, a good buddy during the year they both worked night shifts in adjoining sections of midtown. She tapped on his window. When he rolled it down she said, 'Hey, Artie. You're working east side now, huh?'

'Oh, Sarah, yeah, I am,' he said, surprised. 'How come they called you out on this? I thought you were in Homicide now.'

'I am,' Sarah said. 'Janine's my sister.'

'She is? Well, how about that.' He looked from one to another, puzzled by their expressions and body language. Instead of hugging, the way most sisters would be doing by now,

Sarah was staring at Janine like she was trying to guess what she had for lunch, and Janine looked like a small animal caught in a trap.

Then Janine exploded into sobs. 'Oh, Sissy,' she wailed, 'I'm in an awful mess, somebody took my baby.' She put her head back and closed her eyes. The lights from the store signs gleamed on the sweet curve of her wet cheeks and on her tousled blonde hair. She looked like a beautiful lost child herself. Watching, Sarah thought, *She's covering something. Where the hell is Denny?*

'She's just been giving me Denny's height and weight and so on,' Mendoza said, 'and what she was wearing. We put out an amber alert.'

'I heard it,' Sarah said. 'Artie, is it OK if I just ask her a couple of questions?'

'Why, sure, go ahead,' Mendoza said. 'You want to...?' He started to open his door but she shook her head, walked around the patrol car to Janine's side and opened the door. She put her hand on the top of Janine's head and turned it so they were face to face.

'Open your eyes,' she said. When Janine's reluctant eyes were looking into hers, she said, 'Where's Denny?'

'I don't know! That's what I've been saying for the last hour, didn't anybody tell you?'

'*You* tell me. Denny's missing? What happened?'

'Two guys jumped in my car right out in the street—'

'Which street?'

'What difference does it make?' Janine turned her imploring face toward Mendoza, who was watching the two of them, fascinated and uneasy.

'Look at me, Janine.' *The hell with secrets.* 'Which street?'

'Kolb Road, for God's sake. What's the matter with you?'

'Where in the street?'

'At the light! What are you trying to do to me?'

'What light?'

'You sound like you don't believe me!'

'I believe you. Which cross street was the light on?'

'Whatever's out there in front of the store. I can't think – Golf Links!'

'Were you already stopped at the light?'

'Of course I was stopped, it was a red light! Are you *trying* to be mean, Sarah, or can't you help yourself?'

'Were you going or coming?'

'From what?'

'The store, Janine. Were you headed toward the store, or leaving it?'

'Oh. Well...' Some terrible uncertainty crossed her face, but she gave her head a little shake, swallowed thoughtfully and said, 'I was waiting to turn in.'

'Which way was your car headed?'

'I don't – I was coming from Lurlene Street, so which way is that? Toward the mountains – north, north! God, Sarah, you sound like I'm the damn ... suspect!'

'Never mind how I sound. Two men, is that what you said?' Sarah glanced across at Mendoza and saw him nod. 'And they both had guns?'

'Yes! Yes!' Janine put her hands flat against the sides of her head, closed her eyes and began to cry again. But just then the other patrolman, whose nameplate on his pocket said: E. Merlin, walked up to the car with the box boy following. He stopped by Sarah, leaned down toward the open door and said, 'Excuse me, Ms Lynch?'

Janine's blue eyes popped open, streaming tears. 'What?'

'Ma'am, this is Roy. The boy that helped you before? And he said to tell you he's keeping your beer and stuff in the cooler in the back of the store.'

Fifteen

Ordinarily Hector was good at making up clever lies on the spur of the moment. But having a strange kid sit up behind him like that, for a few seconds it kind of put a lock on his brain. These little eyes were staring at him in the noisy dusk, cars were roaring past him blowing their horns, and he had to decide right there in the middle of traffic what to say. Or do? *Throw the kid out.*

What was the penalty for throwing a kid out in traffic? *Relax, fool, you already killed a man, what could be worse than that?* That thought settled him down, so he could think.

'Your mom, uh,' Hector said, vamping now, stalling for time till he could figure things out, 'your Mom asked me to come out and move the car.' He found a break in traffic and turned right on Stella Street.

'She met you in the store, huh?' The small face flashed a mean little smirk. What was that all about? 'Are you her new boyfriend?'

'Oh, well, not really.' A little chuckle. 'I'm just a friend.' Feeling his way; this was an odd child.

'Oh.' The eyes studied him in the poor light. 'Let's go back and get her now. I'm hungry.'

'Ah, well, see, that's just what she was worried about.' Hector smiled his shit-eating grin and jumped right on the clue. 'She said go on out there and get you something good to eat. So, what would you like?'

The kid leaned forward, interested now, and a braid slid over one shoulder. Good, a girl. Girls scare easy.

'A double bacon cheeseburger,' she said, watching him with measuring eyes, 'and a large coke.'

'We can do that,' Hector said. 'Why not? There's a drive-in right around here, isn't there?'

'Two blocks up Kolb Road from the store,' Denny said.

'Which way's up?'

'Uh ... toward the mountains?'

'This place got a drive-in window?'

'Yes. Go right around there.' She leaned over the seat to point and he saw how small her arms were. She talked older, but she was younger than his youngest sister. He could handle her easy, no sweat. She was asking him now, 'You're not from around here, huh?'

'No, I live, uh, farther south.' He'd get her some food, he decided. Let her eat it while he drove up to Estes' place, got his passport and visa and decided what to do next. Might just put her back where he found her. Get back in Ace's car, go home and get his money and head out. Easiest thing to do, no fighting, nothing tricky about it except getting back on to the Fry's lot without being noticed. That shouldn't be too tough with so many cars around. He still didn't like the idea of taking Ace's big showy car down to Ohio Street, but ... well, he had a while to decide.

'There it is.' She pointed and he pulled in. She unbuckled her seat belt and climbed into the front passenger seat while he was pulling into the drive-in lane. He got concerned for a minute, his grocery bag was open and the gun and the money were right there in sight. But she wasn't looking at that, just staring ahead to the order window, asking, 'Can I have some fries too?'

'Sure,' Hector said. 'You good and hungry, huh?' He reached over and kind of mashed down the top of the Trader Joe's bag before he gave her order to the tinny voice that came over the speaker by his window. Ordered a burger and coke for himself too while he was at it, and then remembered all his money was in the bag, so he had to open it up a little. He didn't look, just reached into the paper envelope and fished out a bill. The car ahead of them got its order and moved, so he pulled up and paid. When the attendant handed out the paper sack of food Hector handed it to the little girl so she could hold it while he parked. She started digging for her sandwich right away. Half starved and no manners; must be some mama she had there in the store.

When he'd put his change in his pocket and parked the car he said, 'Here, lemme have the sack.' He unloaded the rest of the food on to the dashboard and spread the paper bag over the console between them like a picnic table, laid out his burger and her fries and put the drinks in the pull-out holder. They sat together silently, eating, Hector thinking hard. Was she going to raise a fuss about going to Estes' house with him? *Try it and see what happens*. If he had to throw the kid out he'd do it, but it would be better to keep everything quiet right now. He finished the last two bites of his burger, put the trash from his order back into the white paper sack it came in and started the motor.

'Gonna run up the street for a minute,' he said, 'see a guy.'

'We better stop and get Mom first,' the girl said.

'No, she's got some more stuff to buy, she said go ahead.' He didn't look at her but he said in a friendly way, 'You're OK to eat while I drive, right?' He didn't wait for an answer, just pulled right out into traffic. She kind of rolled her eyes sideways at him but went on eating and drinking. Looked like she wanted to get that food inside her before she argued about anything.

Soon as he was squared away in the flow of cars up Kolb Avenue, he dialed Estes. A woman's voice answered and he asked for Bernie. She said he wasn't there.

'When's he comin' home?'

'Who's this?'

Hector didn't want to say his name with the kid sitting there. 'I'm a ... customer. S'posta pick up an order. Didn't he tell you about it?'

'I just got home myself.'

'So you don't know nothin' about it, huh?'

'Sure don't.'

'He said seven o'clock. It's after seven now. When's he gonna be back?'

'Look, I already said I don't know. Do you want to leave a message or don't you?'

'Yeah.' Hector chewed his lip. 'Tell him Hector called, and tell him...' He turned away from the little girl, who was busy sucking on her coke. Talking into the window with his voice just above a whisper he said, 'Tell him if I ain't got my order by eight o'clock he's gonna be one sorry sonofabitch.'

He hit the end button, dropped the phone in his lap and drove a few seconds with his hands gripping the steering wheel, swallowing his rage. When he picked up the phone again he dialed a number but did not hit send. Holding the phone up to his ear, he put on his shit-eating grin and gushed, 'Hey, Buddy, howyadoin'?' He pretended to listen a few seconds, chuckled and said, 'Still burnin' through the plastic, huh?' He clucked a couple of times playfully, tsk tsk. 'Well, listen, my guy is late too, so whaddya say I take this beautiful girl to a movie? Time I finish my business you oughta be done shoppin' and we can all be on our way, right?' He did another pretend-listen, said, 'Fine, fine,' and folded up the phone.

The dubious eyes watched him. 'Was that Mom? Why didn't you let me talk to her?'

'Well, she's just shopping up a storm, she's in a hurry. And she said a movie's OK. What movie would you like to see?'

She shook her head firmly. 'It's a school night,' she said. 'I can't go to a movie, I have to finish my homework.'

What was with this kid? She acted like a grown-up woman with a bug up her ass. His sisters would have been just yelling the names of movies at him by now.

Hector tried the grin his mama could never resist. This strange brat just stared back at him with her stern little jaw clamped shut. 'Look, your mom said it was OK, what are you worrying about? What's your name, by the way?'

'Denny. I need to go home now.'

Well, shit, maybe that would work. Drop her there and... 'Where do you live?'

'It's back there near the store. But I can't go there by myself.'

'Well, no, of course not.' He got into the right lane, ready to turn. 'I'm gonna take you.'

'No, I mean I can't go in the house without Mom. We have to go get Mom first.'

'What, you're afraid to be alone in your own house? A big girl like you?'

'No.' Angry, she shook her head so hard her braids whipped her face.

'What is it then?'

She glared at him. 'There's somebody else there right now.'

'Oh?' Hector saw how her eyes had gone flat and cold, and had a hunch. 'Who, your daddy? Your brother?' She was shaking her head. 'Your Mom's boyfriend?' She didn't say yes but she quit shaking her head and sat staring down at her knees. *Shit. A thousand cars I could have grabbed, I have to pick the Evil Mama's damn car.*

'Maybe I could go to my aunt Sarah's house,' she said, still looking at her knees, kind of talking to herself. 'I don't know if she's home, though. I'd have to call.'

Hector opened his mouth to say, 'Go ahead, call,' but then who knew if Aunt Sarah would recognize Evil Mama's car and raise a stink? So he put on the big-buddy grin that always worked with his sisters, leaned over her and said, 'Aw, come on, you deserve a treat, don't you? Let's go to the movies. You ever seen *Master and Commander*?'

'No.' He watched her trying to resist. 'It's an old movie, isn't it?'

'Havin' a rerun at the Roxy. I already saw it once, but it's so good I'd like to go again.'

'Well...' Finally, the face that turned toward him wore a kid's expression, excited. 'OK.'

'Aw*right!* Oh, you are gonna *love* this movie. Hang on, here we go.'

He drove west to Campbell and past the crowded lot in front of Bookman's, around the corner to the front of the theater and up the ramp to the theater parking on the second level, thinking, *Who's gonna look for a stolen car at a movie theater?* And off the street like this, he really couldn't ask for a better place to wait for shithead Estes.

He grabbed his Trader Joe's bag, said, 'Let's go, Denny!' and walked down the ramp to the theater window smiling down at her, doing his best to make this look like *Uncle* Hector and his little niece with the braids. Denny made it look even better when she looked over the railing, said, 'Look!' and pointed down to the little park on Edison Street where a dozen or so teenage boys in weird pajamas were threatening each other with sticks.

'Aw, don't worry, that's just a dumb slant-eyes game,' Hector said. 'Ain't nobody getting hit much.' The little girl looked at him funny and said something about Ti Kwan-Doh, and Hector thought angrily, *Always somebody wants to correct me.* Wanted to smash her face right there but told himself, *Keep your shine on, kind ol' Uncle Hector.*

He thought he had enough money in his pocket but it didn't quite cover the tickets, he had to reach into the grocery sack again. It was OK though, everybody around him was looking at the times on the board and buying tickets, so nobody watched him.

They grabbed a pair of seats near the back, on the aisle, because the picture was starting. The camera panned across the opening scene, the tall ship in the fog, men and boys on deck with all the sails flapping and the ropes hanging everywhere. Denny was hooked right away, he saw, staring up at the screen with big eyes.

He sat beside her, waiting, and then, oh Christ, his damn cell phone started to ring inside the bag. He thought he'd remembered to turn it off. People all around him were looking, and somebody said, 'Sshhh!' He whispered, 'Sorry!' and fished around in the bag till he found it. But then he couldn't seem to get the motherfucker turned off. He punched where he knew the end button should be, but it kept ringing. Somebody said, 'Will you *please*!' In a panic to get the noise stopped he darted back up to the entrance door and out into the hall where he could see the buttons.

Under the light, he finally found the end button and got the ringing stopped. Then he stood staring at the thing in his hand. *This ain't my phone.* For a second he got that disoriented feeling he'd had when Denny first sat up in the back seat of the car, his brain saying, *This can't be happening.*

Then he realized, his own phone was right where he always kept it, in the holster that clipped on his belt. He checked it; it was turned off all right. This was Ace's phone he was holding. *Man, you gotta get your mind organized, you can't be lettin' little things rattle you like this.*

But when he remembered the Trader Joe's bag back there under his seat, all the money in it and the gun, he got rattled all over again and hustled back to his seat in a sweat. It was OK, though; Denny was sitting bolt upright staring at the screen like it was the first movie she ever saw, and the bag was right where he left it.

He sat through the first scene, then leaned toward Denny and whispered, 'Be right back.' She nodded without taking her eyes off the screen. He walked up the aisle carrying the Trader Joe's bag, stood under the light in the hall while he pulled his phone off his belt and dialed Estes' number.

Estes answered on the first ring, his voice sharp, 'Yeah?'

'It's Hector. My stuff ready?'

'What's the idea hasslin' my wife? We don't have to take that shit from you.'

'You shoulda been there at seven o'clock like you said. You want your money or don't you?'

'You better have it all in cash, putz. I'm not taking any checks from you.'

'Who said anything about checks? I'll be right there.' He walked as quietly as he could down the aisle past Denny, who was so absorbed in the movie she never even turned her head. He pushed the panic bar on the metal door under the lighted exit sign, went out and climbed the cement stairs to the parking garage.

Driving away, he thought once about the little girl sitting there alone in the dark theater. She probably wouldn't even notice his absence till the movie ended. Then she'd look around at the crowd leaving, and wonder ... *Ah, she'll figure it out and call somebody. Ain't nobody ever died from getting left in a movie theater.*

He drove east and then south to Estes' house, watching the streets carefully, checking his rear-view mirror often. He knew he had to be ready to abandon this car at the first hint that a cop was checking his license plate number. That would leave him on foot in a town that sprawled for miles over hot desert. Public transportation was scarce in Tucson and taxis hard to find, but he would figure that out if he came to it. *Long as I hang on to my grocery bag I got money and a gun, what more do I need? Even got my bottle of Gatorade,* he thought – a little joke to cheer himself up. Ace's half-finished bottle was still sloshing around down there in the Trader Joe's bag.

And seriously, maybe he ought to try a swig. Ever since he got back to Tucson he'd been getting so *stressed out,* it wasn't like him at all and he was really sick of it. Things kept happening that he didn't expect, making him feel like he wasn't in charge. He tried saying to himself again, *You already killed a man, what could be so hard after that?* And just like that, it worked again. By the time he parked in front of Estes' house he was a cool dude, ready for his next boss move.

Let's stick to the plan now, he told himself, giving a sharp little rap on the door. Get these papers, roll on down there to Mexico and make that bundle. And then come back to Tucson and show ol' Rudy Ortiz how the big boys do it.

Sixteen

'OK, Janine,' Sarah said, 'they're doing us a favor, letting us talk in here for a few minutes.' They were in the manager's office at the back of the Fry's store – the last stop, Sarah had been trying to get her to understand, before Mendoza took her to the Rincon station for further questioning.

'How about some favors for me? I'm the one whose child is missing.' The glow from the beer and pot was fading fast. Janine looked ragged and ready for a fight.

'Janine, you've got to give me some straight answers now. You hear me? Once Artie takes you to the station you'll be in the system and I can't talk to you any more. You'll be dealing with detectives from the child abuse section. I won't have any more access than any other family member does, till they decide how to charge you.'

'*Charge* me?' Janine stared at her sister and the two uniformed officers with her mouth open, the red coming up in her face. 'You mean you're going to blame the victim? What the hell's wrong with you people?'

She's looking for a scapegoat. Sarah saw it all coming, the indignation and denial, the frantic search for someone to blame. *And here I am, handy as usual.* But Denny was out there somewhere and the games had to stop now. 'Janine, look at me. Look at me! Denny is missing and you lied to the police. Unless you tell me right now where you left her you're going to jail.'

'I didn't lie about Denny! She was in the car with me!'

'You told us you hadn't been to the store. But the box boy said he found you wandering in the parking lot crying, alone, carrying two sacks full of beer and cigarettes.'

'And hot dogs and buns, and mustard and milk. You make it sound like—'

'OK, hot dogs. What else did you lie about? Where was Denny while you bought the beer?'

'In the car! Only somebody moved it!'

'You left her in the car? Janine, were the keys in the car?'

'Well *yeah*. How else was I going to leave the AC on for her?'

'You mean the motor was running too?'

'That's what makes it *work*, right?' She tossed her head, rolled her eyes at the ceiling.

'And the reason you couldn't take her in the store with you was?'

'I was in a hurry! She said she was hungry, I wanted to get home and feed her.'

'Uh-huh. All that beer was for you?'

'No! I was ... doing a favor. For a friend.'

'Where's this friend now? Janine? Answer me!'

'He's at home...'

'Whose home?'

'*My* home! Waiting for me.' Sensing that her friend at home was not being well received, she revised him. 'Or he was. He's probably gone by now.' Met by dubious silence, she tried self-pity. 'Why does everything I try to do just get so damn screwed *up*?'

Sarah took a deep breath, glancing quickly at Artie Mendoza and Ed Merlin, who sat on either side of her watching the two of them, ready to cut this off if it turned into a family fight. They were stretching their prerogatives as a professional courtesy to her but their patience was not going to last much longer. *And Denny's out there*. 'Are you quite sure you parked where you showed us, in the handicapped zone?'

'I never even noticed those stupid little stripes on the ground, Sarah, they should mark those things a lot better than they do.'

'Never mind that now. Just tell me if you're sure you were right there under the store sign, by the stacks of chairs.'

Janine lifted her arms out from her sides, spread the fingers of both hands in a gesture of supreme exasperation, and said, 'Yes!' The three faces in front of her closed up and went bland. Sarah got up, nodded to the two uniformed patrolmen and they all moved to the door. Janine said, 'What?'

Sarah turned, holding the door open, and said, 'Just wait right there a minute.' She closed the door and the three of them stood in the aisle by the deli counter with their heads together.

'OK, she lied, but I'm not seeing any malice here,' Mendoza said. He looked at his back-up.

'No,' Merlin said, 'but there might be an issue about driving under the influence. I've got a kit in the car...'

'We're not going to prove a whole lot now,' Mendoza said. 'I think it's more important to find the kid.'

'I don't see this as an intentional kidnapping, do you?' Sarah watched his face. She was asking, without saying it aloud, if they could keep the FBI out of it for now. 'Doesn't it feel like if we find the car we'll find Denny?'

'Sure looks that way to me,' Merlin said, 'but I guess we ought to see what they say about it downtown.'

'Well, but best chance to find her is in the next couple hours,' Mendoza said. 'Rather than bog down in bureaucracy, why don't we just ask everybody that's got a minute to start driving a grid around this area?'

'We can try that,' Merlin said, 'for a while.'

'Good. Here's my cell number.' Sarah handed out cards. 'Can you keep me in the loop?'

'Count on it,' Artie Mendoza said. They had done domestics and a burglary watch together, broken up bar fights and talked a crack addict down off a roof. They were tight. Sarah knew he would help her in any way he could, within his limited options. Merlin had more reservations, she could see, about the slight bending of rules they had already allowed, but he trusted Mendoza so he was going along. Mendoza punched her shoulder lightly and she held up a thumb to each of them.

They went back in the manager's office where Janine waited. Mendoza, as first responder, explained that his incident report was going to have to include the lie she had told about two armed men. But he and his partner would be searching for her car and her child, and they would enlist as much help as they could. 'Let's see, I already have your address and phone number, and this description of Denny, we can put that out right away. We need to count on you to stay home so we can find you, OK?' He was quiet and polite, but not sympathetic. Janine watched him anxiously, uncertain how to deal with a man who seemed impervious to her charms.

'I'll take Janine home,' Sarah said, as they walked out of the store.

In the car Janine said, in a small voice, 'Will you stay with me tonight?'

'No,' Sarah said. 'I'm going to drive around, look for Denny.'

'Let me go with you! Please?'

'You heard Artie, you have to stay home.'

'Listen, I don't have to do anything just because *he* says it.'

'Janine, weren't you listening to him? They need to know where you'll be if they find Denny!'

'I heard him, I heard him.' She pouted. 'I hate being preached at.'

'He was just telling you how things are. You know yourself, it's possible Denny might just come home.'

'Oh, Sarah, do you think she might? Get away from those two goons?'

'Janine,' Sarah said, 'there aren't any two goons, remember? You made them up.'

Janine waved off the lie. 'However many rotten guys took my car, I bet my Denny can get away from them. She's such a bright kid, isn't she, Sarah?'

'Uh-huh.'

When they turned into Lurline street, Janine began peering ahead toward her house, muttering. Sarah said, 'What?'

'I said I hope he's gone.'

'Who?'

'Uh ... Buster.' They reached her block and she said, 'Good, his car's gone, he must be gone.' Sarah stopped the car. Janine turned with sudden urgency and begged, 'Will you come in with me? Please? Just till I get in the house.'

'Are you afraid of the man you left here? The one you bought the beer for?'

'Kind of. Maybe. I'm not sure.' She looked around. 'Where's the groceries?'

'In the trunk. Why would he be mad at you?'

'Well ... he gave me some money. And then I never got back with his smokes.'

'I see.' Sarah got out of the car, looked around. The street was empty. All the lights were on in Janine's house. Hard to tell. She unsnapped the cover on her holster and folded it back. 'OK, let's go in.' She popped the trunk open. 'Can you carry both of those?'

'Yes. Oh, God, my house key's on the ring with the car keys, though. What if he locked...?' But Sarah was already turning the knob, and the door swung open. The kitchen and living room shared the cluttered space at the front of the house. It smelled like marijuana, Marlboros and beer. Through the open door of Janine's bedroom, Sarah could see her trashed bed, sheets and blankets trailing on the floor.

They stepped inside. On the kitchen table, amongst the empty beer cans, someone had written with a red flare pen: FUCK YOU

BITCH.

Janine set the grocery bags down on top of the message, and began to cry.

Denny's door was closed. Sarah put her right hand on her weapon, stood by the door hearing nothing, turned the knob and pushed. The door would only open halfway. She stepped in quickly, looked behind it, and found Denny's little armchair there. Odd. The desk light was on, shining on Denny's books and papers. The rest of the room was neat and empty. She opened the closet door. Empty.

She checked Janine's room and the bathroom quickly. 'OK, all clear,' she said. Janine was still standing by the kitchen table, sniffling into a tissue. 'Let's be sure the back door and the windows are all locked, OK? Then you lock the front door after me and you'll be fine.'

Janine lifted her woebegone face out of a mound of wet tissue and wailed, 'You're going to leave me here all alone?'

'Janine –' Sarah locked the back door and tested it – 'do you think this man is dangerous?'

'Oh, *I* don't know. I just met him.'

'So you took him right home to bed, huh?'

'What, you always wait until the banns are read?'

Janine had her head up now, glaring, and Sarah's anger flared. *Not too helpless to scratch your sister.* 'Fine. Sleep with thugs, destroy yourself, I won't say another word.' All three windows were locked. Not that they'd keep anybody out if he really wanted to get in.

Going out the front door, she said, 'Come and lock this while I'm still here.'

Janine, looking defiant, stamped over, but then, typically, folded at the door and clutched Sarah's arm, beseeching, 'Promise you'll call me right away if you hear anything.'

'Of course. Try to sleep, it will make the time pass.' She stood outside till she heard the bolt turn.

She was two blocks away, still steaming, before she thought, *Damn, I shouldn't have left her with the beer.* But she couldn't persuade herself to go back.

As she drove out of the dark, narrow street on to Kolb Road, hot and noisy with streaming traffic, she put her sister out of her mind and focused on probabilities. Which way was he likely to go, this kidnapper/car thief?

Where's my Denny?

Seventeen

When she woke up and felt the car moving, Denny thought Mom must have forgotten to put the brake on. Afraid she was rolling around the parking lot, she sat up fast.

The car had a driver, but it wasn't Mom. *Oh, swell, another boyfriend.* What was he doing out in the street though, and why were all the horns blowing?

'What happened?' she said. 'Where's Mom?' The guy stammered something about Mom telling him to move the car. That made no sense at all, was he high? She got ready to start screaming. She'd heard once if you felt uneasy with strange grown-ups, the thing to do was yell till some other grown-up came and helped. The logic of such a move felt a little shaky to her – how could you be sure the second grown-up would be any better than the first? But it was the only idea that came to her so she decided to try it at the next red light.

In the meantime, though, because you might as well try everything, she told the new boyfriend she needed her Mom because she was hungry. And right away, instead of telling her to wait, he asked her what she wanted to eat. Now what was *that* all about? Anybody knew boyfriends thought hungry kids were one of the biggest drags on earth.

But Denny was so hungry by then that just talking about food made her stomach growl, so she pretended to believe he meant it, and asked for two things Aunt Sarah wouldn't allow and Mom usually couldn't afford. And this strange man, maybe he really was from another planet because he didn't even argue, just drove right up to the window and ordered everything she said, even the fries she thought of at the last minute. Then he ordered a second set of everything for himself.

Mom had really latched on to something here – but he was way too young for her, what was she thinking?

An even bigger surprise was how he paid for the food, reaching into that grocery sack on the floor to fish out a bill. Denny had seen plenty of flaky boyfriends but this was the first one that carried his money in a Trader Joe's bag. He didn't bother her while she ate, though, give him that much. He finished his own food first and said he had to go somewhere, and she went along without any objections because the food tasted so good she couldn't even think of leaving it.

He made a phone call while he drove and got mad at the person on the other end. She heard him say his name, too, Hector. As if she cared what his name was, but why was he whispering it? Then he dialed another number but didn't send the call, she could tell by the sound. He sat there like a dork, driving the car and talking into a dead phone, and pretty soon she realized he was pretending to talk to her mother. Mom did have her cell phone in the store, the only phone she had and she carried it everywhere. But what was up with this guy? Even the boys on the school bus didn't act *that* crazy.

She began to be really concerned about being out in the car with anybody so off the wall. It was one thing after another, as soon as he quit pretending to talk to Mom he started talking about the movies. She had to decide fast if she should try to get this nutcase to take her home, or go to his old movie. She didn't really want to go anywhere with him, but compared to that creepy slimeball Mom had left in the bedroom at home, whispering Hector looked like a better choice. At least he bought burgers and fries, and so far his worst fault was pretending to talk into a dead phone. Dweeby but probably harmless, she decided. Besides, she could finish the essay questions on the way to school in the morning, but who knew if she'd ever get another chance to see *Master and Commander*?

He parked upstairs in the parking ramp, another point in his favor. She had always liked that space, it seemed enough like a cave to start her imagination going even before she got into the movie. She felt odd walking up to the ticket window with a man she didn't know, but nobody paid any attention to them. People were all looking up at the schedule and asking each other what they wanted to see. Hector got some more money out of his grocery sack, and their cashier pointed to theater six. Denny could hear the movie starting as they walked toward the door, and her heart leaped toward it crying *yes*! She couldn't wait to get into the glamorous darkness where the brave and handsome people lived, in a world completely unlike her own.

The movie had already started. They took the first seats they could find and she was enchanted at once, in her imagination she got on that ship and sailed away with the sailors in the odd hats.

And then that fool's telephone started to ring. What could he be thinking, coming into a theater without turning it off? He was scrabbling in his bag, trying to find it, but even after he pulled it out he couldn't seem to get it stopped. All the people around them were hissing like snakes. Denny shriveled into an angry lump, pretending she wasn't with him. The ship was moving into the fog ... He jumped out of his seat carrying the ringing phone and ran toward the entrance.

The relief when he was gone felt like a cool breeze after heat. Denny watched the ship move into the fog bank, saw the arms and hands of the brave sailors straining on the lines ... and in her mind, suddenly, she saw Hector's slim brown hand reach into the grocery sack and pull out a twenty-dollar bill.

It only took a few seconds. She leaned sideways into the darkness in front of his seat and slid her hand into the sack. She felt a slippery garment, a plastic bottle, something cold and metallic, and then just as she was losing her nerve her hand felt a paper envelope with the flap open, and inside was that familiar greasy feeling that could only be money.

She meant to just take one or two bills, whatever was handy. But she heard the muffled thud of footsteps coming down the aisle and fear brought blood surging into her cheeks in a hot rush. She had the envelope half out of the sack; she pulled it out and stuffed it under her shirt.

Sitting up trying to look innocent, she faced

the movie as a stranger walked down the aisle and passed her. She tried to get up enough courage to take the envelope out from under her shirt and put it back in the grocery sack, but the space around her seemed bright as day, all of a sudden, and she felt as if everybody was watching her. Then Hector was there, sliding in beside her. Denny sat up very straight so the bulge from the envelope would not show. On the screen, a huge shipload of Frenchmen shot cannons into a smaller shipload of English. Hector got quite excited during the battle scenes, Denny noticed. Remembering the cold metallic thing in the sack, she decided it might be a gun, and as she watched the slaughter on the screen she wished she had put the envelope back.

When the battle scene ended he picked up his sack and walked back up the aisle toward the entrance. While the captain and the doctor on screen played their delicate stringed instruments, so surprising after the bloody battle, Denny sat with a lump of dread growing in her stomach. She expected Hector to come tearing down the aisle any minute and demand his money back.

Instead, a few minutes later he walked right past her with his eyes straight ahead. He never said a word or made any sign to her, just went down the aisle fast toward the screen, opened the exit door under the little light and went out.

Watching the movie, Denny felt her mind split in two. One half longed to get absorbed in the story again and forget everything else; it was mysterious and glamorous, and ordinarily it would have blotted out everything else. But she kept wondering where Hector had gone. When he didn't come back after a few minutes, she began to consider that maybe he had intended all along to leave her there and take the car.

She sat a few minutes nursing sour feelings of abandonment and betrayal. Then she thought, *Oh, well, I didn't care about him while I was taking his money so I guess it's fair.* Eventually, though, she began to wonder, *How will I get home?*

She was still working on that problem when another thought popped up. *If he's gone with the car I guess I can keep the money.* She pressed her arm against her stomach and heard the envelope crackle. *Unless he notices it's gone and comes back.* Fear made her stand up quickly then, and grope along the upward-slanting dark aisle with her left arm pressed against her body, holding the envelope in place.

In the hall she saw the sign for the women's restroom. She pushed through the door and went into a stall. The relief of getting into a private space with the envelope was so great she immediately felt a sharp urge to urinate. She pulled the envelope out from under her shirt and sat down on the stool. While she emptied her bladder, she opened the flap and pulled the money out of the envelope. *Eeee, a whole fistful of money.*

She put the envelope across her knees, set

the bills on top and spread them out a little, and began to look at the denominations. At first she was sure she must be misunderstanding the numbers, but these were twenties, she'd seen plenty of them, and these were fifties, right? So then all these others were hundreds, had to be. In her mind, for the first time ever, Denny used one of Mom's favorite expressions, *Holy shit.*

She got the feeling of eyes watching her and looked up guiltily, but nobody was peering over the top of the stall. She stuffed all the bills back in the envelope, folded the flap over, stood up and zipped her shorts. She slid the envelope in her waistband and was reaching for the door to go out when she thought again about the problem of getting home. She couldn't walk – she didn't really know the way and was pretty sure it was too far. She had to make at least one phone call, maybe more, and that meant getting some change. She took the envelope out from under her shirt, took out a twenty and put it in her pocket.

She closed the envelope and put it back down the front of her shorts, but at her first step, it slid out of her waistband and down the leg of her shorts on to the floor. She scooped it up in a sweat – what if somebody saw all that money? This time she slid the envelope carefully into the front of her underpants, which were tight enough to hold it.

Now, where would she find a phone? She felt conspicuous walking out by herself; she had never been on the street alone at night. At first, in the crowd around the door of the theater, nobody paid any attention to her. But as she walked toward Grant the traffic thinned and people began to glance at her. She stood at the corner, looking around. Walgreen's and Bookman's had lights on. Did they have public phones? Could she find anybody to ask in such busy places? Kids were easy to ignore. She looked across the street and saw a Coffee Xchange with all its lights on, people sitting at tables, a sign in the window that said '24/7'. *They must have a phone.*

She watched many lanes of roaring traffic for a long time before the light changed. She hurried across Grant, terribly afraid she wouldn't be fast enough. But she made it, and then she had to wait again to cross Campbell. It was just as busy but felt a little easier because she'd proved she could do it once. Traffic seemed faster at night, though, the lights were more confusing. Getting all the way to the coffee shop seemed like climbing a mountain.

She felt shy at first, walking in, but nobody looked at her much. The customers were mostly students absorbed in each other and giving a lot of thought to their food and drink orders. There was a counter where a pale, thin girl and a smiling young man with dark brown eyes were serving pastries and elaborate coffees. Denny went and stood at the end of a line of customers, rehearsing the words she would use to ask for a phone.

Idly, she watched the big TV screen in the corner. A news program was on, three reporters sitting side by side at a long desk, talking. Other images appeared, a war scene, a baseball game. The sound was turned down, she couldn't hear it well enough to know what was being reported, but then an image of her mother appeared on the screen. *Mom!* Why was she crying? She was talking into a microphone held up by a reporter. Denny walked quickly to the TV set as a head shot of another reporter came on. Standing close to the set she could barely hear him say, 'Ms. Lynch's original story about how her car was stolen seems to have changed somewhat since it was first reported earlier this evening. But her child is still missing, and Tucson police are searching for Denny Lynch...'

Denny stood watching as her last year's school photo came up on screen. *Why didn't I at least get the part in my hair straight?*

She went back and waited in front of the cash register again, burning with shame. Was everybody in school going to know that her Mom told a lie? Why did she do that?

When she got to the counter the thin girl said, 'What can I do for you?'

'Um,' Denny said, 'I need to use a telephone, please?'

'There's a public phone right there by the back door,' the girl said, pointing. 'Do you need some change?'

'Yes, please.' She put the twenty on the

counter.

'Is that the smallest you've got?'

'Yes.' She tried to look appealing. The young man with the wonderful eyes was watching her now, not exactly in an unfriendly way, just very interested. Young men his age were never interested in Denny, so she didn't know how to take it. He said something softly and the girl turned toward him with her eyebrows raised. Then they both turned back and began staring at her.

'Listen,' the girl said, 'you know you look just like that missing kid they been showing on TV?'

'Oh? Well,' Denny said, 'where did you say the phone is?' When they both pointed to it she walked past the TV set into the back hall and stood looking up at the pay phone, which was hopelessly beyond her reach. *Maybe I could go get a chair.* But then the young man from the counter said, right beside her, 'Shall I give you some help with that? What number do you want to call?'

Denny thought about Mom on TV, looking loony, telling a reporter a story about two men with guns. She had made up her mind not to ask Aunt Sarah for anything more, but this felt like an emergency. She closed her eyes, got a clear picture of the framed card Aunt Sarah had given her to keep on her desk, and read off the number of her aunt's cell phone.

Eighteen

Sarah drove fast into the parking lot behind Coffee Xchange, parked in the first spot she came to and ran around to the front. Through the glass door she could see Denny, small and tired looking, sitting at a table near the window with Artie Mendoza.

'Denny,' she said when she got inside. Her voice had a bad wobble in it so she didn't try to talk any more, just put her arms around her niece's skinny shoulders and held her close. Mendoza got up and moved away a little, gave them some space and waited. Denny trembled and made small noises, trying not to cry. When Sarah could talk she said, 'Are you hurt? Did anybody hurt you?'

'No. I'm OK. I don't know why the policeman came.'

'I called him, honey. He's been looking for you ever since your Mom reported you missing.'

Denny pulled away, looking mortified. 'Why did she do that? She knew where I was.'

'She did?'

'Sure. In the car. Right where she left me.'

'But the car was gone. At least – she said she couldn't find it.'

'Well, what – did she forget she told that man to move it?'

Sarah peered into her face. 'What man, Honey?'

'Hector. The one who took me to the drive-in and—'

Sarah held up one hand. 'Just a minute.' She caught Mendoza's eye and nodded, and he came back to the table. 'Denny, do you feel up to telling us what happened?'

'Well ... sure.' Denny looked from one to the other.

'From the beginning,' Sarah said.

'Where's that?'

Mendoza said, 'Your Mom left you in the car, is that right? In front of the store?'

'Yeah.'

'She left the motor running?'

'I don't know. Maybe. She said she'd be quick, but – I fell asleep.' She told them about waking in the moving car, the unknown man driving. They asked her what he looked like and she tried to remember. 'Brown skin. Curly hair. He smiled a lot.' She did the best imitation she could manage of Hector's oily grin, shrugging her shoulders and looking sly.

Mendoza said, 'So he didn't seem like ... a scary guy?'

'No. He seemed kind of ... silly. He kept saying he was a friend of Mom's so...' She shrugged matter-of-factly. Sarah met Mendoza's eyes and shrank from the contempt she saw there. *Are we always so damn judgmental?* Things weren't so black and white when it was your own sister.

'So then I said I was hungry and he got me a cheeseburger.' She saw the adults look at each other and said, 'What?'

'We're just surprised,' Sarah said. 'Go ahead.'

'Well, then he started to go someplace...' She told them about the phone call, how angry the man got. 'That's when I heard him say his name. Hector.' Mendoza wrote it down. 'He got very mad, but he didn't get mad at *me*.' She made a sound close to a sob and managed to turn it into a kind of chuckle. 'He just asked me if I'd like to go to a movie.'

'A movie?' Mendoza looked disbelieving. Sarah realized she probably looked the same way and tried to make her face neutral.

Denny, looking into Sarah's eyes, raised one hand. 'Swear to God.'

'What film did you see?'

'*Master and Commander*. Just the first part. Hector's phone rang and ... I think he made some calls. Then he left and after a while I decided he probably wasn't coming back so I left too.' She blinked. Her eyes were bright with unshed tears. 'First movie I ever walked out of.'

'Poor Denny. I'll take you again, I promise.' Sarah hugged her again and patted her back. 'You did *very well,* sweetheart. Walking up here and calling me, that was really smart.'

'That boy helped me,' Denny said, nodding toward the counter. He smiled at her and she wrinkled her nose and smiled back.

'One new experience after another, huh?' Sarah looked at Mendoza. 'Just to be sure, maybe somebody should check that ramp for the car?'

'Osterman already did. It's gone. We find the car, chances are we'll find the bad guy.'

'Right.' Her eyes asked him for one more favor as she said, 'I know there's a lot more to clear up, but for now ... what do you say? She's pretty tired.'

'We really ought to take her in for a rape check.'

Oh, Christ. Sarah turned to Denny and asked, 'Honey, did he touch you? Or...?'

Denny, looking stricken, shook her head emphatically. 'No. No, no, Aunt Sarah, nothing. Never. Honest.'

Sarah said, 'She knows the score, Artie. We've talked.'

'OK, if you feel sure. Take her home, get some rest. I'll file my report. Tomorrow ... I'm on again at three. We might have her look at some mug shots. Uh...' He nodded toward the sidewalk.

Sarah said, 'Denny, just sit here one more minute, OK? Then we'll go home.'

Outside he said, 'We're still looking for the car, no sign of it yet.'

'OK.'

'And, uh...' He cleared his throat. 'We tried to call your sister.'

'I did too. Sound asleep, I guess.' She avoided his eyes for a moment, not wanting to talk about Janine. But he had helped her in every way he could tonight. She couldn't stonewall Artie. 'Janine has problems, you could see that. I'm trying to help her, but it isn't easy.'

'It never is, for family.'

'Do you think – could you just drive by Janine's house and make sure she's there?' She told him about Janine not wanting to go in the house by herself, and about the note on her table.

'OK, I'll check on her, sure. But ... I have to tell you, Sarah, they're riding us pretty hard to report these child neglect cases before something worse happens.' Mendoza watched the traffic on Grant Road for a few seconds. 'I know we can't settle anything tonight, but you might as well know that I'll be putting it all in my report just the way it happened. How Janine lied to us, left her daughter in the car with the keys in it, and the fact that she was out buying beer and cigarettes for some guy in her house who's so abusive she's afraid of him herself. If I find out she deliberately didn't answer the phone, after I specifically asked her...' He turned to face her, and his eyes were hard. 'I let it ring ten times.'

'Artie, look, I think she's just asleep, OK? OK, maybe passed out – I'll settle for that if I can just be sure she's there. And I'll take care of Denny.'

'I know. But if you weren't here, Denny would be on her way to a shelter right now, and then she'd be in the system and you'd all have fewer options tomorrow. You ought to think about that, Sarah.' He put his cap on, headed toward his squad, turned back at the edge of the sidewalk and said, 'I'm going to ask a social worker to call on Janine, maybe help her get started in a program, if—'

'She just got out of one. But do what you have to do. And thanks for your help, Artie.'

'Take care.'

Watching him get in and boot up his PC, Sarah swallowed a metallic taste of fear. Walking back into the coffee shop she saw how Denny must have looked to Mendoza, skinny and tired in her ratty T-shirt, hair falling out of her braids. Not like somebody's cherished daughter, for sure. Sarah had spent many hours worrying about her sister, but she had never before faced the fact that Janine's reckless behavior put them all at risk of losing Denny. To what, state custody, foster care? *Not while I'm still breathing.* She walked in and leaned over Denny's chair. 'Ready to go?'

'OK. Is Mom home?'

'I guess. But since it's so late, why don't you stay at my house tonight?'

'Well ... OK.' She almost smiled 'I don't have a nightgown or anything.'

'I'll find you something. Let's just thank these people here, OK?' They stopped by the cash register, where the two clerks were smiling at them, pleased to have played a part in the night's big news story.

Denny said, 'Thank you for helping me

with the phone.'

The young man who had recognized her said, 'You're welcome, Denice. You take care, now.' They both looked at Sarah, obviously curious about her relationship to this child. They could see she wasn't the weeping woman on TV. Another time, Sarah would have taken the time to explain, made sure the picture was crystal clear as far as the department was concerned. Tonight she wanted to get Denny home, so she just thanked them for their help and left them to wonder.

Holding her passenger door open for Denny, she asked, 'Are you hungry?'

'No. Actually that guy bought me a double bacon cheeseburger and fries.'

'He did?' Sarah laughed out loud and then checked herself, shocked at the sound. *How can you laugh when she* ... but it was funny. She checked the seat belt, grinning. 'Boy, Denny, you sure know how to pick your kidnappers.'

Denny said, 'Yeah, dinner and a movie, pretty good, huh?' and giggled behind her hand. But giving way to one emotion somehow jarred a couple of others loose; she hiccupped, gave Sarah one horrified look, and began to cry.

'It's OK.' Sarah leaned in and held her, patted, murmured, kissed her hair. 'You're entitled, sweetheart, you've been brave long enough.' She freed one hand and found some tissue, pressed it into Denny's wet face. When the sobs let up a little she passed fresh tissue and said, 'Want to blow your nose?'

While Denny was busy with that she got in and started the car. 'You know, if we go straight home,' she said, moving into the street, 'maybe you'd still have strength enough to eat a dish of that chocolate ice cream I've got in the freezer, what do you think?'

Denny sniffled once and said, 'That'd be good.' She wiped her face some more and said, 'You don't think that man in the car ... he really wasn't one of Mom's boyfriends, huh?'

'I don't think so. We can ask her tomorrow.'

'I kind of thought he was lying to me. He didn't seem like Mom's type.'

'Oh? What type is that?' As soon as she said it she wanted to take the question back. *God, I'm discussing my sister's sexual preferences with her ten-year-old child.*

Denny yawned hugely and said, 'Big and ferocious. This guy was small and cute. Or he thought he was cute anyway.' She yawned again and added thoughtfully, 'He just wanted the car, I bet. He didn't even know I was there till I started to talk.' She leaned back in her seat, turned a tear-streaked face toward Sarah and said, 'Come to think of it, you know what he smelled like?'

'What?'

'Marijuana.' She shrugged. 'But I guess most grown-ups do sometimes, huh?'

Nineteen

'OK, Bernie, my man,' Hector said, rubbing his hands together, grinning and shrugging. 'Let's do some business, whaddya say?' Estes was scowling in his doorway, his disapproving face puckered up like a prune.

Hector was bursting with positive energy now, focused like a laser on closing this deal and getting on down the road. Bernie had been a real prick on the phone before, but what the hell. The finish line was in sight here, there were only a few obstacles left between Hector and his new life. No use holding a grudge.

But Estes was determined to get an apology. He kept going over and over how Hector had sworn at his wife. *'Language'* he called it, like some prissy professor. Had his nose in the air like he wasn't just some small-time pile-a-shit counterfeiter. 'That kind of *language* is just not acceptable in my home.' *Pussy little fake. Jesus, this guy was counterfeit all the way through.*

'You think I need your stupid job?' Flouncing around like a goddamn ballerina, blocking the doorway so Hector couldn't even get in out of the heat. 'I mean, I've got people *waiting in line* for my work, people who pay in advance and say please and thank you. Then you come around here with this cockamamie pay-as-you-go scheme and swear at my wife? I don't think so.'

'Bernie,' Hector said, and put on as much of the shit-eating grin as he could force out of his face, 'I was out of line, I admit it, OK? I was in a hurry and I just lost it. But I'm in an even bigger hurry now so do we really have to stand out here and talk this to death before we do it? I got places to go.'

But Bernie was having too much fun being the injured party to quit. He had things to say about *respect* and then he wanted to talk about *courtesy*, all this concern for manners while he kept Hector out on the step in the hot night. Then Mrs Bernie backed the family minivan out of the garage, right past them down the driveway, the two boys in pajamas, in their little booster seats in the back. Where the hell was she going with them this time of the night? Not that he cared. The boys were both yelling, 'Bye, Daddy!' Bernie started blowing kisses, saying, 'Take care, sweetie pie,' to his wife and yelling messages for his boys to give to Grammy.

The wife rolled down her window and said, 'They'll be fine, they'll sleep all the way to Pinetop.'

'Good,' Estes said, 'call me when you get there, remember. What's it going to be, three hours?' He looked at his watch.

'Just about. Don't be late Sunday, they like

to eat by one.' A lot more blowing kisses while Hector, the paying customer, stood on the step about to melt. He longed to smash this guy in the doorframe with his own front door, stupid pansy playing Father Knows Fucking Best.

Finally they were in the artsy-fartsy living room under the elaborate chandelier, Bernie's watercolors all around them on the walls, framed in gold. Probably had plenty of them because they never sold, right? Because who'd buy his crappy historical scenes of Old Tucson? They stood under the home-made art and argued some more.

Hector was doing the arguing now because he wanted to see the goods before he paid the rest of the money. Something about the way Bernie was behaving made Hector suspect he hadn't done the job at all and was getting ready to work some new dodge as soon as he got his hands on the cash.

'Absolutely not,' Bernie said. 'I did you a big favor doing this job without all the money up front, and you're not even grateful. You abuse my wife instead.'

'You've had my eight hundred dollars for three weeks, how about some gratitude for that? And I've got nothing. It's just good business, Bernie. You gotta show me the papers before you get the rest of the cash.' He was getting anxious about the stolen car sitting out there in the street too, no question but what the Evil Mama would have reported it by now. Suppose a cop came by and spotted the damn thing? He couldn't stand the thought of ending up in the slammer just for boosting that worthless piece of junk, all his careful plans in the toilet for nothing. But he had to see the merchandise before he paid. Damn, this man had a head like a rock.

Finally Bernie said, 'OK, you can look but don't touch, then I want the rest of the money and I want you out of here, understand?' He went into another room saying, 'You just wait right there.' Acting like a goddamn parole officer, Hector wanted to break his face so bad. But he came back with a plastic box, set it down and took out three cardboard sheets with clear plastic covers. Laid them out on the table, and there they were right there, beautiful, the passport and visa and driver's license, with Hector's picture and Ace's name, Adolph Alvin Perkins, to match the registration papers in the car. Hector got a little light-headed for a minute, looking down at his new self. He started to pick up the driver's license but Bernie grabbed his arm. 'Money first,' he said.

'I was just...' Hector said. He stopped then, because all of a sudden Bernie's watery gray eyes were watching him across the short blue barrel of a Rossi .38.

'Aw, shit, Bernie,' Hector said, 'now what's this about?'

'Keep it simple, Hector,' Estes said. 'Just put your money on the table.' He let go of Hector's wrist and backed up a step, the gun steady in his right hand. Did Bernie have the balls to fire that thing? In his wildest dreams, Hector had never imagined this wussy painter would have a gun. But he was standing there like Cool Hand Bernie, didn't look like he was bluffing. Of course he had himself a cheap little lady's gun, but even so he could have, what, five bullets in that cylinder? Only had to hit you with one. Hector could almost feel himself sucking air through a hole in his chest.

Bernie had a different attitude now, too, not so preachy, just serious and cold. He said, 'Put your money down on the table so I can see it all, and then pick up your documents and get out of here.'

Jesus, another minute he'd be saying what they had here was a failure to communicate. It would serve the little shit right if he got his ass whipped, pulling that thing on a customer. Hector halfway planned how to do it, fake him out with a pleading move and then twist that gun out of his puny hands and pound his face to a pulp with it.

But the new papers were right there on the table, clean and pretty with fresh ink, and they ... damn, they made him feel like a pro. He didn't want to fight with Bernie, what the hell did he need that for? He wanted to take his new identity and roll on down to Mexico, start his new life as a drug lord, save his fighting moves for the badasses down there.

So he set his Trader Joe's bag on the table behind the sofa and reached in for the long white envelope. Couldn't seem to put his hand on it right away. Felt around a couple of times and said, 'Well, shit,' and spread the top open wide. Pulled out the Gatorade and the windbreaker, the cell phone and three little bags of dope and the ... no, not the Ruger.

The money wasn't there. So it was better if Bernie didn't see the Ruger till Hector decided what his next few moves were going to be. He picked up the windbreaker and shook it, felt in all the pockets just to make sure, but he knew he hadn't put the envelope in the pocket of Ace's raincoat, why would he do that? For a few seconds he had one of those wipe-outs like in the car when that little girl sat up. Like looking into a fog bank, and this time it felt like the sun was never going to shine again.

But Bernie Estes was standing right there looking more and more inclined to fire that motherfucking Rossi at him. Hector went back to the last clear thought he had before he hit the fog bank. Grabbed the handles of the grocery bag with his left hand, turned to Bernie Estes with his shoulders raised in a mock-hopeless shrug and said, 'Stupid money musta fell out in the car, I'll run out and get it.' Grinned his shit-eating grin and reached into the bottom of the grocery bag with his right hand, got a firm grip on the Ruger and kept right on grinning while he shot Bernie Estes through the bag. No time to aim but then his target was only two feet away. The shot entered Bernie's chest high, just below the neck, and knocked him over backwards as he was trying to return fire.

Bernie's shot went into the chandelier, made a helluva racket, shattered glass that flew everywhere like bright knives. Hector felt pain on his cheek and knew one of the pieces had cut him. He pulled the gun out of the bag, aimed carefully and fired two more shots into Estes' squirming body.

When Estes lay still at his feet he put the Gatorade and jacket, the phone and the dope back in the bottom of the bag. He laid his new documents carefully on top, and slid the Ruger down alongside everything with the handle up so if he needed it he could get it fast. His hands were shaking a little but he thought he was OK, just had to look cool from here to the car, no big deal.

He walked out of Estes' house carrying the Trader Joe's bag in his left hand, pulling keys out of his pocket. A couple of neighbors came out of their houses and looked around, asking each other, 'You hear something?' Hector walked straight to his car, got in and drove east on Princeton Road the way Ace had taught him, slow as a hearse, easy over the speed bumps. He turned left on Prudence, turned left again on Broadway and caught the light just right.

Cool Hand Hector, right? Damn right. Let's see ol' Rudy top that one.

Twenty

Rudy Ortiz never took a vacation. But sometimes he liked to relax a little after work and for that he usually went to the dog races. Tucson Greyhound Park was on South Third near the highway, an oval dirt track backed by indoor bleachers in an old cast cement building. Its lumpy asphalt parking lot had room for a thousand cars, but usually there were only a hundred or so nondescript older models clustered near the door. Admission was a dollar and a quarter, the program cost a dollar and a half, and there was rarely much of a wait at the betting windows. The clientele ran to janitors, waitresses and cowboys, truck drivers and bartenders, with a sprinkling of sunburned tourists. People often brought children in strollers. Rudy served on the park board because he thought the dog track, like the tire store, was perfect just as it was, and he hoped to protect it from any improvement.

Sometimes on Sunday when the track opened early, Rudy's wife joined him and they had dinner on the second floor near the windows, watching the dogs run. Camille liked to bet the *quiniela* and they spent a lot of time picking the dogs.

During the week he went alone in the evening and sat in the noisy bar downstairs. Besides the dog track out front, on the ground floor he could watch two or three other races from around the country, simulcast on big TV screens. You could bet on horses as well as dogs, and people who had money on a horse at Santa Anita or Pimlico often stood in front of the sets and urged their chosen horses on.

There was no table service on the ground floor. People brought their own drinks from the bar on the back wall and carried baskets of food in from a window in the lobby. All that fetching of food and drink, added to the traffic back and forth to the betting windows and the yelling in front of the TV screens, made the place feel as crowded and busy as a train station. The lack of service meant nobody hassled you. You could sit at a table as long as you liked, alone or with somebody, drinking or not. It was a good place to meet people and do a little business, so public and noisy that in effect it was private.

Tilly found him there at ten thirty Wednesday night. He pulled a chair away from the table next to Rudy's and sat sideways on it, close enough to talk but not to eat or drink. Tilly didn't come to be sociable, he would tell what he had to tell, get his orders and leave.

'OK, like I told you this morning Ace is dead,' Rudy told him. 'And now I got a few more details. The *boca* got back to me after lunch. That John Doe in the paper, that was

Ace. Some runner found him in the park yesterday morning.'

'Mmm.' Tilly could read at about third-grade level, but most of what was in the newspaper puzzled him, like news from a distant planet, so he rarely bothered to look at it. He was not surprised, though, to hear that Ace was dead. He had never figured Ace for a no-show. Man made plenty of money working for Rudy, and he was the only one of Rudy's dealers that Tilly knew he couldn't scare. Guy like that didn't just run off. But he had never seemed like a likely victim, either.

'What makes 'em think it was murder?'

'He was stabbed.'

'Ace? Hard to believe. You see a picture?'

'No. But my mouth saw the autopsy and his prison records. He says they match. They made him offa his prints.'

'Huh. They know who killed him?'

'Not yet. They know he was dealing and they're going through his laptop.'

'You worried about that?'

'Nah. They ain't gonna find much there.'

'You sure?'

'Uh-huh. Ace kept a coded customer list but he blew off all his orders as fast as he filled them. He told me once the reason he left Stroud and came to work for me was he thought Stroud wrote down too much.'

Tilly asked, impressed, 'How'd you get Stroud to let him go?'

'I didn't. Ace did. When he made up his mind to come over to me he told Stroud he kept a list of all his customers and dealers, in a safety deposit box. Said he left instructions with a family member to mail it to the chief of police if –' Rudy squinted, remembering – '"in the event of my death". I think that's how he said it.'

'You know how to find the box?'

'Ace never done it. I told him, I can't have something like that hanging around, suppose you get popped? And he said, "Don't worry, I got no family and I never write anything on paper".'

'Did he tell you who'd be on the list if there was one?'

'No. But if I thought hard enough I could probably sit right here and come up with most of the names myself. I pretty much know all the players. Hell, so do you by now, right?'

'I guess. Tucson's not LA.'

'It ain't even Phoenix. That's what's good about it.' Rudy watched a big gray gelding win by three lengths at Woodlands. When he turned back to Tilly he looked grave. 'Right now, I'm more interested in who capped Ace and why. If it was just some personal thing, well ... he won't be easy to replace but that's all it amounts to, the bother. But if somebody's coming after my dealers, that's different.' He stared into his beer and then reluctantly put his biggest worry into words. 'Or if there's something in that apartment that leads them to me.'

'I can't get in. They got one of them special

locks on it.'

'I know. But keep nosing around. And we'll all need new phones, I'll do that tomorrow.'

Rudy didn't worry about surveillance much. He assumed he was being watched by the local Narcs, but so what? They watched everybody in his part of town. Now and then they nailed a load and put somebody in jail. It never changed anything. He kept most of his business out of sight, but even so he was doing too well in South Tucson not to attract some curiosity. And he was *la raza*, Latino. Cops always suspected them first though they said they didn't.

The trick, he had always thought, was to keep his lifestyle and possessions so low-key that drug interdiction people would think that he was just a small cog in the big wheel of drug traffic that rolled through Tucson year after year. Unless something obvious forced them to come after him, he thought, they'd probably go on waiting for him to lead them to the Big One.

Any luck, by the time they figured him out, he'd be the Big One that got away.

What he did worry about, every day, was the wild card you couldn't predict. For instance, Hector Rodriguez. 'What about that silly-actin' kid worked with Ace, that Hector? You find him?'

'Not yet.'

Rudy allowed himself to look annoyed. Maybe even Tilly needed a fire lit under him sometimes. 'What's so fuckin' hard about finding a snot-nose kid from the neighborhood? Shit, he grew up here, everybody south of Twenty-Second Street must know who he is.'

'They do, and nobody knows where he is today. His old beater car's gone from beside the house where he always kept it. Hasn't been back since we been watchin' the place. His mama says she hasn't heard from him and I believe her. I can see she's worried. He's just *out of town*.'

'You know –' Rudy rolled a toothpick from the left side of his mouth to the right, thinking – 'he might be gone in Ace's car. The cops haven't found it.'

'How would he get Ace's car unless...' Tilly shifted in his chair, looked at Rudy and then away. 'There's no way Hector is tough enough to whack Ace Perkins.'

Rudy took a sip of his Dos Equis. The skin of his face seemed to be growing darker. 'Didn't you check this kid out after Ace hired him?'

'I did and there was nothing. One little stretch in juvie, otherwise he boxed up groceries, worked at the car wash, lived home with Mama.'

'But now he's starting to look good for Ace's killing?'

'Rudy, I don't think that figures at all. Ace was too smart—'

'It figures if he's got Ace's car.' Rudy set his glass down sharply and stared at Tilly. Red veins had begun to show in the whites of his eyes. 'What's the use having you for a fixer if I gotta find out everything myself?'

'I ain't done yet, Rudy.'

'You ain't even started as far as I can see. What about Hector's mama? Any chance she's pushin' for somebody else?'

'Rudy, she lives in a mud adobe down on Ohio Street, she ain't in the life. She does laundry for Anglos and sells Amway products. Combs her little girls' hair every morning on the step, gives them a coin for the half-price lunch at middle school.'

'A ton of dope gets pushed through Tucson every day by housewives and janitors. Get Sanchez to ask around, see what else she peddles besides soap.'

He turned away from Tilly Stubbs toward the bank of large-screen TVs on the wall across the room, and watched eight horses bolt out of the gate at Palm Beach. A youngish man in tight black jeans stood watching the race intensely. When the number six horse won he walked past them tearing up tickets, and sat down at a table by himself, cursing bitterly.

'I got a better idea,' Rudy said, turning back. 'Never mind farting around with Sanchez. All he brings back is stupid gossip. You go on over to that Rodriguez house yourself in the morning, put the arm on those two little girls and get their mama to tell you where we can find Hector.'

'Rudy, these are people with a lot of friends, the neighbors ain't gonna like...' He quit talking when Rudy Ortiz slammed his beer glass down on the table so hard it broke.

Very red in the face, paying no attention to the tableful of beer raining on to his knees or to the blood running out of the cut on his hand, Rudy leaned across gleaming shards of glass and hissed, 'I lived in this town all my life, asshole, you think you need to tell me what people here don't like?'

'I'm just sayin'—'

'And I'm sayin' don't say. Who needs you to fuckin' say?' His voice had become a raspy whisper, he seemed to be choking on his rage. 'I pay you top dollar to be my enforcer, now get your candy ass on the street and start breaking bones. Next time I see you,' he wheezed as Tilly got up and employees in aprons came running with towels, 'you better be handing me Hector Rodriguez.'

Twenty-One

Hector pulled into a Super K-mart on the north side of Broadway and parked. He needed to sit still a minute and think. It was getting harder and harder to keep his plan straight. Really, now that he'd killed Bernie, he should get out of town *right away*. But first he had to drive this old Dart back to the Fry's store and pick up Ace's SUV. Then he'd go home, peel his money off the bottom of that loose tile under the bed, pack a few clothes. From there he could roll right on to I-19 and be on his way.

That was the plan. But now he had this problem: Ace's money was missing. His mind kept asking, *Where the fuck? How the fuck?* The money envelope had been in the Trader Joe's bag, no question about that. He hadn't taken it out of there because he hadn't had time to find the shoulder pouch he wanted to carry it in. And he hadn't let the bag out of his sight since he picked it off the ground by Ace Perkins' body. Had he?

Well, except ... With sudden perfect clarity he remembered running up the aisle at the movie theater with Ace's phone ringing in his hand. *But then I turned the phone off and went right back in, and the bag was exactly where I left it, in front of my seat.* The little girl was still sitting in the seat next to it with her eyes glued to the screen, looked like she hadn't moved or even breathed, hardly, since he left.

Anyway, come on, it was beyond crazy to think that a grade-school girl in braids could have grabbed his money. She wouldn't have dared!

But who else had access? He had bought tickets with that money when they entered the theater, and the only time it was out of his sight after that was when he stepped outside with the phone. He was sure of it now.

So it had to be her. *Shee-it.*

I find that fucking rotten brat I'm gonna

strangle her with her own braids.

How was he going to find her, though? He didn't even know her last name.

He rocked in his seat and ground his teeth from the aggravation of having his plan screwed up like this, time after time. After he'd worked so hard and been so careful, why did everything have to get so – *wait.* He stopped rocking and made a small happy sound, 'Ooh!' *You're sitting in her Mama's car, dickhead.*

He punched the button on the glove compartment. The door dropped open but of course no light came on, stupid pile-a-shit car. But the registration was in there, all right. The dome light didn't work either, so he got out and walked over to the light from the front of the store to read it. It was made out to Janine Lynch, with an address on Lurlene Street. Couple blocks south of the Fry's store, just like the kid said. He folded the registration, stuck it in the cargo pocket of his pants, and got back in the car. In less than a minute he was back in westbound traffic, looking for a place to make a U-turn and go back to Kolb Road.

The clock in this heap was running, but of course the time was wrong. It said ten minutes to nine and he knew it had to be later than that. He looked at his watch, squinted and looked again. Ten minutes to nine, was that possible? It seemed as if hours had passed since he left that little girl sitting in the theater.

Well, but then ... girls that age, he knew from his sisters, they really got *into* a movie, and *Master and Commander* had at least another half hour to run. Denny would still be sitting there, staring up at those sailors on the screen. Why go to her house and wait when he didn't even know how she'd get there, or when? *Wake up and smell the coffee, Hector.* All he had to do was move his ass and he could still find her where he left her.

Less than half an hour after he shot Bernie Estes, he was back in the Roxy parking ramp, parking the old Dart again. *Goddamn, I'm glad I don't have to explain this to anybody*, he thought as he walked down the cement slope. *Hector Rodriguez, gonna be a big man in the drug trade but right now he's chasing the cash that was swiped from him by a little girl with braids. Shee-it.*

He fished his ticket stub out of his pocket, lucky thing he kept that at least. He walked in the front door and straight across the lobby, showed it to the ticket-taker at the podium on the far side. Said, 'Hadda run out for a minute,' and got an impatient nod. Padded softly up the carpeted stairs to theater six, holding his breath.

He had thought hard during the drive about the quietest way to take the money away from the kid. *Get a hand over her mouth and pat her down quick.* People right close around might notice, but he could be out of there before they decided what to do about it. It wasn't as if he had to kill her. Even if she had the nerve to complain to anybody, who was going to believe a wormy-looking little brat had stolen all that money?

And grabbing it away from her would be easy. No purse, no jacket, the money had to be right there in her clothes.

But when he got inside he couldn't see her. He knew exactly where they'd been sitting and she wasn't there. Why would she move? He patrolled both sides, walking quietly down the aisle and then really taking his time on the way back up, scanning the faces carefully in the light from the screen. The theater was less than half-full, it was a school night so there were hardly any children. In a couple of minutes he had satisfied himself that she was gone.

He stood behind the back row for a few seconds with rage burning a hole in his gut. He had seen how she looked at the screen, as if she wanted to crawl in it and live there. She would never have left the movie, he felt sure, for anything but that money.

Well, so Evil Mama had Evil Child, that figured. But what, he asked himself in a hot surge of self-pity, had he ever done to deserve the rotten luck that led him to their worthless car?

Well, he would just have to do it the hard way, go to her house and take it away from her there. He walked down the aisle one more time, and opened the door under the light. Then for reasons he didn't want to think about he resurrected an old trick from the days when he and his buds used to skip junior high and sneak ten little gang-bangers into the movies on one ticket. He pulled Denny's ticket stub out of his pocket and inserted it carefully between the latch and the doorjamb. Just in case. Because things had been happening very fast, the world was getting a kind of a flaky feel to it, so you just never knew.

He walked up the stained cement stairwell, heard a funny sound, and stood still on the third step from the top, listening. After a few seconds a bad knot of pain began to grow in his stomach, and he decided that in some weird way, maybe sometimes you did know. He was hearing the unmistakable static-infused crackle of a police radio.

A loud but hard-to-understand dispatcher's voice said something like, 'Fifty-two, say again your location?' And a voice nearby responded, deep and clear, 'Copy, I'm on the top level of the Roxy Theater parking lot, corner of Campbell and Grant. Looking at the brown 1976 Dodge Dart, license...' He read off the letters and numbers and continued, 'Mentioned in tonight's BOLOs as the car stolen out of the Fry's parking lot on Kolb Road.'

The static voice said something and the nearby voice went on: 'Affirmative, I have it in sight. You want to send a tow? Uh ... no, no keys. Locked, yes. Roger, I'll hold.'

Hector eased up in the stairwell till he could just see over the top step. A young officer stood by the open door of his squad car, facing away from the stairs with the mike in his hand. He looked relaxed and easy, chewing gum. Hector thought about Ace's Ruger right here in the bag, eight rounds left in it. *I could blow his head off right now*. He held the thought for about ten seconds, enjoying the feeling of power it gave him, before he told himself, *Forget it. They'd follow you forever*.

The officer was looking around the parking ramp, and as his head turned toward the stairwell Hector ducked and went quickly back down to the door and pulled it open. The ticket stub fell to the floor as he went through. He closed the door quietly, walked back up the aisle and went out through the lobby into the still-hot night. He turned away from the bright lights to his right, around the corner on to darker Edison and into Tahoe Park where, earlier, Denny had pointed to the pajama-clad boys practicing Tae Kwan-Do.

The tiny park was dimly lighted, but empty and quiet now. Hector moved into the shadow of some bordering bushes, took his phone out of its holster, pulled up his speed-dial menu and called a cab.

Ace had made him put that taxi number on there. 'If I ever need to pull out and leave you I will,' he said on their first night together, 'and then if you're lucky you might need a ride home.' *Good ol' Ace, all heart.*

Waiting for his cab made him wonder if that little girl named Denny had found her way home yet. Was she sitting in her house, holding his money in her thin hands, smiling? He got mad all over again, double and triple mad from having to squat in the bushes listening to that police radio – he could still hear it up there on the top level of the ramp, the radio squawking away.

The tow truck arrived while he waited for his cab. There was a lot of talk and maneuvering, the *beep beep beep* of the truck backing up, and then the whole procession came down, the tow truck pulling the old brown Dodge backwards, the squad car behind with its roof lights flashing. Hector watched, burning with anger, longing to put a shot through the cop's windshield. He hugged himself, trying to calm down. *Be cool. You still got your papers and your gun and Ace's car.*

Ace's car. He said it over and over, as he walked around the block to wait in front of Bookman's, where he'd said he would meet the taxi. *Long as I got Ace's car, I'm still in business. Just gotta revise the plan a little. Take this cab home, get my gear and money outa there. Go get Ace's car, drive it to that address on Lurlene Street and find the freaky kid with the braids. Get my money back from her – the easy way or the hard way, however she wants it. And then get out of this town.*

Twenty-Two

Didn't it just figure? All the other aggravations he'd already dealt with today, and now he got one of them funny-sounding immigrants for a taxi driver. Had on some kinda long gray dress with a vest thing, a full beard and bushy black hair around a white cap. Kind of a guy Hector and his buds called Ali Outzenfree from that kids' game they used to play. Indian from fucking India for chrissake, not one you could talk to from down here on the rez.

Hector said, 'You know where Ohio Street is?'

'South of the highway, is it not?' Talked English like the Queen of England with a lilt.

'Uh-huh. Take I-10 to I-19 and I'll tell you from there.'

When they got to his neighborhood Hector had him drive right past his house, turn left on Fifteenth and come back up on Missouri. Most of the yards looked like trash heaps, car bodies sitting on blocks, piles of lumber and old furniture. Hector's house was old and beat-up, but Mama kept it neat.

He didn't see anybody watching the house, so he directed the driver back to Sixth

Avenue and got out in front of Playa de Mariscos. When he paid the ten dollars he owed, almost all the change he had left on him, he said, 'Fifty more in it for you if you'll wait for me here.'

'I cannot wait more than fifteen minutes.'

'That'll do.' Hector walked back down Ohio, circled into the alley, unlocked the little iron gate and moved silently into his own back yard. His mother had a ramada in the yard where she did some cooking and laundry and sometimes snoozed in a hammock. Hector sat among the pots and jars for two minutes, listening. Nothing moved. The only sound was a dog barking a couple of blocks away.

He turned his key in the back door and eased inside, moved past the soft breathing of his sisters on the daybed and stopped by his mother's open bedroom door. She turned over and groaned in her sleep; he stood listening to the whir and trickle of the swamp cooler in her window till her breathing was regular again.

The hinges on his bedroom door squeaked a little. He took his time and closed the door from the inside before he turned on one tiny lamp on his dresser.

First the money. He was a little too big to get all the way under his bed, but he knew exactly where the loose tile was. He stretched, and in a minute had the tight roll of bills in his hand. He sat on the floor by the bed to unwrap it – his own two thousand, saved up one bill at a time over four months. The cash in Ace's bag, unexpected riches, had felt like good times. This money still smelled like baking soda, sweat and fear – afternoons in the single-wide, nights in the car with Ace. It was wages, earned the hard way with hustle and worry, and as usual not nearly enough.

For now it was all he had, though, and losing Ace's white envelope had taught him something: keeping all your money in one place was bullshit. He stuck a fifty in each of the two big cargo pockets of his pants, slid a couple of bills into pockets in Ace's windbreaker and zipped them up. The new canvas duffel he had recently bought and sneaked into the house was under the bed in its box. He slid it out carefully, trying not to scrape, and opened it on the bed. He was packing, sliding hundred dollar bills into socks and underwear and tucking them into neat zippered pockets in the bag, when his door swung open and there stood Mama with the hammer in her hand.

'Hey Mama,' he whispered, pushing money under a pile of shorts, getting his smile started, 'did I wake you up?'

'What's going on?' Tiny and wild-eyed in her blue nightgown, hair flying around, toenails long and ragged on her bare feet, she stared at the half-packed bag. 'You getting ready to go someplace, Hector?'

'Mama, put the hammer down, I'm sorry if I scared you.' He reached out for it but she backed up a step.

'What happened to you Monday night?' If she got mad enough she still might hit him with that hammer. She had not raised three kids by herself in south Tucson without having plenty of juice. 'You forget where you live?'

'Hey, I called you Tuesday morning, remember?'

'Uh-huh. From Benson. Said you'd be home in a few hours. What, Benson got moved farther down the road?'

'Well...' He shrugged helplessly, his hands held wide.

'Well...?' She imitated his gesture. 'So now it's almost Thursday morning and I'm asking, where you been? And where do you think you're going?'

'I been around, Mama, right around here in Tucson.' He tried a lofty tone. 'I had business.'

'Oh, business, listen to the big tycoon. I had a call from your parole officer, that's what I had. You forget you were suppose to check in yesterday?'

'Guess I did.' It seemed like a hundred years since he had cared about that nagging little prick. He pulled a couple of new shirts, still in their plastic wrap, out of the back of the closet. Didn't care if she saw them now. He had been hiding his preparations for weeks, but now he tossed in the new chinos he had clipped to the coat hanger inside his raincoat. 'Don't matter, I'm leaving anyway.'

They had started out whispering but

Mama's whisper had quickly turned into her normal voice so Hector spoke up too. As they got louder, his sisters appeared in the doorway, clinging to each other, their eyes wide with fear. 'What's happening?' Luz asked, and then, relieved, 'Oh, Hector's home!' They ran to him with hugs. They imitated Mama, who usually acted as if he walked on water. Mama followed the old Mexican ways that said the man should be king in his house. Till she got angry – then you better be ready to duck.

Hector had worried so much about what Mama would say when she found out he was leaving, that in the end he'd decided it would be better for everybody if he didn't tell her. Without really admitting it to himself in so many words, he had intended to sneak away and call her later from Mexico.

But now the taxi was waiting, Evil Mama's car was in the hands of the police with, come to think of it, his fingerprints all over it, and the neighbors on Princeton Drive might decide to report those gunshot noises any time. And he had just realized he never thought to pick up the shell casings from the last two bullets he fired into 'Estes the Bestes'. So his mother's anger was no longer his biggest worry. He brushed his sisters aside, walked past his mother without looking at her, went into the bathroom and got his shaving gear and toothbrush and came back and put them in another of the clever little pockets in the new duffel. He took the Gatorade bottle out of the Trader Joe's bag, folded the bag as flat as it would go with the gun and wallet and jacket inside, and laid it on top of the rest of his gear. The duffel wasn't quite full, so it sagged a little when he zipped it shut.

'Mama,' he said, 'I gotta go.'

She was still holding the hammer, but Hector watched her expression fade from rage to sorrow and knew she wasn't going to use it on him. 'Twenty years' hard work since I started to carry you,' she said, 'all I get is, "Mama, I gotta go"?'

Damn, why did everything have to be so hard? He remembered one of his uncles saying, 'Women always want more.' He picked up the new duffel and walked to her side, gave her a quick hug with one arm and moved away fast so she couldn't grab him. Didn't need to worry about that, though, her body felt stiff as a stick and she never moved. 'I'll call soon,' he said, 'take care now.' She stared past him into the closet, didn't even turn her head when he walked away.

Maria Elena said softly, 'Bye, Hector.' Luz ventured one quick, scared little bye-bye wave, watching her mother covertly.

Hector moved quickly through the back yard, stopped to lock the back gate, and still got back to the taxi in fourteen minutes. The driver was hunched over the wheel with all the doors locked, spooked by the neighborhood. Hector knocked on the back window and laughed when the guy jumped. When Ali finally got a rear door open Hector got in and said, 'OK, my man, time to go get my wheels.

Take me to the Fry's store at Kolb and Golf Links.'

'First I must get my fifty,' the man said, and Hector, grunting with irritation, dug one out of his right-hand pocket. The driver grabbed it and drove out of there fast. Hector sat back against the seat and let his mind go blank. No use figuring out anything more till he was in the Excursion and ready to hit the road. Then he'd decide how to get his money back from the hellcat with the braids. But he wanted that feeling, of the big powerful car under him, before he forced himself to decide anything more. All he knew right now was that it had to be quick.

Pulling into Fry's lot, he told the cabbie to drive around to the back of the store.

As soon as they rounded the corner he could see the big shiny rear end of the Ford poking out between a couple of employees' cars. And right behind it, *shit shit shit!* Another one of those blue-and-white patrol cars was pulled up crosswise, fucking light strip flashing like a goddamn merry-go-round, pale green light inside from the PC screen on the dash. Behind the wheel was a big motherfucking goddamn shit-for-brains Tucson cop talking on his fucking cell phone, stupid fuckhead!

Hector's brain ran out of obscenities and hit pause. Hunkered in his private dead zone, he watched the patrolman close his phone and get out of the squad car. In his neat blue uniform, in no hurry because he had a badge and a gun and all the power of the city of Tucson backing him up, he walked around his vehicle. Just beyond his own rear bumper he stopped, tall and strong, weight-lifter's shoulders bulging out of his bulletproof vest, and beckoned to the tow truck that was pulling around the corner.

The Indian cab driver was watching the tall cop too, Hector noticed as his brain came back to life. He could see that old Ali wanted to jump out and run over there, yelling for help. *He'd do it right now if he wasn't afraid to leave me with the cab.* Better get him the hell away from the cop and the tow truck while he was still dithering, Hector decided. He chuckled a little, trying to sound like the SUV had nothing to do with him, and said, 'Well, hell, looks like we gotta detour around this mess, don't it?'

'I do not understand,' Ali said. 'I thought you said your car was back here.'

'Well, I did have one here,' Hector said, still in that aw-shucks voice, 'but I guess my friend just took it on home with him. That's OK, I'll go get my other one.'

The driver went along with the story, probably because he didn't like being back there in a tight space, in the dark, with a man who was obviously lying to him. He had to back up and pull forward a couple of times to make the tight turn. Then he wheeled around the Dumpsters and drove to the front parking lot. In the back seat, Hector was near tears, thinking how close he had been to driving away from here in Ace's SUV. Part of his mind was already vaulting on ahead, telling him to forget his rage and go get his old Subaru Brat from Ace's single-wide in the trailer park up on Ruthrauf. A future kingpin in the drug trade couldn't operate out of a taxi. And he couldn't be seen with tears running down his face either, but oh, *fucking Goddamn it, if he'd just been a few minutes earlier!*

Ali didn't ask where he needed to go next. He pulled into a parking spot near the front of the store and turned off the motor, and Hector knew from the way he squared his shoulders that he was sick of worrying about this fare and had decided to blow him off. So he wasn't surprised when the little guy twisted around in his seat, not really looking at Hector but past him out the window while he said, 'Very well, sir, we have used up the fifty dollars, now I must go home.'

'Bullshit.' Hector knew that cop was going to be busy at the back of the store for a few more minutes, so up here in front he and Ali were alone in the cab together and Hector was the one carrying a Ruger with eight rounds left. 'I still got at least thirty dollars' worth of time coming,' he told the driver, 'and what you're gonna do with it is take me to the Desert Oasis mobile home park up on Ruthrauf.'

But old Ali seemed to have grown bigger *cojones* up here in this lighted space with people milling all around them. He shook his head and said, 'No, sir, we are all done.' And right then, fucking Christ, Hector remembered that his gun was inside the Trader Joe's bag that he had zipped inside the duffel.

But you had to keep on keeping on, wasn't that what his parole officer always said? So he leaned across the back of the driver's seat flashing the shit-eating grin and in the voice of a wheedling boy he said, 'Aw, c'mon, man, we couldn't of used up all that money just coming up here from Ohio Street, did we?' He didn't mind the contempt gathering on the cabby's face because by then he had his boot knife in his left hand behind the seat. Keeping his face forward in the light so the cabby could see his foolish smile, he passed the knife to his right hand.

When he was ready he grabbed Ali's hair at the back, just below the white cap, keeping his own smiling face up there in the light so anybody passing would see only a Hispanic passenger joking with his Indian driver, probably say, Is this a great country or what? He slid the knife along the top of the seat under his hand, stuck the sharp point in the driver's throat and said, 'You wanna die right now?'

Ali sucked in air and rolled his terrified eyes back toward his passenger silently, shaking his head emphatically, though Hector could see it hurt his scalp.

Hector said, 'Then put this fucker in gear and drive west on Golf Links to Aviation Highway, take that to Euclid and turn north and from there on I'll tell you where to go.'

'I cannot see if you hold my head...'

'You rather I cut your throat?'

Ali shook his head again, pleading, 'No, no, please, I have three children!'

'Better drive if you want to see 'em again.'

It was over fifteen miles from the grocery store to the mobile home park, and Hector was shaking with exhaustion by the time they reached it. Ali was right about one thing, he couldn't see very well with Hector holding his head like that. So they had several near-collisions, and Ali cried the whole way and prayed in some funny language. Just north of Davis-Monthan, with the big jets roaring over their heads, after narrowly missing an eighteen-wheeler, Ali pissed his pants. Hector gritted his teeth and tried not to breathe till they reached the crumbling gate of the Desert Oasis.

'Stop right here,' Hector said, and slid off the seat fast, dragging his duffel behind him. The park was poorly lighted at night. He kicked the cab door shut, trotted through the gate and ducked behind a Dumpster in case old Ali had a gun stashed somewhere in that front seat. Apparently he didn't; he hit the gas and took off east on Wetmore laying rubber on the street.

Walking along the lumpy asphalt driveway toward Ace's lot, Hector felt used up and disgusted. He knew he should have kept the taxi with him till he was sure his Brat was still in the carport and fit to drive. But in that small, urine-smelling space with the weeping, praying driver, he had found himself longing to kill the man just to shut him up. He could have done it too, nothing to stop him, except right then some voice in his head said, *That's enough killings in Tucson for now, just get your butt out of town*.

And for a minute it felt like good sense maybe turned his luck, because there was his old Subaru Brat right where he'd left it, facing the dying bougainvillea vine at the end of the carport. All four wheels still on it and no flat tires. Key turned in the lock just like always, motor started right up and there was even half a tank of gas left, all *right*!

The park was quiet for once, lights off in most of the units around him. Sitting in the dim light coming from the street, listening to the quiet hum of his old, well-cared-for motor, he rubbed his tired arms and began to cheer up a little. Everybody hits tough times, he told himself, you just have to get through it. He thought about the frantically weeping, praying cab driver, and chuckled. *First time I ever actually scared the piss out of anybody*.

Before he pulled out on the street, he dug Evil Mama's car registration paper out of his right pocket, turned on the dome light and read the address on Lurlene Street. Just off Kolb Road. Wasn't this weird? Sometimes he went months without even *thinking* about Kolb Road, now for two days he'd practically lived on the damn crazy street. A few minutes later he turned south on it again and saw it was still full of traffic roaring both ways, an endless river of noise and light.

After Kolb, Lurlene Street seemed unbelievably quiet. Dark, too. Hector saw one light, way at the back in the brick duplex on the next corner, but the house was silent, nothing moving. Different strokes, man. His part of town would just be starting to jump about now.

He strained to see house numbers, followed them as they grew larger. Evil Mama must be one more block east. One car was parked on the street up there about the middle of the block with the parking lights on, but ... oh motherfucking shit it was another blue-and-white. What was *with* those fuckers tonight, were they just *attached* to him or something?

The patrolman was out of his vehicle, standing by the front door of a house under an overhang with a little light shining down on him. Hector could see the house number now, same as the paper in his hand. The uniformed officer was beating on the door with his fist relentlessly, *bam bam bam*, the noise like cannon fire in the quiet street. While Hector watched, dogs started barking and lights came on in surrounding houses. The cop was looking around, scanning the way cops did, and when his eyes got to Hector's slow-moving car they stayed on it. His fist never stopped pounding on the door but Hector could see his little computer brain taking in the make, model and color as Hector approached. Hector sped up and rolled by. In the rear-view mirror he saw the cop's head swivel, still watching him, memorizing the license number now. Hector turned left at the next corner, kept on going down Birch Avenue to Stella Road and turned left again.

He watched his mirrors. No squad car appeared. Two more blocks and I'll know he's not going to follow, he promised himself. He kept checking the mirrors and when no lights appeared by the end of the second block he said, *'Yeah!'*

But as soon as he was sure he was safe he felt the last of his energy draining away, like water from an open tap. In the last two days he had killed two men and threatened to kill a third, kidnapped a small girl by mistake, and had two vehicles and a fistful of cash snatched right out from under his eyes. And now, in the least likely place, he had been blindsided by still another cop. It was too much. He had to sleep or die.

Kolb Road was beginning to feel like the punishment for every sin he'd ever even thought about, but he maneuvered his way on to it one more time. He drove south to I-10 and underneath it to the frontage road, and rented a room at one of the ten interchangeable motels in a three-block area with signs reading: $36.95 and up. The clerk said that would be $48.35 with tax, and Hector, too tired to argue, paid it and went upstairs to a room that smelled like cigarettes and sweat. The couple next door encouraged each other loudly in the pursuit of pleasure, banging their headboard against the wall, but Hector was past getting turned on or even irritated.

The image that came into his mind after he closed his eyes was of that tall, big-shouldered police officer, standing behind Ace's SUV and beckoning to a tow truck. *Tomorrow I'm going to Mexico*, he promised himself as he drifted away, *where at least I know I can turn around without bumping into fucking Tucson police.*

Twenty-Three

'This T-shirt's pretty shabby,' Sarah said, 'but I guess it'll cover your bones, won't it?'

'Sure. Thanks.' Denny held it up. 'Hey, the Diamondbacks. I didn't know you were a baseball fan.'

'Oh, that's an old shirt of Andy's, I found it in a box of stuff from the other house.'

It had not been old the day she pulled it out of a box she thought held only sheets. Suddenly smelling Andy where she least expected him, she'd given a great cry of despair and spent the next half hour curled around the shirt on the bedroom rug, howling like a hurt dog. Hardly the brave start she'd intended for her newly single life, the episode shamed her so much she added it to the grudges she held against Andy, disregarding the fact that he knew nothing about it. He had been an ardent lover once, lavish with flowers and kisses, and even after he began malingering he always won his way back with sweet praises for 'my wife with the traffic-stopping legs' and 'my girl with the barn-burner smile'. She had thrown him out, but his absence cut like a knife.

Having stained his shirt with make-up and tears, she wore it like an angry battle flag while she pruned bushes, cleaned gutters and painted the back fence. When it was stiff with sweat she washed it with bleach and afterwards wore it for all her hardest chores, relentlessly punishing the shirt for its owner's offenses. Turning it over to Denny would be the first kindness she'd ever shown it. Seeing its blurred colors hanging limp on Denny's slender hands, she decided it was high time she let her grievances against Andy go too. She and that shirt had both suffered enough.

Denny wasn't making any move to get into it, though, she was standing awkwardly, looking at her toes. Was she going into shock? 'Would you like to take a quick shower while I dish up the ice cream? You might sleep better.'

'OK.'

Why was she standing by the bed like that, not moving? Sarah said, 'You need any help?'

'No, thanks.' She shook her head so sharply that her braids swung wide. Sarah could see she wanted to be left alone to undress. She walked out to the kitchen, wondering, *Isn't it a little soon for that?* The idea that Denny might be approaching puberty, becoming shy about her body, was sharp as a sword in her chest. *She's hardly had any childhood yet! Can't this kid ever catch a break?*

Getting out dishes and spoons, she remembered she'd promised to call her mother as soon as she had news about Denny. She pushed the speed-dial on her cell phone, pulled the ice-cream carton out of the freezer while she listened to three rings, and opened the flaps while a lot of labored breathing sounded in her ear. Finally Aggie said, just above a whisper, 'Hello?'

'Mother, I've got her, she's here with me.'

'Oh, thank God. Oh, Sarah, is she all right?'

'Yes. I'd let you talk to her but she's so tired...'

'I bet she is. My God, I feel like I can breathe again. Where did you find her?'

'You're not going to believe this. She called me and asked for a ride.'

'She what? I don't understand.'

'I don't understand it all myself yet, but you can hear the whole story from her tomorrow, if you want to. I'd like to keep her home from school for one day. But – could you come over so I can go to work?'

'What, you want me to stay with Denny? Well, I – where's Janine?'

'Well, Mother, that's another long story that I don't think we want to get into right now.'

'Oh, God, she's run off again, has she?'

'Not exactly, but – the main thing is,

Denny's OK, and I'd really be grateful if you'd spend tomorrow at my house. Can you do that?'

'Well – of course I'll come if you need me. It's just...'

'What? Have you got a date?'

'No, but my car has. It's in the garage getting its steering gear fixed. I should have taken a rental but I got chintzy and said I'll just stay home a couple of days ... and wouldn't you know, Sam's gone fishing. But maybe I can find somebody else in the morning...'

'That'll be too late. Can you stand it if I come get you about six thirty?'

'Oh, sure, I'm always up early. Shame you have to do all that extra driving, though.'

'No problem. I think Denny's about ready for her ice cream now, so ... see you in the morning, OK?'

'I'll be ready, honey. Oh, Sarah, I feel like you gave me my life back.'

'I know. I feel the same way. Sleep well, mother.' She punched the 'end' button and stood holding the phone a moment, struck by the change that had taken place in Aggie's voice between the beginning and the end of the conversation. She had sounded frail when she answered, but became strong and able as soon as she heard there was work to be done. *Maybe she needs more than just games.*

The phone rang as she was folding it up. 'Sarah, it's Artie. I just left your sister's house, she's there.'

'Good. Was she ... all right?'

'I had to pound on the door quite a while to wake her up. She may have some angry neighbors for a while. All the dogs started to bark.'

'But she's OK?'

'Far as I could tell. She must have had some of that beer after you took her home, she was pretty vague. But she just shrugged when I asked her about the man you said she was afraid of, so I guess he never came back.'

Sarah had been too busy to think about the man who wrote on the table, so now the big surge of relief surprised her. *He didn't come back*. And right behind the relief, the shadow of guilt that always seemed to hang like a dust cloud between her and Janine. *He could have, though. I should have gone back there myself.* And behind the guilt came the anger. *She's responsible for her own life. I can't take care of everything, damn it.*

The family two-step.

'Thanks for checking, Artie. I know you have more than enough else to do.'

'About twenty calls on the screen right now. But hey, it makes the time go quick.'

'I owe you a big one, pal.'

'Nah, we pass it around, right? Talk to you later.'

Denny came out to the kitchen with wet hair hanging down her back as Sarah was dishing up. She ate a spoonful of ice cream, said, 'Mmm, good.' She ate another bite and said, 'How will I get to school in the morning?'

'Well, I've been thinking. What would you say to taking a day off tomorrow?'

'Oh … why? I'm all *right*, Aunt Sarah.'

'I know. But I think one day of rest might be a good idea. Grandma said she'd come over and stay with you.'

'She did?' Denny frowned. 'Does she have time?'

'Mm-hmm. She's looking forward to it.'

Denny put down her spoon. 'Are you worried about the man who took the car?'

'No. And you don't need to be. We'll find him. Soon. With luck, maybe tomorrow. Our guys have the license number and a full description of the car.' Denny was watching her with that measuring look she got sometimes. 'You've got good grades, you can afford one sick day, right?'

'I don't want to get marked down for skipping.'

'I'll call your principal and get you excused.' Denny still looked dubious so she said, 'If he gives me any trouble I'll sic the chief of police on him, OK?' Finally, that got a giggle. Pleased by the happy noise she grinned back and said, on impulse, 'Boy, it's good to see you there in that chair. I've missed you around here, sweetheart.'

Denny gave her such an odd look, then – what was it? Dubious, Sarah thought. *If she were older I'd even call it cynical. What did I say wrong?* Confused, she fussed with her dessert, scraping the last spoonful as if she was still hungry. As soon as she saw Denny take the last bite she said, 'Are you finished? Let's call it a day.'

'Ah, my good old futon,' Denny said, climbing in. Sarah was already thinking about what she could afford to replace it with, but Denny seemed to think the present accommodations would do fine. She yawned and stretched in the clean sheets, turned on her side and said, 'Oh, *man*, am I tired.'

Sarah picked up the pile of dirty clothes Denny had left folded neatly on her chair. 'I'll wash these so you have something to wear in the morning.'

''K. Thanks.' Her eyes were already closed. Sarah went out and started a load of laundry, came back to check and found her sleeping soundly.

In the living room, she glanced at the phone, saw she had a message and pressed the button. The answering tape beeped and then a quiet voice said, 'Sarah, it's Will Dietz. It's, uh, almost nine thirty. I just saw this story about your sister's child – is there anything I can do to help you? Please call me if you have time, I'll be here at work till ten thirty, and home by a few minutes after eleven. So call me if you can, doesn't matter how late.'

Her watch said eleven twenty. He might be home and he wouldn't be asleep yet. Even if he was, she told herself, a cop can go back to sleep after anything.

'Hey,' she said when he answered, 'hope I didn't wake you.'

'Not even close. This thing with your niece, anything I can do to help?'

'Oh, I guess we're over the hard parts for right now, but thanks. It's been a crazy night.'

'Tell me about it, somebody stole her mother's car?'

She told him about seeing the story on TV, her run to the store to find Janine, hearing the false report of two carjackers with guns and the way her sister's story fell apart under scrutiny.

'Why did she, uh...?'

'My sister has substance abuse problems as well as other issues.' It was a psychobabble summary, but she felt too tired to go into a full explanation.

He just said, 'I see. So, how did you find her child?'

So kind, to let a guarded answer lie. She described her lonely search through dark streets, talking to patrolmen in other cars. Then the strangest twist of all, Denny's phone call from the coffee shop.

'What did she say?'

'She said, "Um, Aunt Sarah, I'm sorry to bother you, but could you please give me a ride?"'

'Wow,' Dietz said, 'some kid.'

'For sure. And some strange kidnapper, Will. Or car thief, whatever.' She told the story of the cheeseburger and the movie. 'What in the holy living *hell* do you suppose he was up to in that movie theater?'

'Making phone calls, sounds like. Waiting

for something. Looking for somebody?'

'Uh-huh. And the question is, did he find that person? And what are they doing as we speak?'

'In your sister's car.'

'If we're lucky. We still might get him that way, everybody's looking for it.'

'So ... what about tomorrow? Will your niece go to school?'

'I decided she needed to stay home a day.'

'Sounds like a good call. So you're taking the day off?'

'No. My mother's going to come over and stay with her.'

'You're sure? You've talked to her?'

'Three times tonight, in fact. A record for modern times.'

'Uh-*huh*. And she drives, there's no...?'

'Like a pro, but her car's in the shop, so I have to go get her. I'll be watching the sunrise for the second time in two days.'

'Sarah, isn't that something I could help you with? Why don't I pick up your mother?' As if they were old neighbors who traded favors often. When Will Dietz set out to give comfort he didn't skimp. His voice had no tremor tonight either, come to think of it.

'Oh, Will ... she's way out in Marana.' Sarah got a sudden distinct vision of Will Dietz helping her mother into the front seat of his car, standing quiet and straight by the door, his hand under her elbow, and thought how much Aggie would like that. *Who wouldn't, actually?* 'Are you serious, could you really do that?'

'Of course. What's her address?'

She gave it to him and said, 'Can you have her here by seven thirty? It's going to take about forty-five minutes each—'

'I know how far it is. No problem. Will she answer if a strange man rings her bell at dawn?'

'I'll call her in the morning so she expects you. This is very kind of you, Will.'

'Not at all. I'm trying to curry favor with her daughter.' His voice warmed up a little when he said it – though it was probably said in kindness, she reminded herself, to make the favor seem smaller.

Even so it made her cheeks flush. She said, 'Well, you know what? You're succeeding nicely.'

'I am? Good, then, let's have dinner together some night soon and I'll try to succeed a little more.'

'You will? I mean, I'm sure you will.' They both laughed nervously. *I sound like an idiot.* 'Soon as I get my niece settled.'

'And I get a regular shift again, so I know what I'm doing.'

'Oh, is that happening soon? Back to Narcotics? Good for you.'

'Hope so. Let's see, I take the Ina Street exit, is that the best?'

'Cortaro's closer.' She took some time describing the best route to her mother's house, because the streets in these suburbs wind around so ... It was comforting to talk to a person who understood so much about the night's problems without having them explained. Dietz seemed happy to chat, too – he described some of the shifts he'd been working, subbing for duty sergeants at the various stations. He told a funny story about a surge in DUIs after a huge family reunion at a midtown hotel, another about a ridiculous argument in the patrolmen's break room over the relative merits of the Diamondbacks' pitching staff. 'Yelling at each other as if their own futures were at stake.' They chuckled together softly, and went on to comment about tomorrow's weather and the construction on various Tucson streets. They had both had years to find out how empty a room could feel after you hang up a phone.

When they finally said goodnight she moved the clean clothes into the dryer, set a pot of coffee for six and got ready for bed, still smiling. A conversation that had begun between colleagues seemed to have ended between slightly-more-than friends. Sarah found rueful amusement in the reflection that their relationship had taken a step forward, after all these years, thanks to the screwed-up train wreck that was her sister's life. *Gee, thanks for revving up my social life, Janine.* She knew at once what Janine's response to that would be – how she would flick her hair back and say defiantly, 'Well, somebody had to do *something*.' Only a sister could be close enough to ridicule both sides of a fight.

In bed, drifting toward sleep, the cop in her

surfaced and popped her eyes open. *OK, the keys were in the ignition, but even so, who'd pick Janine's old heap out of a big lot full of better cars?*

She answered herself, staring into the dark, A guy who just needed a ride in a hurry.

To go where? And coming from where? How'd he get to that parking lot? People didn't walk on busy, treeless Kolb Road in the summer heat. Where's the car he came in? Did he say to a friend, 'Just drop me off at the Fry's store so I can steal a worthless car?'

She tried to picture the shrugging man with the oily smile that Denny had imitated. A man who found a helpless child in the back seat, didn't abuse her as a monster would have, but didn't take her back where she belonged either. *What he did,* she said carefully to herself, trying to get her mind around it, *was buy her a cheeseburger and take her to a movie.* And then leave her there, a ten-year-old alone in a darkened theater at night, and drive away in her mother's car.

What kind of a man is that?

Denny, who in her short life had with reason watched a good many men carefully, had said of him, 'He thinks he's cute.'

A sociopath with a Paris Hilton smile? Sarah scrolled through mental pictures of men she'd arrested. She found one or two sneaky smiles and several mean ones, but none that even at a stretch came close to cuteness.

Drifting off again, she saw a vague image on the insides of her eyelids: a brown-skinned male smiling and shrugging the way Denny had done.

You're not really on my job sheet, you odd piece of work, but if I find you first you're going to feel major pain.

Twenty-Four

Tilly groped for the ringing phone in the dark. While he was still lifting it, before he'd had time to say hello, a man's voice began talking, high and fast. By the time he got the speaker up to his ear, the caller was in mid-sentence, words tumbling over each other, and all Tilly heard for sure was: '...find some way to make it our fault.'

'Who is this?' He sat up and fumbled for the light switch.

'It's Brody for chrissake. Somethin' wrong with your phone?'

'My phone's all right.' The light came on, hurting his eyes. 'Hell, what are you calling me for in the middle of the night?'

'I'm scared, that's why I'm calling you. Shut up and listen, now, because you need to hear this. I can feel it coming, I seen it before. He's got his nuts in a pucker.'

'Who has?'

'Rudy, Rudy, who else? Will you listen to

me? Rudy's on the prod on account of Ace getting whacked, and he's looking around for somebody to blame.'

'What time is it? The sun ain't even up, can't it wait till daytime?'

'It's almost six o'clock for Chrissake. Willya wake up and smell the coffee? Them apes from Old May-Hee-Coe are gonna be here with the snow in a couple hours. And Rudy's gonna be there, so before we meet them guys we need a strategy, because I'm tellin' you, he's on the warpath.'

'So he's jumpy because of Ace, so what? He's jumpy about everything lately. Ain't nothing for you to worry about.'

'He says it is. Called me last night at midnight, gave me hell for not finding that Rodriguez kid that worked for Ace. I said, "I can't find him because he's gone, I told you that, Rudy." And then, my Christ, he started yelling and raving – talked like I had something to do with capping Ace, you ever hear anything so crazy? I think he figures I took the money, for fuck sake.'

'He was probably drunk,' Tilly said. He peered at his watch again. Talking to Brody was tough enough even after a good breakfast. Getting personal wake-up service from him was cruel and unusual punishment. 'I seen him at the dog races last night, he was drinking a lot of beer.' *Spilling a lot, anyway.*

'Rudy don't get drunk,' Brody said. 'Ten years I worked for him, I never seen him with a load on yet. He gets crazy, is what he gets.

When he gets mad. And right now he's mad at me.'

'Tell him Sanchez did it,' Tilly said, and chuckled in a comfortable way so Brody'd know it was a joke.

'That won't fly,' Brody said, and Tilly realized with a little tingle that Brody had seriously considered it. 'Sanchez is from the neighborhood, he's a Mex.'

'So?'

'Mexicans stick together, don't you know that? Jesus, how long you been in Tucson?'

Too long, I'm starting to think. He got out of bed. 'Brody, I gotta get going, I got things to do before I meet you at the store.' He hung up the phone before Brody could say any more. Fucking Mick would talk all day if you let him.

He showered and dressed, drove to HoJo's and ate the three-egg special with sausage and country fries. Usually he took his time, enjoyed his food, got two refills on coffee. Waitresses in the southwest corner of Tucson went out of their way to give Tilly good service. He was weird-looking but he behaved himself, didn't grab at them and left a decent tip. They all knew him by now since he ate three meals a day, by himself, in the half dozen fast-food places within a twenty-block area that he could replicate in any city in the country.

This morning he was even quieter than usual, ate with scant attention to his food and took only one coffee refill. He sat for some time over the second cup, staring at the condiments holder as if he expected the catsup bottle to tell him how much physical abuse of Hector's small sisters would persuade their mother to tell him where Hector was.

If she knew. If they all got to screaming that would be a problem in that neighborhood where the houses were so close together. He would have to grab the smallest girl as soon as he got inside and threaten to break her arm if they screamed. Then he'd promise to break it anyway if Mama didn't talk.

He went over the scene carefully with his friend, the catsup bottle, including the message from Rudy about a bonus for Hector that he was pretty sure would get him in the door. When he felt ready he put his standard tip under the saucer and paid his bill, agreeing with the counter guy that yes, it looked like another hot one.

Twenty-Five

'Well, I could certainly get used to *this.*' Aggie Decker's smile lit up Sarah's doorstep at seven twenty-four Thursday morning. 'Getting chauffeured across town by a polite attractive man who knows his way around all the westside bottlenecks, what's next? Is a fat lady going to sing?' Her hair had been blow-dried and sprayed, and she was wearing the pink blouse with pearl buttons.

Dietz stood quiet beside her, looking amused.

'Coffee's hot,' Sarah said. 'You're both nice to get up so early.'

'I'm always up early,' Aggie said. 'It's one of nature's little jokes: by the time you're old enough to retire, you can't sleep late any more.' She walked into Sarah's kitchen, picked up a mug and smiled across it at Dietz. 'Want some?'

'Thanks, I better get to work.' He looked at Sarah.

'Right.' She put her hand on his arm and walked him back out the door, closing it behind her. 'You drew an early shift after a late one?'

'My skej is kind of crazy right now. Lot of

people sick, I guess.'

'And fetching my mom made your night even shorter.'

'Oh, that was a pleasure.' His plain face creased in a smile. 'Any time.'

What did she say to him, I wonder?

'Sarah?' He looked at her in a searching way, and gently touched her face.

'What?' she said.

'I just ... I like seeing you in the morning.' He leaned forward and kissed her quickly on the lips.

Struck dumb by an overwhelming desire to grab him and make love in the carport, Sarah stared at him in silence as he turned away and opened the door of his car. At the last minute, she heard herself say stupidly, 'See you later.'

'Count on it,' he said, as he climbed in.

She watched him back out and drive to the end of the block. As he turned he hit the horn one little tap, *beep!* She waved at his disappearing taillight and went back in the house.

'So,' Aggie said, without looking up from the paper, 'you finally found a keeper, hmm?'

'Just like that, in one ride in from Marana, you made up your mind?'

'It didn't take the whole ride, for heaven's sake. This one's the real deal, isn't he? Not a bartender, hmm?' While his marriage to Sarah lasted, Aggie had doted on Andy Burke, called him 'my son, the restaurateur'. Sometime during the divorce wars, she had begun to call him 'that bartender'.

'Definitely not a bartender,' Sarah said. 'Dietz is a cop.'

'Oh dear. Well, you can't have everything.' She set the paper down and met Sarah's eyes. 'Janine's disappeared again, is that it?'

'No, she's over there on Lurlene Street, last I knew. But her mind's not exactly in the game.'

'I told you she was drinking again. Is she using too?'

'Beer and pot for sure, I'm not sure what else. I know you deserve the whole story and I'll tell you everything I know, but can we wait till tonight? I need to get to work.'

'Sure. Shall I let Denny sleep as long as she can?'

'Yes. And when she does get up, maybe just ... sit around, talk, read books? A long hot bath and a nap would be good this afternoon, I think. She was completely exhausted last night.'

'What if Janine shows up?'

'Ask her to stay for dinner.'

'Seriously?'

'Sure. I'll bring home plenty of pork chops. Just don't let her leave with Denny, OK? We've got to get a few things straightened out before Denny goes back over there. I'm going to try to talk her into another go-round in detox. You'll back me up, won't you?'

'You bet. Not that she ever listens to me.' She looked at Sarah, shrugged her desperation shrug and said, 'Forget it, go to work. I'll take a broom to her if I have to.'

Sarah went in her bedroom, changed into work clothes, came out and stood by the counter adding watch, Glock, shield. 'Help yourself to breakfast, will you? You remember where everything is?'

'I'll muddle through. And Denny will help me after she gets up. Have you noticed how she always knows where everything is?'

'Yes. She has the makings of a good detective, I think.'

'God forbid.' Head on one side, Aggie produced one of her rare, beautiful smiles of unmitigated pleasure. 'That's a good outfit, blue's really your color. If I just don't look at that miserable gun, you look very nice.' Thirteen years of commendations and merit raises had done nothing to alter Aggie's opinion of Sarah's career choice.

'You do know how to wreck a compliment, don't you, Agnes Veronica?' She repeated her father's goading use of his wife's full name and was rewarded with a flash of blue-eyed irony over the top of the paper. 'Call my cell if you need anything. The number's – here, I'll leave my card by the phone.' She looked around. 'What else? I'm sorry the best reading light's by the chair in there where Denny's sleeping, but...'

'Don't worry about me, babe. Go to work; I'll be fine.'

Her phone buzzed as she backed out of the driveway. Artie Mendoza, pleased with himself, said, 'Hey, Sarah, we found your sister's car last night.'

'You did? Where?'

'Would you believe it was back in the ramp at the Roxy Theater?'

'You're joking! What've we got here, a car thief with a passion for movies?'

'Looks like it. I almost didn't look up there, it seemed too crazy, but then I was passing so – and there it was again. I thought about searching in the theater – the bad guy was probably in there. But all I had to go on was a brown-skinned guy with a silly smile, so ... I just went ahead and had the car towed to East Impound.'

'Have you requested fingerprints yet?'

'You bet. I got high priority status for 'em, too, called him a suspected abuser. I couldn't very well claim kidnapping since we never turned it in.'

'Good thinking. Hey, you're good to call me. Shouldn't you be sleeping?'

'Oh, in a few minutes. I like to work out first. See you, Sarah.'

So, the system had worked for her while she slept. It was so gratifying when it felt big and effective, instead of just big and out of control. *They could have a match on those prints by tonight.*

Headquarters station at 270 South Stone was noisy and crowded, with a tour and a class waiting. The building served so many functions it was always busy. People came there to be deposed, too, and to reclaim evidence after a case ended, so the reception desk hummed with traffic. Sarah wedged into an elevator and went up to the evidence room, where she found Eisenstaat at the window, signing the checkout sheet for Ace Perkins' computer. 'Morning, Harry. How're you coming with that thing?'

'I only got a few minutes with it yesterday. Give me another hour.'

'Fine.' She checked out the small box of miscellaneous items from Perkins' desk. 'I'm going to take another look at this desk diary and the stuff out of the drawers.' They waited together through three full elevators before they got a ride back to third floor.

'Hey, Sarah,' Ibarra said, without looking up from the mounds of paper on his desk, 'I'm almost ready with the phone bills.'

'Good. Soon as I look at my messages – about ten minutes, OK?' She was sorting messages at her desk when the phone rang.

Delaney said, 'We caught a break on the victim's car, Sarah.'

Sarah opened her mouth to say, 'No, no, that was my sister's car,' but Delaney, oblivious to the personal problems that had swamped her the previous evening, went right on. 'A uniform named Morrissey, do you know him?'

'No.'

'Neither do I but he does nice work. He got a call last night about an Excursion parked in an employee space behind the Fry's store on Kolb Road. Noticed fresh bolts on the plates so he checked the VIN, and it turned out to be Ace Perkins' car.'

'Well, hoo-ray for Morrissey. Where is it?'

'Downtown impound. Will you write up the requests for prints and DNA?'

'You bet. Nobody's looked at it yet?'

'No. How'd you make out at the victim's apartment?'

She told him what they brought back. 'We're going through records now. We should know a lot more in a couple of hours. I'll try to get out and take a look at that SUV, too.'

She hung up wondering about the odd coincidence, Ace's SUV found at the Fry's store at Kolb Road. *Could there possibly be any…?* She shook her head. *Nah, come on. Too weird.*

Ibarra walked into her cubicle a few minutes later, chuckling over a thick folder. 'Ah, Sarah, some days I think I'd do this job for nothing. Don't quote me on that, now.' He was grinning in the super-tickled way he had, round cheeks, dimples, gold tooth and pink ears all glowing.

Sarah said, 'I do like a man who can get his jollies off a stack of phone bills.'

'Well, when the phone's owner was a pusher, there's this nice odor of scandal that hangs over everything…' Ibarra demonstrated titillated sniffing as he pulled a chair around beside Sarah, plunked on to it and spread messy marked-up sheets of paper all over her desk. 'Just look at this – week after week, the same local calls over and over, all a minute or less. Customer calls, see? All business.'

'Ah. And I bet you looked up some of

the names.'

'Better believe it. You ready for my list of frequent flyers?' He pulled a handwritten sheet out of the stack and the two of them bent over it.

'My, my,' Sarah said, reading, 'what a lot of stockbrokers.'

Ibarra chuckled. 'Who knew they were such party types?'

'These down here are all lawyers, aren't they?'

'Oh, yes, indeed,' Ibarra said. 'This one handled my cousin's divorce.'

'Oh my God, these two are good customers of Andy's,' Sarah said. '*Shee*, he's fed plates and plates of pasta to these coke-heads. They probably couldn't even taste it.'

'Wanna see something disgusting?' Ibarra said. 'Here's my wife's periodontist.'

'Now you know what those high fees are for.'

'Last powder he buys with my money,' Ibarra said, 'I'm gonna get her pearly whites out of *his* office.'

Sarah tapped the paper, thinking. 'Our victim had a very high-end list of customers, didn't he? You suppose somebody got envious?'

'Ah, wouldn't we like to have access to *that* kind of gossip.'

'Yeah, why don't our undercover guys ever bring us the juicy stuff? Oh, here's something really shocking,' Sarah said, 'a personal trainer!'

'Why is that so surprising? They work under stress and charge ridiculous rates.'

'You're right, that's the classic combination, isn't it?'

'Then there's this one call,' Ibarra mused, 'every day to the same unlisted number.' Contemplating his trove, he massaged the back of one hand with the palm of the other, looking inscrutable and wise. Sarah half expected him to start saying, Think about it, grasshopper.

'You called it?'

'Several times. I get an answering machine that says ... I *think* it says, "Swing". Something like that.'

'Just that one word?'

'Uh-huh. Go ahead, try it.'

Sarah dialed the number. A man's voice, quiet and very fast, said one word. She hung up and wrinkled her nose at the phone. 'He says "Swing", or maybe "Swain". A signal to leave a message, I guess.'

'Right.' Ibarra flashed his devil-made-me-do-it smile. 'Wanna try leaving an order for a couple of eight-balls?'

'Great idea,' Sarah said, 'have 'em delivered to Delaney's office.'

Ibarra turned pensive. 'I'll pass that number along to Narcotics, but how much longer do you think it'll get answered?'

'Couple of hours. I might want to talk to some of these people.'

'For what? Users don't kill their suppliers.'

'Probably not, but somebody must have a

name, a make of car ... anything.'

'The department doesn't favor harassing taxpayers about their personal habits.'

'Until something else comes up. I'm keeping this list.'

'OK,' Ibarra said, 'I'll call my man at Verizon and get the skinny on this unlisted number.'

'For sure,' Sarah said. 'And you asked them to monitor Perkins' account, right?'

'Yeah ... we didn't find the phone yet, did we?'

'Sure didn't.'

'So possibly the killer's got it.'

'*Quite* possibly. And a lot of dope, I suppose. And some guns?'

'Oohh, yeah.' Ibarra whistled softly through his front teeth, making a note. 'Three guesses and the first two don't count. In which other country would we be likely to find Ace Perkins's murderer residing at this moment?'

'You're probably right, but let's not give up on him yet. What else have you got there? Personal calls?'

'There aren't any.'

'Aw, come on. Everybody makes *some* personal calls.'

'You got any friends you talk to once a week for forty-five seconds?'

'Really, that's all there is?'

'Really.'

'So he's got another phone someplace.'

'There aren't any other phone bills in those files we brought back. Four months on this number, that's it. Ace Perkins sure kept his files neat.'

'Good, he gets A-plus for filing,' Sarah said. 'But what did he do for a *life*? Have you been through the rest of his records?

'No.'

'Can you give 'em another hour or so?'

'I guess. Looking for what?'

'A girlfriend, a boyfriend, a dear old mom? Something to put a face on this guy. I'm going to go see what Harry's got.' She walked along the row of workstations to where Eisenstaat hunched over Ace Perkins' laptop, his long hands crowding each other on the small keyboard. 'How's it going?'

'Damn toys, I hate 'em. You want to look at this now?'

'If you're ready for me.'

'Now's as good a time as any, and it's not gonna take long. This guy let most of his gigabytes go to waste. Here, take my chair, I'll sit by you and tell you what to poke.' She sat in his warm chair as Eisenstaat guided her quickly through the contents of a nearly empty machine. The email program held ten messages in the inbox, nothing in the sent file, nothing in the trash.

'Just these ten? And they're all clusters of letters and numbers,' Sarah said.

'Some kind of code,' Eisenstaat said. 'Customer number first and then an order. And he must have blown off every message as soon as he'd read it. These are all from the last two days.'

Sarah said, 'Any idea how much he was moving?'

'Well ... a guess. No way to know if these two days were average, but...' He guided her to an account in another program. 'This looks like his re-orders for the last couple of weeks.'

'Have you figured out the symbols?'

'I'm guessing CO is cocaine, and HE is probably black tar heroin – they tell me that's the joyride of choice this year. Jimmy thinks, based on his customer list, he wasn't peddling much hemp. I'm not really schooled in this crap, though, Sarah, you should get some help from our guys at the undisclosed location.' Detectives at 270 South Stone had adopted the vice-president's supposed hide-out after 9/11 as an ironic address for their own narcotics squad.

'I will. But let's try some ballpark figures, for now.'

'Well, say this biggest amount is coke...' He did some math. 'Somewhere between three and five thou, his cost, every week.' He looked up over his glasses. 'Double on the street, right?'

'Oh, triple,' Sarah said. 'Or more. Delaney's rule of thumb is, just crossing Tucson, the wholesale price doubles. And then retail, it'll double or triple again.'

'What's that thing Johnny Carson used to say?' Eisenstaat pushed his glasses up on his long nose. ' "Sure beats selling shoes at Thom McAnn, doesn't it?" ' He made a derisive noise. 'Kind of hard to match it in the police department, too. Not that I'd ever say a discouraging word.'

'Keep thinking how lousy his long-term benefits were,' Sarah said, scrolling. 'What else is in here, Harry?'

'Games. Solitaire, chess, bridge. A couple of crosswords.'

'Personal correspondence?'

'None.'

'I swear, Ace Perkins had less fun pushing drugs than I have hooking.'

'What?' Eisenstaat peered through his bifocals.

'She just makes rugs, don't let her start,' Ibarra said, walking by.

'Let's look at his favorite sites,' Sarah said. She tapped. No list came down. '*Nada*. This man has more in paper records than he has in his computer.'

Eisenstaat chuckled. 'A horse-and-buggy drug dealer, don't you just love it?'

Sarah pushed her chair back impatiently. 'I feel like we're stuck in the mud here – I'm going to go order print and DNA testing on the Excursion.'

And while she was at it she could nose around a little about Janine's car. It was officially none of her business, of course, somebody in Auto Theft would have that folder. But as long as she was over on that side of the building, there was no harm in schmoozing with a receptionist named Lois, who told her a crime scene specialist was working on the Dodge 'as we speak'.

'Terrific. Who's on today?'

'Gloria Jackson. And she told me a few minutes ago not to expect her back for a while, she's finding plenty of latents.'

'Well, fine. Who's got the theft?'

'Nobody yet. All the detectives have so many cases already – but this one has a priority rating, they'll get to it pretty soon.'

'Uh-huh.' Car theft was like sunburn in Tucson, an affliction so common people hardly bothered to complain about it. *If I'd reported Denny as a kidnapping the FBI would be all over this car. But then so would the media.*

'Of course, if some prints match up with other cases,' Lois said, 'whoever's working those will grab it.'

'Sure. Now, how about these work orders on the Excursion? How much of a delay am I facing there?'

'Oh, we might have somebody to put on it by afternoon.'

Back on her floor, Jimmy Ibarra followed her into her workstation and stood by her desk looking incandescent, saying, 'I offered my man at Verizon a great big kiss but for some reason he wants it from you.'

'What's he got?'

'Wednesday night, at twelve minutes after nine, Ace Perkins' phone received a call from this number –' he showed her the slip of paper – *'and somebody answered it.'* He gave her one of his hot-salsa super-smiles. 'Couldn't have been much of a conversation, three seconds. But still.'

'But still is right. Oh, this is very nice, Jimmy, somebody's carrying that phone around and you know what? It just might have a GPS on it and – and—'

'And we could do some electronic stalking, how cool is that?' Ibarra said. He did a little dance before he added, uncertainly, 'Tell me again, how do we do that?'

'Well, you know what, I think this is why God created support staffs. I'm going to call my favorite geek.'

She got Tracy Scott on the phone and explained their request while Ibarra jittered happily beside her. Listening to Tracy's reply, she said, on a descending scale of happiness, 'Uh-huh, uh-huh, uh-huh,' and hung up scowling.

'What, what?'

She put her fingertips on her forehead and closed her eyes while she recited the difficulties. 'Our telephone system is Verizon which doesn't support that service. But Nextel does but he doesn't think our software interfaces with theirs. But he's also heard we can rent the equipment from the Feds when we need to but he thinks it's too expensive for anything but high-profile cases, so he's going to ask around and get back to me, blah blah blah. Why are all the phones ringing?'

'Probably if you answered it...' Ibarra sprinted for his.

She picked up hers and Delaney said, 'Sarah, we just got a new case and it sounds like a messy one. Is everybody out there on the floor?'

'Uh...' – she stood up and looked over her divider walls – '...yes.'

'Good. Tell me, are you making any progress on the Perkins case?'

'Yeah, we've got several good things going.'

'Well, what I was thinking, I can manage this one I just got with five guys, if ... would you be able to keep going by yourself?'

'Oh, sure.'

'OK, I'm going to try it that way. If I get there and decide I need you, I'll call you from there. Switch me over to Ibarra now, OK?'

For ten minutes, there was a great clatter of phones, desk drawers, briefcases and Glocks all around her. When they were all out the door, Sarah sat down in the echoing silence, telling herself not to start imagining that Delaney was starting to isolate her from the rest of the section. He had a new case, he needed everybody but decided to make do with one less so the primary on yesterday's case could keep some momentum going.

To quell her screaming paranoia, she started a list.

Twenty-Six

After breakfast Tilly drove to Ohio Street and parked across from the Rodriguez house, two doors east where he could see most of the west end of the block. He had been in this neighborhood a half-dozen times in the last three days, looking for Hector, so he had it pretty well memorized.

It was crowded but not complicated, old adobe single-story houses with open patios and junk-filled yards. The occupants lived precarious lives, paycheck to paycheck when they had jobs, scratching and grabbing when they didn't. People here weren't looking for any trouble they didn't already have.

By now, Tilly figured, he could not be the only one checking on Hector's house. So, before he went after Hector's mama and sisters he needed to sit quiet a minute and see if anybody was hanging out on the block today that didn't belong.

While he watched he thought about Rudy, who was beginning to worry him. *He's had it too good for too long*, he decided, *he can't stand the thought of losing anything now*. This was the same Rudy Ortiz who had once stuffed money into the mouths of two bloody heads and shipped them to Mexico. Now, because one of his dealers had been capped, he was breaking beer glasses in public and accusing his hired hands of conspiring against him? Pitiful.

Tilly had watched Rudy Ortiz trying to keep up as the drug culture became increasingly corporate, suits coming up from Mexico to talk about 'building a customer base' on the junior high playgrounds. He had been afraid Rudy was passing some kind of a tipping point the day he began trying to say 'potential new revenue stream'.

Man with money and power starts losing his confidence like that, trying to impress the sexy new girlfriend and the hip haircuts from Cancún, the next place he's going to be is up to his eyeballs in shit. And anybody standing too close is going right down into the slime with him.

The neighborhood looked quiet enough, the usual dogs barking, a boy riding his rusty bike toward middle school. Just beyond the Rodriguez house, a car with bald tires and one door that didn't match backed out of the driveway where it was parked, and drove east. As soon as it was out of the way Tilly saw the car turning the corner out of Fifteenth, a new Impala carrying two men with short haircuts, neat shirts and ties and impassive faces. They drove slowly toward the Rodriguez house and stopped at the curb in front of the next house to the west.

Just then the door opened and Carmencita

appeared on the step with her two daughters. Tilly watched while she tied up their hair with rubber bands strung with bright beads, straightened their clothing with a couple of little jerks, checked their book bags and handed each of them a coin. The men in the maroon Impala were watching her too.

Tilly had quit paying attention in school a couple of years before he dropped out in sixth grade; both the little girls he was watching now could undoubtedly read better than he could. Life had been his teacher and even at that he had been a slow learner. But over the years he had developed good instincts on a narrow range of subjects. He usually knew who was high and on what. He was good at spotting a weapon, could smell when a fight was likely to start, and knew all the ways to win if you had to get into it.

He was muscle. He made his living in whatever illicit activity was happening nearby when he needed money. He kept a small bag packed at all times, and had more than once left even that behind. One of the first things he did after his arrival in any city was find all the ways out of it.

He knew when, as now, he was looking at cops. These two had the tightly wound but confident look he associated with Feds. DEA, he was guessing – that would figure. And what Tilly knew best of all was his bottom line: he had been in prison twice, and he was never going back.

So as Hector's sisters walked away waving

goodbye and the two self-possessed men got out of the Impala and introduced themselves politely to Carmencita Rodriguez, Tilly made up his mind. *Fuck it. Time to go.*

He drove quietly to Fifteenth Street, watching his rear-view mirror to see if the cops made a note of his license-plate number. They never even glanced his way. He thought he probably had time to pick up his grab-and-go bag, but as he turned into the street below his apartment building he saw a couple of cars he wasn't sure about and decided, once again, *fuck it*. He drove quietly away from his few possessions and was rolling northwest on I-10, passing the cement plant in Marana, by the time Hector's sisters had begun to recite the pledge of allegiance at Apollo Middle School.

Who needs Tucson anyway? Fuck the whole fucking desert. So what if it's dry heat, it's still heat.

He had done well for himself in Tucson, his money stash was bigger than when he came. Only thing he regretted, he decided as he passed the Red Rock turn-off, was never meeting that policewoman again, the one that looked at him that day in front of Ace's apartment. He had thought of her several times since that day, and each time he found himself wondering, *What would it be like to do a woman like that?*

Tilly's entire knowledge of sex had been gained with prostitutes and occasional free-lancing druggies willing to trade sex for his help getting a fix. He knew what his face looked like, people had been making fun of his looks ever since fifth grade when his stepfather put him in the hospital the second time. So he had always treated sex as a fair-traded commodity, tried to get what he paid for and didn't expect extras. He never risked the contempt he was likely to get from an approach to an unpaid woman, and judging from the endless bitching of men in bars about their women, he had concluded he wasn't missing much. But ever since he'd seen that woman detective ... He didn't even know how to say it, exactly.

Passing that weird-looking mountain with the funny name, Picacho, he figured out what it was that made her face stay in his mind: that woman had been looking straight at him and thinking about him. Like she thought he was ... interesting. She wasn't afraid, and she wasn't coming on to him. She wasn't hostile either, she was just ... thinking about him.

Now why the fuck is that a turn-on? He didn't know but it was, his crotch had warmed up and he was squirming in his seat to get some more room in his jeans.

Maybe I could get me a regular job of some kind, he surprised himself by thinking as he approached Eloy. *Work daylight hours, have more of a life.* It was his second radical thought in the space of a few minutes and it made him feel ... warmed up even more.

Tilly cranked the AC down a notch, put the Escalade on cruise control and aimed its nose toward his bankroll in LA. He tuned the radio to a hip-hop station, nudged the sound up a little and nodded to the beat, thinking about the possibilities of life in the slow lane.

Twenty-Seven

Hector woke slowly, out of a dream of being in a car in the rain. Somebody in the car with him kept yelling, from the back seat, 'No, stop, oh, please stop!' But Hector laughed and said, 'What are you talking about? It's hardly raining at all,' which it wasn't right then, just a sprinkle. A minute later, though, he felt his car lurch out of control and saw they were floating down a big wash and into a river. It was the Rillito, he saw, usually just a dusty ditch but now full of dirty water, right up to the top of its banks. As the torrent flowed past the back doors of stores and restaurants, people called out to him from their open doors, saying things he couldn't quite hear.

His passenger kept on screaming, but Hector, still cool, said, 'Don't worry, I got a plan for this.' He rolled down his window and each time they came to a bend in the stream he leaned out and grabbed for a branch or a fencepost. But he was never quite close enough and the water was flowing so fast, when he grabbed for something it slid through his fingers. The person in the back seat got louder and louder, other people were yelling too and then Hector noticed that the car was sinking, he was going under.

He sat up in bed, suddenly awake. But the screaming went right on, a woman's voice crying out in rage and pain. Her screams were punctuated by sounds Hector had never heard before, insane animal grunts, and after every grunt came more thumps and crashes and another scream.

The couple next door were having a raging fight. Last night's fun was all forgotten, they were trashing their room and there was more yelling, now, from the manager who was knocking on their door. Hector knew right away he had to get out of here, this kind of a fight made people call the police.

His pants and sandals were on the chair by the bed, he was dressed in a few seconds. He grabbed his duffel and had his other hand out, reaching for the door handle, when the noises changed. There was harder knocking, now, next door, and a deep voice yelling, 'Police! Open up!'

Hector froze. The knocking and calling continued until one of the occupants, the man, opened the door and muttered something like, 'What's up?' Hector had watched this scene more than once in his neighborhood and knew how it was going to go: the person answering the door always said something utterly stupid like, 'Whaddya need?' and then stood there, wavering, convinced he looked so innocent he could bluff his way out of breaking up a roomful of furniture and putting lumps all over a woman.

Listening, Hector longed to fast-forward this idiot's life so he wouldn't have to wait for it to play out – the sobs of the woman, the denials of the man, their joint declarations that nothing at all was going on. You don't have to put those cuffs on him, the woman wailed, he'll be fine as soon as he sobers up. But the patrolman had back-up now and besides the empty vodka bottle in the room the officers found weed, and then a lot more weed and some heroin and the paraphernalia for that and soon the woman was in cuffs, too, still weeping.

Hector pressed against the door, afraid to peek out through the blinds for fear the officers would spot him and want to ask questions. Cops loved witnesses. And what if they noticed his car? It wasn't connected to Ace's murder in any way that he knew about, but what if his parole officer had a search order out for him? He was afraid to move for fear of attracting attention to himself.

He kept looking at his watch, in agony as the digital numbers showed eight thirty, nine, nine thirty. The motel manager got back into the mix, wanting to be paid for the damage to the room. They tried to leverage some cash out of the couple, but the man let them go through all his pockets to prove he had hardly any money left on him and the woman couldn't even find her purse.

Standing by the door grinding his teeth, Hector listened as the motel manager signed the damage report, complaining to the cops that you never got paid for the time it took or the inconvenience to your other guests. *You hit on something there, my man.* His cheek against the door, Hector closed his eyes and told himself to stay cool. Finally they were all going down the stairs together toward the squad cars, the two prisoners unsteady on their feet, the man cursing.

Hector risked a look when he heard car doors slamming. Each officer had one prisoner in the back of his patrol car and they were pulling out of the lot. Finally Hector opened his door a crack. Nobody moved in the rooms around him, so he carried his duffel out on to the walkway. He could see the top of his car below him, and was starting down the stairway when he wondered, *Why was the hood popped like that?*

He ran down the steps, noticing as he did that the Brat was sitting funny, too. He had parked at the end of the row, against the corner formed by the L of the building. At the time he had been too tired to think about the fact that one side of the car was in the dark and out of sight of the office. Not that anybody in this two-bit fleatrap ever checked the lot anyway, probably.

Hector had often joked with his friends that even south of Twenty-Second Street, his car was perfectly safe because it was too worthless to steal. But he had bought new tires and a good battery for it, in case he might be driving it to Mexico. Now he saw that the good battery was missing and on the side away from the office, not just the back tire but the whole fucking wheel was gone.

He had been awake and anxious for hours without any breakfast, hunger was growling in his gut. But he found the strength to hurl curses at all the rotten fucking bad luck that had robbed him of Ace's car and the quick easy start out of town that he had worked for and earned. Red tongues of rage danced in front of his eyes as he thought of all the work he had to do next: hunt through salvage yards – fucking Rudy's stupid salvage yards – for a wheel for this old Brat, and then buy a new tire, and a battery, and get it all installed.

Even as he cursed, though, he knew that in another minute he'd get at it, because he didn't have the juice left to steal another car. He didn't know why but his luck was all gone in this town, his bad moon had risen, his plan was shot to hell. There was no way to know how many people were looking for him, and he was running out of time and money. He would have to use all his poor boy skills, beg rides and borrow tools from friends, sweat and humble himself all morning, into afternoon if it took that long, maybe even stay in this lousy excuse for a motel again tonight – he knew he couldn't go back to Ohio Street.

And now it wasn't optional any more, he

absolutely had to get Ace's money back. As soon as the Brat was running again he was going to find that rotten skinny grade-school girl and put a hurt on her she'd remember for the rest of her life. He let his mind linger for a minute on the pleasure of doing that, because Christ knew he had a little pleasure coming. The sounds he had heard from the room next door came back to him, and the muscles in his shoulders quivered. He imagined Denny with tears running down her face, begging him to take his money and go.

Twenty-Eight

Is this whole department stuck in a swamp? Sarah rubbed her hands together, pulled her earlobes and did a restless sitting tap dance. She was waiting for fingerprint reports, a search warrant, the final on the autopsy, the decision on the GPS tracking. *I could try looking through that computer again by myself.* She knew she would have to be very lucky to find anything Harry Eisenstaat had missed.

Where else could I look? She needed to know much more about Ace Perkins, the squeaky-clean seller of illicit street drugs, whose lifestyle was so wrong for his modus operandi. A tough ex-con – Ace Perkins wouldn't go down easy – who lived, if that was the right word, with a nearly empty computer in an apartment as uncluttered as a monk's cell. A snitch who took meticulous care of his classy wardrobe and read library books. *I could find out how long he's had that card.* Was he a native Tucsonan, come to think of it? Almost everybody in Tucson was from someplace else, but, what if there was family nearby?

Perkins, Adolph Alvin didn't come up in city directories past or present, or as an alumni of any school in the Tucson Unified School District. He was not listed as a member of any local club or fraternal organization. His Arizona driver's license and his car registration dated from the day before he rented the apartment. Same week he opened that account at the bank.

Let's see how he was doing the month before that.

She got an outside line, dialed the Florence prison, and asked for Warden Cluff. A secretary said, 'He's away from his desk today, can anyone else help you?'

'Uh ... sure, I should think so.'

'Hang on, I'll see if I can locate Deputy Phelps.' She clicked off and the phone system treated Sarah to several verses of a canned Roy Orbison ballad. Finally the song cut out and a very deep, cordial male voice said, 'This is Sergeant Phelps, how can I help you?' Sarah identified herself, explained she was investigating the murder of a former inmate, gave Ace's full name and told Phelps she was looking for additional information about the prisoner.

'You bet,' Phelps said heartily, 'hold on.' She ground her teeth while Orbison finished saluting 'Calypso' and Kaye Starr started bargaining for a doggie in the window. Why did the very worst songs have the longest half-life on Muzak? When Phelps came back on he said, 'Adolph Alvin Perkins was in detention here from eighteenth August two thou—'

'Wait, wait. I have his detention records, that's not why I called.'

'Oh? Well ... why did you call?' Phelps's voice had frosted over; he didn't like being interrupted.

'I was hoping to find somebody who remembered the prisoner. Anyone who dealt with him and could give me some, you know, *insight* into his, um, personality. How he got along while he was there, who his friends were. Anything like that.'

There was a pause before Phelps said, 'Well.' Then a longer pause until his deep voice, now mournful, said, 'You know, we have over three thousand inmates incarcerated here, coming and going constantly.'

'I know. But the guards work certain buildings, don't they? They must get to know—'

'They're not allowed to fraternize in any way, ma'am.'

Sarah opened her mouth, closed it again, took a deep breath and asked the warden's assistant, 'So, you don't think you could find anyone there who might remember Adolph Alvin Perkins?'

'I think that would be highly unlikely, ma'am.'

'I see. Well ... thanks for your time, Deputy Phelps.' Sarah hung up and spun around on her chair, muttering dark oaths. Through the open door of her cubicle, on the second turn, she caught the level eye of Kyle Ost, a Gang detective who had just walked in and was standing by his desk looking cheerfully disreputable, wearing a black T-shirt with a portrait of a vilely grinning pirate and the message: Anything you want from shipping?

'How you doin', Sarah?' He re-settled his reversed baseball cap. 'You look like your blood pressure just spiked.'

'I just got treated like the village idiot by a total stranger.'

'Pass it along,' Ost said. 'Best way to get rid of shit is let it run downhill.'

Life lessons from a gang squad member, what next? She went and got a Styrofoam cup half full of almost-acceptable coffee from the break room and sipped it while she dialed the support staff phone. 'Scott Tracy, please,' she said, feeling good about remembering his name for once, till the girl who had answered the phone reminded her, for the third time this week, that his name was Tracy Scott. When his uppity drawl finally sounded in her ear she said, 'Genius Geek, I'll bet you're the resident expert on how the state of Arizona software works, right?'

'Well, I exhibit varying degrees of brilliance, depending on the day. And the night before, actually.' He snickered. 'What do you need?'

'I need you to evaluate a prison record.'

'Evaaaaluate, omigod, a task worthy of my mettle at last. Lay it on me, what do you need?'

'I'm looking for something I can't quite describe, you know what I mean?'

'Um, no.'

'I'm fishing for information, how's that?'

'Usually called surfing, but OK, what information?'

'I've got this homicide victim who's a known drug pusher, the records show him getting released from Florence last February.'

'Uh-huh.'

'But a couple of things about him seem, uh ... offbeat. So I was wondering, could you take a look at his prison record and tell me if anything about it seems out of line?'

'You mean with his sentence? I wouldn't know—'

'No, GeeGee, with the records, the records. I just want you to look at the records for Adolph Alvin Perkins and tell me if you see anything that looks ... I don't know ... odd. I told you, I'm fishing. Surfing, whatever.'

'Oh-*kay*.' Genius Geek didn't bother to hide his suspicion that Detective Burke was a few grains short of a spoonful. 'I'll, um, call you back, OK?'

'Good.' She hung up, re-checked her email but found none of the messages she was waiting for. Read through her crime scene notes again, glancing at the clock every few seconds. *I should have asked him how long it would take. Now I don't know when to start complaining.* She was considering one more cup of bad coffee when the phone rang. Tracy Scott's boyish voice, a notch higher than before, said, 'Well, *this* is funny. The DLMs are all the same.'

'Oh? What's a DLM?'

'Date last modified. It's a marker that's hard-wired into the entry so people can't tinker with the records. But it looks like somebody tinkered with this one anyway.'

'I'm not sure I understand.'

'Normally a prisoner's record gets added to each time his status changes – when he enters the system, or gets sent to the hospital, or moves to a different wing, or gets paroled. Every time anything changes, he gets a new entry in his record. We keep it right up to date because wardens, doctors, attorneys, everybody in the system needs to know these things. So the entries almost always have a DLM the same day of the status change or the day after. But Perkins' records all got put in at once, eight entries showing when he entered, went to the hospital, moved to a different cell, got a new cellmate, got a demerit, was assigned to the laundry, when he applied for parole, and when he got out. All that information was entered last February twenty-second, within two minutes either side of two a.m. Two days after he actually *got* out.'

'Uh-*huh*. Well ... why would that happen?'

'I have no idea. It's the first time I've ever seen it.'

'How come my report didn't show that?'

'Oh, well, you just put in a standard report request I expect, an email asking for his records?'

'Actually we searched on his fingerprints.'

'Well, there you go, you got the canned report the system kicks out – when Perkins was sent to prison, what his crime was, when he got out. I went to the database and did an operator's query, asking for all the entries pertaining to Adolph Alvin Perkins. The output isn't pretty, but if you know how to read it, it gives you the straight scoop.'

'I see. A nether world of information known only to the righteous.'

'The righteous, how perceptive you are. What I don't understand is how you knew there was something skanky if you don't even know your way around the system?'

'I just got a feeling there was something funny about this guy and I decided to start with his prison records.'

'*Shee*. That's a killer instinct you got there. You figure out how to burn *that* on to a CD and I want to manage your worldwide distribution, OK? Sarah,' he said, clearly paying her a rare compliment, 'you could be a db auditor!'

'Wow,' Sarah said, wishing she had any clue what he was talking about. 'Does your query show who entered the information?'

'Has to. Yes. It's not a full user name, though, just a login ID, usually three initials and one number. This one is, uh ... EAG2.'

'So who goes with those initials?'

'Uh ... I don't know. Which is kind of surprising but it could be a temp, I guess. You could probably find out by calling the prison.'

'Well ... I don't seem to have the skill set that gets information out of prisons. Do you know anybody on the Florence support staff you could ask?'

'Let's see. Oh, well, there's Stevie ... uh ... Bergen? Durgin? – I'll think of it in a minute. He used to work here. I'll email him and get back to you. While I'm at it would you like me to do a systems search and see what other records have been entered recently by EAG2?'

'Oh, that's a brilliant idea. You really are a genius geek, aren't you?'

'Between us girls it's really not rocket science. You want to come down some time and let me show you how to do some of this stuff yourself?'

'Oh, sure I'll do that. When pigs fly.'

'What, you don't like to hack around?'

'I have to take anger management classes every time they upgrade the software.'

'Huh. I thought all cops these days were card-carrying nerds.'

'Some of the new kids are. I still like people stuff. Eyes and ears on the street.'

'Aw. Maybe you should start a club for geezers, get together and schmooze about the good old days with carbon paper.'

'Tell you what, GeeGee, I think I'll hang up while we're still friends.'

She pulled out the bottom left drawer of her desk, propped her feet on the front edge, and sat back with her arms crossed behind her head. The workstations around her were empty and quiet, and gradually the talk and clatter of the Gang detectives in the next pod and the Aggravated Assault squad beyond them faded into white noise. Isolated in her own mental space, she sat staring at her desk pad until the lines on the calendar blurred.

Somebody fiddled with Ace Perkins' records. The information carried a satisfying buzz, like finding the missing piece of a jigsaw puzzle under the sofa. *Why would anybody do that?* From the start, this victim's appearance and personal habits had seemed out of sync with his life. A street dealer should have been scruffier, messier, have a loud wife and smelly brats, or sordid habits and ugly pals. Ace Perkins was too scrubbed up.

This new piece fit the pattern of nothing-quite-right. 'Within two minutes either side of two a.m.,' Scott had said. *You work odd hours, EAG2, who are you?* Her mind sizzled with questions.

Her phone rang. Tracy Scott's voice had risen another notch. 'EAG2 doesn't show up on any other records in my systems search. You got that, Shylock? *EAG2 didn't enter any other records*.'

'I hear you.'

'Good. Also I just got this answer to my email.' He cleared his throat. 'Quote: "There's only been three of us doing data entry since the first of the year, and none of us log in as EAG2." Unquote.'

'Well, now,' Sarah said, 'isn't that special?'

'Fact. More fun than a weasel in a mouse-trap.'

'Tracy,' Sarah said after a little pause, 'what's your hunch about this?'

'Offhand, I'd say the system's been majorly borked.'

'Which would translate into English as...?'

'Breached. Screwed over. VIOLATED.'

'Dear me. Right here in the Old Pueblo.'

'How much do you like me now?'

'Genius Geek, write the commendation letter of your dreams and I'll sign it.' She hung up and pushed her desk drawer shut in one decisive move, jumped up and began digging through the box of small items she had checked out of evidence earlier. The keys to Perkins' apartment were in a little manila envelope tucked into the corner of the box, right where she'd left them. She dropped them in her purse and fished out her own car keys, put on her weapon and checked herself out on the duty board.

I can pick up the warrant for the bank on my way. Heat was already rising in waves off Stone Avenue and the tires made a sticky hissing sound on the asphalt. Fidgeting in the check-in line at the underground parking garage near the courthouse, she tapped her foot, drummed on the steering wheel. *Rotten waste of time.* But there were no available spots on the street. She pushed her way through the usual crowds, grabbed the closing doors on an almost-full elevator, jumped out on the third floor and trotted into a judge's office to get the signed search warrant she had requested for Ace's bank records. Another jumpy wait in the echoing marble hall for a down elevator and finally she was back in her car, rolling up the parking ramp, damning the driver ahead of her as he fumbled for change. Finally at the gate, she looked at the ticket and saw that only nineteen minutes had elapsed since she checked in. *Maybe I better lighten up a little.*

Paseo Redondo had more trees and felt cooler, and the traffic was slower. Sarah fed the meter, put gloves on outside the door and walked in slowly, luxuriating in the silence and the sharper focus she got by being alone in Ace's apartment.

They had taken everything from the desk, and the long counter between the kitchen and living room as well, so the apartment looked even more spartan than before. The crime scene crew had taken the clothes from the closet, too, and run a fingerprint check; there were traces of magnetic powder on the furniture and window sills.

She stood in the middle of the living room and turned three hundred and sixty degrees, twice, taking her time. Nothing jumped out, so she started at the windows and did a rigorous search of the backs of drapes, picture and mirrors, edges of carpet, undersides of tables and chairs. When she finished all three rooms she started on the desk drawers they had emptied yesterday, taking each one out and looking at the bottom. She went on to the kitchen drawers, which still held a few utensils and supplies.

She found what she was looking for in a drawer under the counter by the kitchen sink. It held six cheap forks, three spoons and a tall stack of paper napkins. She looked at the stack a few seconds, shrugged, and began holding them up, a dozen at a time by the folded edge, watching how they swung. When one bunch separated at the middle she pulled out the heavy one and opened it. Smiling, she peeled the scotch tape off a flat skinny key. *You were such a clever fellow, Ace Perkins, I almost wish I'd met you.*

She dropped the key in her purse, went back out to her car and drove to the address printed on Ace's bank statements. There she showed her shield and search warrant to the bank manager, who quickly passed her along to his formidably sleek assistant, who led her to the pious lady who guarded the vaults. After brief conversation in churchy tones and a good deal of signing, she was left alone in a cubicle with Ace Perkins' most carefully guarded possessions.

She had expected one of the big drawers, filled with stacks of large bills. Instead she was handed the long, slender drawer of the average householder, packed with neat manila envelopes. She scooped them out and opened an evidence bag, getting ready to carry them back to the station. But her curiosity was piqued by the care with which he had hidden the key to this trove, so she told herself that having sweated and crawled on the floor to find it, she deserved the first, uninterrupted look. There would be discreetly numbered bank accounts, surely; diamonds; perhaps the deed to an offshore villa.

What she found instead made her catch her breath and say, 'Oh.' After a few seconds she whispered fiercely, '*Shit.*' She went through the items for ten minutes, making small sounds of shock and dismay. Then she packed everything into a plastic evidence bag, made one phone call, signed out and left the bank with a somber face.

Twenty-Nine

Delaney told her to meet him at the Wendy's closest to the crime scene he was supervising. He was there ahead of her, blinking at the two cups of coffee on the table in front of him and clenching his jaw rhythmically, making a muscle jump in his cheek.

Just a little tense, are we? He looked at her,

when she walked up to the table, as if he was trying to remember who she was. Then he came back to planet earth and said, 'Thought you forgot me.'

'No, but I forgot the construction on Swan.' She gulped her coffee. 'Man, that tastes good, thanks. I'm sorry to call you off the job.'

'S'OK,' he said. 'What have you got?'

'It's in my car,' she said. 'Will you come outside? I need to talk to you where nobody can listen.'

'Why all the cloak and dagger?' he said, standing in front of her car, grumpy and impatient.

'Get in and I'll show you.' She flipped the locks open and got in the driver's seat without waiting for him. *Growl if you must. I need answers and I'm going to get them*. She fished a glassine bag out of her briefcase and held it up.

'What's that?'

'A key to a safety deposit box.'

'OK. So?' He glanced at his watch.

She told him where she found it.

'You actually went through all the paper napkins?' He snorted. 'Jesus, I've sorted a lot of garbage in my time, but ... why'd you go back there?'

'I decided there had to be something we missed.'

'Why?'

'Well – after you left me alone this morning, I got to thinking about Ace Perkins, how he didn't match the profile of a street dealer. He wasn't into nightlife, he didn't seem to have any bottom crawlers for friends. So I called a guy I know on the support staff.' She told him about finding the anomaly in Ace Perkins' prison records.

'Goddamn. You're saying he's a plant?'

'Yes. This was in the box.' She patted the long brown evidence bag.

'What is it?' He was watching her face now, he'd forgotten about the time. 'Sarah?'

'A forty-caliber Glock, just like ours. A notarized will and sealed letters for his wife and children, and a wallet with the ID and shield for Special Agent Douglas MacDougal, detached from DEA in Denver for assignment in Tucson. His picture matches Ace Perkins' prison photo.'

Delaney turned his face away and said softly, 'Aw, shit.'

'Yeah.'

'Well, but...'

'That's what I said, "Well, but." He's been dead since early Tuesday morning, why hasn't DEA been all over us by now? Don't undercover agents have to carry a monitor? Don't they check in every day? Come to think of it, I bet that's the unlisted number.'

'What?'

'There's an unlisted number on his phone bill. He'd been calling it every day. Jimmy's been spinning his wheels trying to identify it but it's behind some kind of a firewall, the company rep can't find it either. See how this wastes our time?'

'Well, don't start that rant and waste some more.'

'OK. But here's what I really don't get: what use is this wonderful system if his contact doesn't care that he hasn't called since Monday?'

'Good question.'

'Oh, I've got plenty more.'

'I really don't have time for all of them right now.'

'I *know* that, boss, but there's one answer I have to have before I go any further. Is this something you're in on? I suppose if you were you wouldn't tell me, would you? I hate these things!'

'Sarah, I'm not in on anything, forget that. You did absolutely right to call me out on this. And before you do anything more, I agree, we need some answers.'

'Boy, do we. Like, why were they using a guy from out of town? Does that bother you as much as it does me?'

'Oh, you mean ... oh.'

'Yeah. Our guys work with DEA all the time. Auto Theft guys, Gang Squad. Everybody helps DEA whenever they ask. I know a fireman who went undercover for them for two days, posed as a meter man to watch a couple of stash houses. So how come all of a sudden they need a guy from out of town?'

'Sarah, let's not get all excited till we know something. Just ... hold on a minute.' He had his cell phone off his belt, punching in numbers.

'You calling DEA?'

'Damn straight.' He raised one hand in a fend-off motion as somebody answered. Sarah listened as he asked for somebody, waited, and finally said, 'This is Ross Delaney. I – fine, how are you? Yes, well –' He cleared his throat and began to describe what she had found. An outburst of fast questions exploded at the other end. Delaney fired back answers, mostly, 'Yes', 'No' and 'Yes'. Then he was silent through a long speech that seemed to require only the occasional 'Uh-huh'.

After five minutes he said, 'Right. Yes. I understand,' folded up his phone and turned toward her, rubbing his ear and looking thoughtful. 'Sarah, you know where the DEA building is?'

'Yes.'

'Good. Take everything you just found in the bank down there.'

'Shouldn't I check them into evidence first?'

'No. I know it's not kosher but – they specifically asked us not to, and they say they'll give us all the justification we need.'

'See, this is what I was afraid of. I hate this! Withholding evidence – it means they're afraid the department will leak, doesn't it?'

'Look, will you just come down out of the trees till you hear what they have to say? We don't *know* what it means yet.'

'Yes we do. It means they think we're a bunch of retards. Or crooks, take your pick.'

'Sarah, damn it, shut up and listen to me now. You have to have them sign a transfer of evidence form. Have you got one with you?' She didn't. He went and got one out of his car and they filled it out together.

'There,' he said, reading it over, 'That should cover our butts all right.' He blinked at it a few times and added, 'And when you get back to your office I want you to enter the story of your second search in your work log. Describe everything you found, where you found it. Include your reasons for going back for a second look, and a detailed account of this meeting you're going to. Get all the names down, who took the evidence from you and why.'

'I'll do it, boss, but I don't like it.'

'Yeah, well, you don't have to like it. You're following orders and that will cover you.' Seeing her frowning, still dissatisfied, Delaney flushed bright pink and vented some anger of his own. 'How about if I swear on my dead mother's grave, will that be good enough for you? Your objections will be duly noted in *my* work log, OK? Now quit ragging on me and get your butt down there as fast as you can, because they're waiting for you and it sounds like their hair is on fire.'

'I know just how they feel, I'm pretty hot myself.'

'Sarah, this is a direct order now: *chill out*. We stumbled into the middle of something big here, and we need to help the folks with the clout whenever we can if we want to prosper, surely you remember that, don't you?'

'Yes.' When he continued to stare at her anxiously she said, 'I hear you!'

He opened the car door and got out, leaned back inside and told her, 'Special Agent Morrell or Special Agent Cruz, that's who you're going to see. They'll ask you a shitload of questions, I guess, but then they promised to brief you on what's going on.' He cleared his throat. 'Take notes if you can, will you? I didn't get many details.'

'Right.' *This morning we weren't talking, now he wants notes.* She settled the evidence bag carefully into the warm hollow Delaney's backside had left in the seat, backed out of her slot and pulled out into traffic. As she moved to the inside lane, getting ready to turn south, her stomach growled. *Five hours since breakfast and no lunch in sight.* She found an energy bar in the side pocket of her door and devoured it ravenously, sipping lukewarm water from a bottle in the console. 'Pretend it's steak,' Ibarra always said when the schedule drove them to trail food.

As soon as she turned west on Valencia she began muttering to herself, 'Now where's that funny little turn...' She missed the DEA building on the first pass and had to come back to it, a featureless cream-colored square with retro color blocks, squatting on its own big asphalt parking lot.

She pressed the bell on the front door, gave her name and said she was here to see Special

Agent Cruz. A buzzer sounded and she opened the door. Inside was a small tiled lobby with white leather couches, a couple of fake trees. It could have been a dentist's office except that the pretty girl in a red dress at the phone console was behind bullet-proof glass with a small pass-through at the bottom.

A dark-eyed man in jeans and a knit shirt stepped through the door beside the receptionist's window two minutes after Sarah walked in. The name tag that hung around his neck on a cord read: Special Agent Philip Cruz. He didn't smile when he said, 'Detective Burke? Phil Cruz, how are you?'

'Sarah,' she said, and put out her hand.

'My boss's office is right down the hall.' He opened the door he had just come through. 'You can sign in here if you will.'

The ledger was on a high counter that walled off the girl from the hall. In her tiny, isolated space, she seemed to be almost as protected from the occupants of the building as from outside visitors.

A sandy-haired man, large-boned and gaunt, stood up behind his desk when they entered. He was dressed like Cruz but his whole outfit was upgraded in subtle ways Sarah didn't have time to analyze. Cruz said, 'Sarah, this is Special Agent Morrell.'

'Mark,' he said, and shook her hand. 'Thanks for coming so promptly.' They all sat down. Sarah put her purse on the floor and her package in her lap.

Morrell nodded toward it and said, 'Is that the ... uh...?'

Sarah nodded. 'I brought this transfer of evidence form. Can we—'

'Oh, right, sure. Let's see...' He leaned back in his chair to read Delaney's neat block printing, taking his time. Finally he said, 'Fine. Here we go.' They both signed, each took a copy and she put one on top of the package. 'Now –' he looked at her searchingly when she handed it over – 'you haven't shown this to anybody but Delaney?'

'No.'

'Or checked it into your system?'

'No.'

'Right. And –' that look again – 'you haven't told anybody else what you found?'

'I called Delaney as soon as I saw what was in the bank. When I told him what I had he called you. He said tell no one, come straight here, so that's what I did.'

'Good. No offense meant, Sarah.'

'None taken.' *My boss says chill.*

'Good. I think –' he rolled his chair back from his desk a little, rested his elbows on his chair arms, tented his hands in front of his chin – 'what I need to hear from you, Sarah, is what made you go back and search that apartment again?'

'Too many things about the victim didn't fit the profile of a street dealer.' She told them about identifying the body off prison records, and her growing curiosity as the investigation revealed quiet personal habits, regular hours and scrupulously organized records, extreme neatness. 'He seemed all wrong for his life. So I got a bright kid on the support staff to scrutinize the prison records and he found the funny business.'

'The funny...'

'The DLMs were all the same.' Just for a second, Sarah saw Morrell and Cruz exchange a silent *oops*.

Cruz asked quickly, 'Besides your computer guy, who knows about the records?'

'Delaney.'

'You didn't talk to anybody else?'

She shook her head. 'My whole crew's out on a new homicide. I decided there must be something in Ace Perkins' apartment that we overlooked, so I went back by myself.' She told them about the key in the napkins and they traded another of those looks. 'I expected to find a box full of money in the bank. When I found these things instead, I called Delaney.'

'Uh-*huh*. Well, we're certainly grateful you did that, Sarah.' Morrell had been cutting the tape on her evidence bag while they talked. Now he pulled out the long manila envelope and opened it. His face remained impassive when the gun and shield slid on to his desk. Sarah wondered if he knew he had made a small, sorrowful sound.

Cruz stood up and leaned over the desk, swore under his breath, and sat down. The gold second hand of the electric clock on Morrell's desk made a complete revolution inside its gleaming lucite case while they sat in silence.

Finally Morrell said, 'Sergeant Douglas MacDougal, as you see here, was a DEA agent detached from his home office in Denver. He was helping us with a ... a job we've been working on. Been here a little over four months.' He cleared his throat. 'Unusually long for an undercover assignment.' His bland gray eyes searched her face. 'You're the primary, right? You're running the case?'

'Yes.'

'You found him Tuesday morning, is that what Delaney said?'

'Yes.'

Cruz's phone buzzed at his hip. He answered quickly, said, 'OK,' and then, to Sarah, 'Excuse me,' and left the room.

Now, Sarah thought, and leaned toward Morrell. 'I have to ask you, didn't you know he was missing? I thought undercover agents had to carry a monitor.'

'They do. But he was just finishing up here and starting on a week's leave. Originally the job he came for was supposed to last three months, tops. But things got a little more ... complicated than we expected ... so it took longer than it should have and he was in a hurry to get home, said there were things he couldn't put off any longer. We wanted him to stay for the round-up but he said you've got all my information, you don't need me, I'll come back to testify but right now I need some time off. We owed him a ton of leave so we agreed that after the Monday night run he wouldn't call us any more and his monitor would be off.'

'I was at his autopsy. We didn't find a device on him.'

'Oh, they make them so small these days ... Doug's was in his phone. That's not here, have you got it?'

'No, but...' She told him about the phone call that was briefly answered and immediately cut off. 'Did he have a GPS in the thing, too?'

'Oh, yes.'

'We wanted to try tracking it but we don't have the gear yet.'

'We can do that.' He made a note. 'We'll get right on that, thanks.'

Sarah chewed her lip and decided, *Oh, what the hell*. 'Uh ... we still have his homicide to investigate.'

'I know you do and we want to help, believe me, we want his killer caught more than you do. But, uh –' he smiled at her, very collegial – 'starting tomorrow, OK?'

'Oh? Well – could I just ask you about something in the autopsy?' She told him about the burns, the broken fingers.

Morrell's face grew sad. 'Doug was captured a couple of years ago, by the drug ring he was investigating. They took him into the desert across the border and ... did some very bad things before his unit could arrange a rescue. By rights he should have quit after that, but ... Doug was a very dedicated agent.'

Obsessed, Sarah thought. 'One more question?'

Morrell, watching her face, said, 'What?'

'Well ... am I right that you're scooping up a lot of the people Ace was dealing with? Forgive me for calling him Ace, I'm afraid—'

'That's who he is, to you, huh? Yes ... um ... I can't tell you everything but today is the day we're hoping to put the whole ring away.'

'So can I get that list when you're through with it?'

'Absolutely. And we'll tell you everything we've learned that might be of use to you. In fact ... as long as you're here would you like to see the two we've got in interrogation right now?'

'Could I?'

'Don't see why not. We've got their cases made. Right this way.' He led the way down a cement-block hall, their footsteps quiet on tight-weave carpet, to an office-like door near the back of the building. He walked past it and opened the drape on a one-way window next to it. Sarah looked into a room where Cruz and another agent faced a red-faced, indignantly gesturing middle-aged man across an empty granite table. The blue-suited man beside him had to be his attorney.

'Uh ... is that Pappy Grimes?'

'Sure is.' Morrell had a little trouble holding his cooler-than-thou look; a touch of pride kept leaking out.

'The great philanthropist pushes coke on the side?'

'No, he's the money launderer,' Morrell said. 'He was the toughest nut to crack, the reason the operation took so long.' They walked around a corner, past another bank of work stations, to another window in a wall. 'Here's the other one.'

'Oh, now, wait,' Sarah said, staring, 'Anthony Delarosa?'

'I hope he isn't a particular friend of yours.'

'No, I just know him in the department. But—'

'I know it's hard to believe about one of your own.'

'How – who'd he sell to?'

'Oh, he wasn't dealing,' Morrell said, 'just servicing his own habit. Reporting Ace Perkins as his snitch gave him cover. That's been his MO for some time, arresting pushers and turning them into his own private source of coke.'

'But he must have had to turn in some information sometimes, didn't he? To keep the game going?'

'Oh, sure. Some of it was pretty good stuff, too. Delarosa was an accidental find, by the way, we weren't looking for him. MacDougal came back laughing after one of his nights on the street and told us how he got turned and then turned again by the same cop.'

'So,' Sarah said, with a bitter taste in her mouth, 'Delarosa's been furnishing the comic relief, huh?'

'In drug interdiction,' Morrell said, 'you'll take a laugh any place you can get it.'

'Uh-huh.' She had not even liked Tony Delarosa, but now, seeing him gathered up into a heavy-muscled lump with his thick arms across his chest, his ruddy cheeks purple with rage, Sarah turned away in sorrow.

'Well,' she said, 'I don't suppose, though, that *he* killed Special Agent MacDougal.'

'No, not much chance he would cut off his own supply.'

As they walked back toward Morrell's office Sarah asked, 'Will you notify next of kin?'

'Yes, we'll take care of that. The body's at the, let's see, is it Pima County...?'

'Forensic Center, yes, on East District.'

'We'll need to see him, ID him for the Denver office. Can you arrange that? Thanks. How far has the investigation gone? I mean ... have you got a suspect list?'

'No. We have one print, that we lifted off his leg the day we found him. We haven't matched it so far.'

'What about the money?'

'The what?'

'He should have had a lot of cash on him. We did wonder why he hadn't made the drop. Might have been as much as eight or ten thousand dollars.'

'We found ninety cents in his pockets. And no wallet.'

'So ... I guess that's what he was killed for.' Morrell's face became briefly a mask of regret. 'The money.' He sighed. 'It's hard to understand, though. He was a highly skilled agent with a great deal of field experience.

What about his weapon?'

'Nothing on him. Do you know what he was packing?'

'Yes, a Ruger nine ... uh ... P95C, I think. The car, did you find that? A Ford, uh...?'

'Excursion, yes. That was missing too, when we found him. But one of our street patrolmen located it last night behind a Fry's store.'

'Strange. Any sign of Hector Rodriguez?'

'Who?'

'His gofer, driver. You don't know about him?'

Did Denny say his name was – well, but it can't be? 'No.'

'Local boy. Phil and I were dubious about him but Doug felt he could control him and he said a runner from the neighborhood helped his cred. Now I wonder.'

'Hector Rodriguez? Usual spelling?' She looked up from writing. 'What have you got on him?'

'Um, a stretch in juvie for car theft that won't come up on your records, but you can get it, of course, if you have the name and a ... never mind, I'll fax it to you. We're very anxious to find him, but he hasn't been home. Will you let me know if you come across anything on him? There might be something, another address or a phone number, in Doug's laptop. You did find that, I hope?'

'Yes. We'll take another look.'

Cruz came down the hall looking for him,

and Morrell asked him, 'Was that...?'

'Yup. The next load.' Sarah became aware of a great deal of foot traffic, doors being opened and closed, voices.

'I guess,' Mark Morrell said apologetically, 'that I have to cut this short for now, Sarah. There's a lot going on here today. Did I give you my card? Good. We'll be in touch, hmm? You think you can find your way out?'

'Yes,' Sarah said, 'I'm sure I can manage that.'

His smile acknowledged the irony. His handshake was firm but not overpowering as he said, 'We're really grateful to you, Sarah.'

Mark Morrell, she decided, probably had calibrated handshakes for men, women and children, and goodbye smiles graded precisely by degree of warmth. He kept his seamless cool while he was facing her but as soon as he turned away he asked Phil Cruz anxiously, 'Which rooms?' She could see, as he walked away, that he had already forgotten her.

A door had opened beyond him, at the back of the building. Three men were briefly silhouetted there, against the light, two officers with a prisoner between them. Something about the silhouette of the officer on the left held her attention, and as the door closed and the overhead lights revealed his features she saw that the man was Will Dietz.

Surprised once too often in a single day, Sarah felt hot blood surge into her face. She remembered his words in her driveway this morning, 'Skej is kind of crazy right now. Lot of people sick I guess.' *Kissed me and lied to my face.* As the whole crazy week's frustrations found a focus point, unreasoning rage flooded her brain. *Everybody I care about jerks me around.*

Dietz looked past Morrell at that instant and met her blazing eyes. He recognized her anger at once, and lifted one hand in a pleading motion just as she turned away.

Sarah walked steadily, not allowing herself to look back, along the carpeted hall to the high desk by the window. She signed out in the ledger, her hand shaking a little from the pressure of blood roaring in her ears. The girl in the red dress was very busy with the phones now, and the whole building had a beehive feel, quiet scurrying going on all over it. There was a distant hum of many motors at the rear of the building, and once an outburst of loud talk cut off by a closing door.

The lot in front was empty of parked cars but not quiet. One after another, vehicles turned into the driveway with shackled passengers in the back seat, and disappeared behind the building. Sarah sat in her car with the door open, letting the fans blow hot air out, wishing she had something to break.

Her phone rang.

Thirty

Rudy watched them cross the street, step on to the parking lot and stand a moment, scanning the signs in the front windows of the tire store. The uniformed patrolman was from the South Tucson Police Department, what was his name? Manuel Torres. His uncle was an old friend, Raymundo Torres, but in one electric oh-shit instant Rudy knew that family connections would not help today.

The two plain clothes detectives with Torres had pared down bodies and eyes like one-way windows. They wore that air of carrying powerful secrets that he associated with federal officers. He knew without looking that there would be back-up somewhere nearby.

His mind had always accepted that arrest and conviction were possible components of drug-trafficking. Most of the dealers went to prison sooner or later, it was reasonable to assume that his day would come. He had watched plenty of dealers go in and come out and start over. It didn't seem too hard. Cost of doing business, they said with mingled contempt and humor.

But this morning as he saw the threat closing in, he learned that what his mind had accepted, his gut could not abide. His grandfather's battered old tire store, Sunday dinners at the dog track with Camille, even the silly clatter of the crowd of young relatives hanging out at his house grew in importance as the officers approached his shop, reminding him that he had status in this community, long-standing ties of great merit. A stone grew in his chest.

He forgot that he had made careful plans to abandon Camille and go traveling with a high-spirited pole dancer. The bank accounts in the Caymans, and the plans for travel and frolic in faraway lands with Steffi, that part of his dream was easy enough to let go, he admitted now. But what he had in Tucson was real, and in a hot sweat of shame he imagined he saw his wife's eyes demanding, Get it back.

They'll take the house. He knew how these things worked. Once they made the case they took everything they could lay their hands on, all the businesses, houses and cars and boats, bank accounts and jewelry, even the house you were living in. They took as much as they could find and they split it with the local police departments, to pay back the community, they said, for the terrible expense of making the case against you.

He pictured Camille's face the day they told her that she would have to leave the nice house on Thirty-Second Street, the High Resolution TV and the shining kitchen with every gadget ever invented for the care and feeding of relatives. Conveniently disinterested in the bars and body shops that were the ostensible source of his wealth now, Camille concerned herself entirely with the life in her comfortable house, the barbeque out back and the walk-in closet that held her fifty-odd pairs of shoes. For a crazy moment Rudy longed to put his arm over her soft shoulders and tell her, 'I'm sure they won't take your shoes.' It seemed to him he was tough enough to take whatever was coming to him except the shame of what this would do to his wife.

So as he watched the men with the closed faces come through the door, he began to wonder what he had that he could trade them, to let Camille keep the house.

He had heard other dealers' stories, he knew what the Narcs would say – that they had all the proof they needed, he had better just cooperate and hope it would help him with the judge. But he knew they could not have found everything he had, and that cops always had lawyers on their backs, demanding more evidence.

He should probably call his own lawyer soon, but not right away. *Might want to play the dumb Mexican for a while yet.*

He watched them pull their shields out, getting ready to show him they had every right to take away his restaurants and bars, the eight cars he had bought from Pappy Grimes and the old farmhouse down by Three Points crammed to the ceiling with

Mexican Gold and Blue Thunder. In his mind he moved away a little, put some distance between himself and the store's clamor. He got as cool as he could inside his personal oasis, set his priorities, and faced the ominous assurance of the Feds.

They don't know the name of my boca. He ought to be worth a house.

Thirty-One

Sarah saw her home number in the caller ID window and answered while she closed up her car. 'Hi, Mother, how are you doing?'

'Well, just fine. But I don't know what to think about Janine.'

'Oh? Why?'

'Well, I waited till eleven thirty – I know she was bent out of shape last night but I expected her to call here as soon as she woke up. But she never did, so I called her. Her phone rang once, and she picked it up so I know she was there, but she didn't answer and in a couple of seconds the line went dead. Since then I've called three times and never got an answer.'

'Huh. Funny.' *I don't have time for Janine right now.*

'Where do you suppose she'd go?'

'She can't go any place. She doesn't have a car.'

'Oh, that's right. Well, then ... why doesn't she answer the phone?'

'Mother, how could I possibly know that?' Her answer came out sharper than she intended and elicited total silence at the other end. She couldn't even hear breathing. Had Aggie fainted, had a stroke? *Damn, she doesn't even have to talk to pull my string.* 'Look, I never got a lunch break, I'll take one now and swing by there.'

'Oh, honey, could you?'

'Sure. How's Denny doing?'

'Quite well, I think. She slept till almost ten o'clock. Since then we've had scrambled eggs and cocoa with marshmallows and an apple and a couple of cookies.'

'OK. You two stick to your diets and I'll get back to you.'

Out of dubious-cop habit she dialed Janine's number herself as she turned south on Hemisphere Loop. After five rings she closed the phone and turned east on Valencia. Overhead, clusters of sleek jet fighters augmented the hot urban commotion, making tight co-ordinated turns at breathtaking speeds and shooting touch-and-go landings at Davis-Monthan airbase to get ready for the real deal over Iraq. Sarah turned up the radio and took Kolb north, squinting into afternoon brightness.

Turning on to Lurlene Street, she was almost wiped out by an old red Subaru Brat that cut the corner so short he left her no place to go but the curb. Ordinarily she would have hit the siren and arrested his ass; she had no mercy for reckless drivers. Today she had too much else on her mind; she hid out in the anonymity of her unmarked vehicle and let him go.

Lurlene Street looked empty, everybody at work or school. Sarah drove past Janine's house to the end of the block, did a U-turn and came back to park a couple of doors to the west, facing east with a good view of the street all the way to the corner. Visiting Janine lately, you just never knew – the man who left that message on her table could have come back.

She walked silently on the weedy grass next to the sidewalk. Two strides on tiptoe took her from the sidewalk to the front door, where she flattened herself against the stucco wall.

Janine's house had a sidelight as tall as the door and a foot wide. It was covered by an old lace curtain on stretchers, supposed to provide privacy for the people inside but limp with age now and hanging a little crooked. Peering in along the right-hand edge, Sarah could see most of the front room.

Janine was sitting in there, on a scuffed wooden chair, close to her round dining table but facing the front door. Her arms were tied to the chair with striped cotton dishtowels. A leather belt held her left leg tight against the leg of the table, and she had a gag in her mouth.

Sarah took one step across the door and tried the door handle with her left hand. It turned. She pushed the door open and stepped inside with her weapon braced at shoulder height, expecting to confront whoever had tied her sister to the chair.

There was nobody in sight but Janine, who began making frantic sounds through the gag. With her eyebrows raised, Sarah nodded her head toward the bedrooms. Janine shook her head vehemently and made more get-me-out noises through the towel.

Sarah lowered her weapon and pussy-footed around the house for a quick survey. The front room and Janine's bedroom were only slightly messier than usual, but Denny's room, usually the neat one, had been thoroughly trashed. Papers, books and clothing lay in random heaps, and the desk drawers had been emptied on to the bed. Whoever did the trashing was gone, though, Janine was right about that.

'OK, kid,' Sarah said, back at Janine's chair, 'hold still, now, I'll have you out of this in a minute. Man, these are killer knots, have you got a knife? This drawer?' Janine was nodding frantically. 'OK, here we go.'

Janine began to retch when the wad of cloth came out of her mouth. 'Hang on a couple more seconds,' Sarah begged, pulling rags off her sister's arms as fast as she could, 'try not to barf on me, baby.'

Janine bolted for the bathroom as soon as

she was free. Sarah went back to the cluttered counter by the sink, found the phone lying in a stack of dirty dishes, and put it back on its charging stand. She called home on her own phone and Aggie answered in the middle of the first ring, soft and short, 'Hello?'

'Anything wrong?'

'No. Denny's taking a nap.'

'Oh, good. Janine's OK, but – somebody invaded her house and tied her up.'

'Oh, my God. Is she hurt?'

'Just scared, I think. I'm going to take her to the emergency room, though, I think she ought to get checked out.'

'Good. Her life is all messed up again, isn't it?'

'Looks like it, but – we'll see.'

'I'm afraid we will. You'll stay with her, though, will you?'

'As long as I can. I'll see she's in good hands, Mother, don't worry.'

'That's good. See you tonight.'

'Sarah?' Janine stood in the bathroom door, so pale she was almost green. 'Was that Mama?'

'Yes.'

'Has she got Denny?'

'Yes. They're both at my house.' Janine seemed to be sliding down against the door-jamb; Sarah grabbed her and helped her wobble to a chair. 'The man who tied you up, was he the one you were afraid might still be here last night?'

'What?' Confusion showed through all the

other terrible emotions on Janine's face and then it came back to her. 'Oh, no, Sarah, no! This – I can hardly believe it myself but this was the same lunatic who stole my car.'

'What? Why did he come to your house?'

'Looking for the money, he said.'

'The money?'

'That's how he said it, "The money". Not *some* money but *the* money, as if I'd know all about it. I said, "I don't have any money, what are you talking about?" And he said, "The money your kid stole from me".'

'Your kid? Is he talking about Denny?'

'What other kid do I have? Oh, Sarah, listen to me, Sarah!' She clutched her sister's arm and shook it. 'You need to send somebody to your house right away! Because I think he's going there!'

'What? Why would he go there?' Janine's face somehow made room for still another emotion: shame. 'Janine, you didn't tell him where Denny is, did you?'

'I didn't *tell* him, I didn't even know where she was! But ... he figured it out! He saw that card you had framed for her desk and he – apparently she said something about her Aunt Sarah when they were together in the car. So when he found that thing saying "Aunt Sarah's Numbers" he came out here carrying the damn thing and yelling, "Is this where she is?" He had that *knife*, Sarah, a long terrible thing and he said he'd cut my throat! You can't imagine what it feels like to be tied up and have somebody threaten you with a – all I said was "Maybe",' she wailed after her sister's retreating back. 'You're not going to just leave me here alone, are you?'

'I'll send somebody to help you,' Sarah yelled back over her shoulder. She took the fastest way to midtown and used the siren for all but the last six blocks, working the phone while she drove. Dispatch first, where she described the knife-wielding car thief she suspected was headed for her house, gave his ETA as eight to nine minutes, and asked for back-up.

'Do my best,' Dispatch said.

'Hey, come on, this is an emergency! A known felon is almost certainly heading for two very vulnerable people.'

'I'm way behind on emergencies that have already happened,' Dispatch said. 'We'll get to you as quick as we can.'

She thought of calling Delaney then, but felt overwhelmed by the prospect of trying to explain her family's predicament while she sped through traffic with the siren wailing. She pushed the rules about slowing down for intersections as far as she dared, and had a little luck on Alvernon, where several lights turned green as she approached and a few alert citizens actually got out of her way. Even so it felt like swimming in glue.

The tacky old red Brat was parked at the curb in front of her house. Sarah memorized the license as she drove by it but didn't take the time to call it in. She pulled past it, turned the corner on to Olsen Avenue and parked by the easement that ran through the middle of the block. All the backyards in her block had five-foot cement-block walls, heavily weeded on the outside and overgrown with vines. Trotting along past the garbage cans, she knew she couldn't be seen from her house till she opened the gate. From there, she took her chances and sprinted for the back door.

Nobody shot at her. With her hand on the knob she paused two seconds, took a deep breath and drew her Glock. Inside, she heard a man say something and her mother answer.

Kitchen cabinets lined the wall opposite the back door; the opening into the living room was offset five feet to the right. Sarah took back every hard word she'd ever said about this barely adequate duplex, in that taut instant when she realized she could get in without being seen. Fussy about keeping her hinges oiled, she knew they wouldn't squeak. When the door was ajar three inches she heard her mother say, 'Don't you understand English? There is no child in this house.'

'I understand plenty,' the man said. 'You gonna get outa my way, Aunt Sarah, or do I gotta blow your head off?'

Sarah sidled through the half-open door, crossed her tiny kitchen in one long stride and eased back along the counter toward the opening. She heard Aggie give one small, startled squeak, and the man say, 'Believe me now?'

Sarah was one step from the opening when

she heard Denny's voice say, 'Leave her alone!'

Shit.

Ready to step out and shoot, Sarah risked one quick peek and saw that the three of them were hopelessly bunched. The young man, not tall but strong, with beefy shoulders, was clutching Aggie to his side with his left arm. His right hand held a serious handgun. *Ruger, I think.* They were both watching Denny, who stood beyond them in the opening to the hall.

'So,' the man said, 'here she is after all.'

Denny looked small and frail, barefooted in Andy's shabby old T-shirt. 'Let her go,' she said, with a small quaver in her voice, 'and I'll show you where the money is.'

'Deal,' the man said. He walked Aggie to an armchair, said, 'Stay here and be good, Auntie, so I don't have to shoot you,' and gave her chest a shove. She flopped on to the old Morris chair with a yelp. The chair back collapsed and she was trapped on her back with the high armrests in the way of her escape.

Denny turned her back on them and walked across the hall into the den. Sarah watched her walk around the end of the futon, which was still made up as a bed with the covers turned back. The man kept his big gun trained on her as he followed her to the doorway. From the kitchen, Sarah had no shot that wasn't likely to hit Denny.

Aggie was still sprawled in the chair, struggling to sit up, when Sarah passed her, moving silently and fast.

Just inside the door of the den, the intruder's whole attention was fixed on Denny, who was on the far side of the futon, her small face set like an ivory mask. She slid one hand between the mattress and frame of the cheap little bed, and pulled out a fat white letter-size envelope. As she straightened she saw Sarah, standing behind her tormentor in the hall. Holding her breath, Sarah shook her head a bare inch each way and Denny, with no change of expression, moved her eyes back to the man with the gun. She held the envelope up, just out of his reach.

'All *right*,' the man's voice turned boyish with pleasure. 'More *like* it.' He stepped forward with his gun lowered a little, his left hand outstretched across the bed toward the money. Keeping her eyes on his face, Denny turned the envelope over. The man yelled, 'Hey!' as twenties and hundreds cascaded across the bed, and in that moment Sarah sprang.

She hit his gun hand hard with her Glock and yelled, 'Police! Drop the gun!' His weapon fell from his deadened hand. Sarah kicked it under the bed, pulled his right arm up high behind him as she pushed her Glock into his ear and yelled, 'On your knees right now!'

As his knees buckled, Hector tried his last play. Watching him sink, Sarah saw his left hand move toward his pants leg. When he tugged, light glinted on the handle of a knife. She put her weight on her right foot and kicked hard with her left. Her shoe sole hit his wrist with a sickening crack. The second pain disabled him, temporarily; he sank to his knees, whimpering, with his wrist against his mouth.

Needing a solution to the problem of having only two hands, Sarah knelt on the backs of his legs, yelling, 'You put that hand behind your back right now or I'm going to shoot you!' Weeping, protesting that she was killing him, he put his left arm behind him and she holstered her gun long enough to pull his two useless hands together and clamp the cuffs on.

'Ow, ow, ow, that hurts, you're killing me!' he roared.

'You hold still so I can get this knife off your leg, maybe I can help you with that,' Sarah said. When the scabbard was off she tossed it on the bed in front of Denny's round, astonished eyes and asked her, 'What did you say his name was?'

'Hector,' Denny squeaked.

'The more you wiggle around, Hector,' Sarah said, 'the more this is going to hurt.'

He got his voice back then, called her a bitch from hell and promised a slow death at the hands of his buddies while she fished a plastic cuff out of her back pocket and tied his ankles together. When she was done she stood up, leaned toward the back of his head and said, 'One more word out of you and I tape your mouth shut.' In the gratifying silence that followed, she asked Denny, 'Is this the man who bought you the cheeseburger?'

Denny nodded and swallowed.

'And took you to the movie?'

Again, the quick nod. Her hands were clamped into her armpits to stop them trembling but some color was coming back in her face.

'How'd you get his money?'

Denny wiggled her butt nervously. 'He left it by me in a grocery sack.'

'Rotten little shit,' Hector ground out. His jaws were locked against the pain in his wrist. 'You grabbed it when the phone rang, didn't you?'

'Uh-huh.' Denny gave him a look that split the difference between guilt and triumph.

'And *you* got it,' Sarah said, 'by killing Ace Perkins, right?'

'Don't know what you're talking about,' Hector said.

'You will, soon enough. And you're not going to be so pleased with yourself after the Feds explain how you killed an undercover Narc.' His head snapped around and she smiled and nodded into his horrified eyes.

There was noise in the living room, somebody coming through the front door. Sarah heard her mother say, 'In there.' A young patrolman she didn't recognize edged in through the door with his gun braced, looking handsome and strong in a fresh uniform.

'Hey, thanks for coming,' Sarah said from the floor.

'Dan Daly,' he said, looking around. 'You're Sarah Burke?'

'Yes. This is my niece, Denny Lynch.'

'Hey, Denny. You having an exciting day?' He holstered his gun. 'Sarah, you didn't leave me much of anything to do here, did you? Shall I take this piece of trash out of your house?'

'Yes, could we put him in your car for a few minutes? I need to make a couple of phone calls.'

'You gonna ask Delaney for permission to shoot him?' Daly said, putting leg and belly chains on Hector and clipping them together. 'I'll be glad to help you with that.'

'We might not want to shoot him. This little thug may be more important than he looks.' She could see that Hector, even as he shuffled out to Dan's car in full chains, got kind of a boost out of hearing that.

Standing at her curb behind the Brat, Sarah called the DMV. 'Dolly? Sarah Burke. I'm fine, you? Good. Run this for me, will you?' She recited the license number, adding, '1987 Subaru Brat, one of those stupid things that looks like a sedan that lost a fight with a chainsaw.'

'Or a pickup in fancy dress.' Dolly had an enviable ability to talk and giggle while typing accurately in machine-gun bursts. 'Here you go,' she said after a few seconds. 'Hector Rodriguez...' She read off a birth date and an address on Ohio Street.

'Hah!' Sarah said.

'Oh, you like that answer, huh?'

'Yes, indeed. That is an excellent answer, thank you very much.'

'Hey, we aim to please,' Dolly said.

Her phone rang. It was Delaney, wondering where she was. It took her a few minutes to explain how, more or less by accident and acting with perhaps slightly less than text-book caution, she had just captured the killer they'd all been chasing.

Then she dialed the number Morrell had given her an hour earlier. The red-dress girl was polite but cool, explaining that Special Agent Morrell was away from his phone. 'Would you like to be connected to his voice-mail?'

'No. Find him as fast as you can and tell him I just arrested Hector Rodriguez. Rod-riguez, yes. Trust me, he wants him. Tell him I've got the missing money, too, and he should call this number within fifteen min-utes if he wants to talk to me about him. After that I'm going to be on my way to the Pima County jail to charge this man with ... oh, kidnapping and assault and murder, just for starts.' She had to say her number twice; there was a good deal of noise around the phone at the other end.

Dan helped her with the detail work, then, bringing in gloves and evidence bags. They bagged and tagged Hector's gun and knife, and counted the money together. Sarah looked up once and met Denny's watching eyes, and Denny looked away.

The handsome patrolman kept his expression stoic but his eyes indicated that while a thug on the floor with a detective straddling him was no big deal, a skinny child standing nearby in a man's T-shirt, a granny struggling out of a collapsed recliner, and a significant quantity of large bills drifting around their modest dwelling made this an interesting crime scene. 'So,' he finally ventured, 'this guy broke into your house and brought his own cash, huh?'

'Yeah, in this neighborhood we make 'em wipe their feet before they come in, too,' Sarah said. She knew he deserved to hear the whole story but she wasn't in any position to chat. She watched Denny sneaking peeks at Dan, the studly showboat cop. *Wow, she looks like Janine right now. Our next family disaster's growing up before my eyes.* A corner of her mind not completely absorbed with police work ran off alone on its own track, wailing a warning. *She stole all this money, hid it in my house and never said a word. What kind of a kid is she turning into?* The answer stared her in the face: *the kind whose mother brings home a new boyfriend every week and frequently gets stoned out of her mind. Denny needs to be rescued from her life!*

A DEA van pulled into the carport behind Dan's squad. Two DEA agents got out of it and knocked. When Sarah opened the door, the taller one held out his phone and asked her, politely, to push button number one.

'When it answers, ma'am,' he said, 'will you ask for the director, please?'

Morrell said, 'Well, from now on, Sarah Burke, I'm going to be very careful what I ask you for.'

Thirty-Two

After lengthy phone tag and dickering, about the time Sarah began threatening to die of impatience the DEA took Hector to Hemisphere Loop. Delaney got his firm understanding that Tucson PD would get him back as soon as DEA had picked his brain clean. As the van pulled out of her driveway, Sarah's phone rang and it was Delaney again, saying, 'One more thing—'

'Boss, they're just leaving,' Sarah said. 'I don't think I can—'

'It's not about DEA.' Delaney made the funny noises, *mmp mmp*, that she knew meant he was pulling his nose and thinking. 'I just thought you might enjoy knowing that Bud Ganz just matched the fingerprints we found at this morning's crime scene to that same one you and Gloria lifted off Ace Perkins' leg Tuesday morning.'

'Oh, so ... Hector did today's homicide too?'

'Looks like it. Too bad you didn't know that when you ran into your house after him without waiting for back-up.'

'Boss, he had a gun pointed at my niece. What would you have done?'

'Just what you did, I guess. The best police work I knew how to do. And you did very well with it, but I want you to think about it, Sarah.'

No, I'm going to try to put it right out of my mind that my Denny faced up to that double murderer a few minutes ago. Otherwise how will I get through all the work I still have to do today?

She hung up and hurried back into her house, where Denny was replacing the broken peg on the Morris chair. Aggie sat erect by the dining table, fanning herself with the paper. Sarah leaned over her and asked, 'Are you OK?'

'Oh, sure. Never a dull moment around my daughter, the cop.'

'Well, I don't usually do law enforcement from my home. You need anything? Drink of water?'

'No, I'm fine.'

'I'd like to stay and look after you but I have to go and file a lot of reports to keep that bad guy in jail.'

'Where we all devoutly want him to stay forever. Don't worry.' Aggie's eyes glinted. 'Denny's here, what could go wrong that she can't handle?'

As if on a signal, Denny pushed the Morris chair back into its upright position and said with a flourish, 'Ta-dah!'

Aggie said, 'Beautiful. Come here to me, child.' She put her arm around Denny and pulled her close. 'Seems like the day before yesterday I was holding you on my lap, reading you stories.' She made a little clucking noise, *tsk*. 'Maybe from now on you should read to me.'

Denny giggled nervously and said, 'Well, I can do that, I guess.'

'I'm sure you can. You're a lot like your Aunt Sarah, I'm starting to think.'

Sarah said, 'She did all right with that Hector, didn't she?'

'She did, and so did you. Honestly –' Aggie smiled ruefully – 'all these years I've given you grief about your career ... you know what I thought when you went past me like a panther with that gun in your hand? I thought, *Thank God, Sarah's here*.'

'Ah, Mamadiddle.' She patted her mother's hand. *Still a little tremble. Not bad*. 'I better get to work. You two take care of each other, hear? Eat some comfort food.'

Denny said, 'Grilled cheese sandwiches?'

'Why not?' Sarah said.

As she walked out she heard Aggie say behind her, 'What was all that talk about money, sweetheart?' She closed the door quickly, not wanting to hear Denny's reply.

As she drove to Stone Avenue along the sleepy streets of mid-afternoon, she felt her energy sag sharply and her legs began to shake – a reaction to the extraordinary effort of subduing Hector. She pinched her cheeks to stay alert till she could park, wobbled into the break room on rubber knees and grabbed a sports drink and a banana. When her hands were steady enough, she fixed a coffee with two sugars and walked calmly into her section sipping it, doing her best to project *no problem*.

'Here she is,' Ibarra said, as she walked past his desk. 'Now, guys, come on, help me tell Sarah what she missed at this morning's crime scene.' He got up and followed her into her workspace with his dimples flashing.

'Did Delaney tell you,' Eisenstaat said, following him in, 'what a piece of work the wife is?'

'I haven't heard anything, I just got here,' Sarah said.

'Oh. God, it was so much fun,' Ibarra gleamed.

'The neighbors saw all these flies collecting on the windows and got worried when nobody answered the phone,' Eisenstaat said, 'so they called 911—'

'And the first responders broke in the house and found the body,' Tobin said, crowding in. 'So the neighbor's wife called Pinetop and found the victim's wife.'

'You guys think this is funny? *Yech*.'

'Well, not the first part, but wait.' Eisenstaat raised a magisterial hand. 'The widow arrived just in time to identify the body before they moved it. She went through all the requisite weeping and gnashing, but then, you should have seen her recovery speed, Sarah! In five minutes, she was doing this elaborate song and dance about why she couldn't let us into the back room...'

'The back room that just happened to have a padlock on it,' Greenaway tittered.

'Three verses and a chorus about priceless art works that mustn't be disturbed.' Eisenstaat looked genuinely happy for once, Sarah thought.

Ibarra said, 'So, Delaney started looking at that door like a dog at a bone—'

'Finally he says –' Tobin did his blinking imitation of Delaney – '"You want to give us the key or shall we break it down?" But really polite, like a deacon in church.'

'OK, enough already,' Sarah said, 'what was in the room?'

'His printing press!' Ibarra said. 'And all these special papers ... this victim was a first-rate counterfeiter.'

'Oh? I haven't heard *that* word for a while.' Sarah looked at Eisenstaat. 'You used to say it was Tucson's fall-back cottage industry.'

'It was, in the old days. Right behind smuggling dope and people, and boosting cars. You don't hear about it much any more.'

'Whaddya mean?' Greenaway said. 'This town is crawling with fake driver's licenses and green cards.'

'Offa computers, sure,' Eisenstaat said. 'Computer software's so good now, nobody does it the hard way any more. Hell, you can make yourself the King of Romania in two minutes if you want to, and it'll look *almost* right. But this guy was a throwback, everything the old-fashioned way, beautiful etching tools, great paper.'

'Why'd it get him killed, though?' Sarah asked.

'We don't know *why* yet,' Tobin said, 'but *how* is sure no mystery. Three slugs from a nine mil, and we brought back the casings.'

'No kidding, they left the casings?'

'Two of 'em, anyway. And Gloria got some good latents off the table by the couch. And she told me this morning they don't match the victim *or* his clever wife.'

'No, they match the fingerprint Gloria lifted off Tuesday morning's victim,' Sarah added.

'They do?' They all turned disappointed faces toward her. Tobin said, 'I thought you said you didn't know anything about this case.'

'Just that one thing. Delaney told me on the phone.' But he hadn't had time to tell them about the goings-on at her house, apparently.

'So we got the same killer at both scenes? Well, hidee ho,' Ibarra said. 'We ought to wrap this one up in a hurry.'

'But rather than break with precedent like that,' Eisenstaat leered, 'we'll no doubt find some way to snatch defeat from the jaws of victory.'

'Tsk. Who's got the lead?'

'Yours very sincerely,' Ibarra said. He shrugged. 'Delaney figured I didn't have enough to do.' He looked over her shoulder at someone standing in the hall and asked, 'Help you guys?'

Sarah turned and saw that Phil Cruz and a man she didn't know were standing outside her workspace, looking in. Meeting her eyes, Cruz nodded gravely but didn't speak. Sarah stared back, wondering if her quick hit of sugar was making her hallucinate. What would Phil Cruz be doing in Homicide? Then he said, 'Detective Ibarra, could we speak to you out here, please?'

All the investigators who were crowded around Sarah's desk turned to look at Ibarra. He moved stiffly away from them, toward the agents. But he was making avoidance moves – not flashing his usual dimpled smile but looking at his watch and patting his wallet pocket, feigning relaxation like a boy on his first date. *What's going on?*

He stopped in front of Cruz and echoed her thoughts. 'What's going on?'

'Detective Jaime Alfonso Ibarra,' Cruz said. 'You're under arrest for conspiracy in the sale of illegal narcotics. Will you put your hands behind your back, please?'

'Oh, come *on*,' Ibarra said.

'Phil, what are you doing?' Sarah stepped toward them but Cruz put up a warning hand, shook his head and said, 'Sarah, no.'

'What? This is a mistake. You've got the wrong person.' She looked from one to another of their strangely closed faces, till Cruz said softly, 'Sarah, it's no mistake.'

'Let's go,' the other man said. She remembered him now; he was from Internal Affairs. She noted the name on his badge: Sergeant Early. He opened his handcuffs, clamped one around Ibarra's right wrist and reached for the other, but Ibarra swung his left arm away and tried to punch Phil Cruz, who ducked.

Early seized Ibarra's swinging arm, held it steady and spoke to him in a conversational way. 'Think about it, detective. You don't want to add resisting arrest to your other charges, do you?' The two of them stood a moment, eye to eye, Early holding Ibarra's hand and arm close against his body, as if to comfort him.

And maybe in some strange way it did, because Ibarra stopped struggling, sighed once profoundly and relaxed his hands behind his back. Early fastened the metal cuffs on his wrists and Jimmy Ibarra, without a backward glance, walked away from twelve years in law enforcement, from the bowling trophies and shooting awards hanging all over his workspace and the pictures of his children sweetly smiling from his cork board. His crew-mates watched him go with the shocked faces of disaster victims.

A frozen silence held them for ten seconds. Then they all began to talk fiercely at the same time.

'What is this bullshit?' Tobin asked.

'Arrogant bastards at Internal Affairs,' Eisenstaat said, 'like to kill 'em all.'

'What's it all about?' Greenaway asked,

‘What?’

‘I have no idea,’ Sarah said.

‘Well, we’re sure as shit going to find out,’ Eisenstaat said, resettling the small cap he always wore in the department because the air-conditioning made his bald head cold.

‘Somebody’s got the wrong name, that’s all,’ Tobin said. ‘They’ll let him go when they see they made a mistake.’

‘It’ll still be in his jacket,’ Sarah said, ‘unless we do something. I’m going to talk to Delaney.’

‘I’ll come with you,’ Eisenstaat said.

‘Me too,’ Tobin said. Greenaway and Menendez came along, the five of them muttering along the corridor like the advance guard of an uprising.

Delaney was standing in his doorway. ‘I saw them,’ he said, looking at their faces. ‘Come in.’

His office was not much bigger than theirs but had the luxury of a door. He closed it and they all talked at once. Finally he shouted, ‘Hold it!’ and then, ‘Sit down and let me talk.’ They listened, twisting in their seats.

‘We’ve known for some time we had a mole in the department.’ He scratched his red cheeks, his skin irritated by the hot sun outside and now aggravated further by their angry faces staring at him. ‘Our Narcs kept saying shipments were getting moved just before they came to grab ’em, stuff like that.’

‘That don’t mean it’s Ibarra,’ Tobin said. ‘What’s Narc problems got to do with Homicide anyway? Why are they picking on us?'

'Nobody's picking on you. And you know as well as I do it's irrelevant which section he's working in. We all move around and have friends in other sections. All of us know what anybody knows. We email, go to lunch, have coffee. I heard somebody making jokes around here yesterday about this being the best news service in the world.'

'So we gossip,' Eisenstaat said. 'That does not prove Jimmy did anything wrong. Are you just going to let them haul him away without defending him?'

Delaney smacked his fist on his desk. 'I already defended him! I defended him plenty!' His eyes got a wet look and Sarah realized he had hurt his hand. 'But this last sweep at DEA ... for months they've had a phone tap on the big guy's phones – what's his name? Ortiz – and a mike in his car and Christ knows, maybe a bug up his ass. They've even got conversations he's had in bed with his wife and his girlfriend. And they've got Ibarra on tape telling the bastard all about every move we make around here. Everything you learned about Ace Perkins, as fast as you got it,' he said, glaring at Sarah.

'You heard this? They played it for you?' Sarah asked him.

'Last night. At home, right after supper, when I should have been reading the paper and watching the ball game, I got to listen to that.'

'You're sure it was Jimmy's voice?' Eisenstaat asked him. 'They can fake anything now.'

'It was his voice. You know that tricky thing he does with his esses? Only part of the accent he's got left. I'd know it anywhere.'

Watching them, Sarah thought, *This would have been so much easier to believe about Eisenstaat. He's got the right face for a spy and he's so easy to dislike.* She asked Delaney, 'They came to your house?'

'Two DEA agents and that Early guy. Quite a delegation. My wife told me later, "For a minute I thought *you* were getting arrested." How's that for faith?' He was trying to make them laugh. They looked at him stone-faced.

'They didn't have to come into our section and arrest him in front of everybody,' Sarah said. She was having trouble controlling her voice. 'Early held on to his arm and they put *cuffs* on him, boss, right there by his own desk.'

'Like he was some goddamn rapist or something,' Eisenstaat said. 'Fucking pansies couldn't walk him out to their car without *restraints*?'

'Yeah, how chickenshit is that?' Greenaway said.

'The entire procedure was by the book,' Delaney said. 'They just did what they always do. What all of us do,' he reminded them, 'when we have to.' He looked around the circle of his detectives, blinking. 'You just don't like it now because it's happening to one of us.'

When he had blinked at each of them once, Sarah got up silently and walked back to her own desk. She sat there alone, listening as the other four detectives came back along the hall, bunched together, talking in angry undertones about the defiant, rebellious moves they would make next. We'll take it to the Union rep, one said, and another added, I got a friend who can put some heat on the chief.

As soon as they were back at their own desks, though, they sat down quietly and began making phone calls, pulling up email, typing. They had good jobs with seniority and benefits, retirement funds growing, everything to lose. To deal with the pain and frustration of not doing anything, they settled back quickly into the reliable comfort of the work, the many tasks that were always there waiting.

And Sarah, after the burning knot in her throat dissolved enough so she could swallow, got ready to go back to work too. She pulled up the report forms she needed for the arrest of Hector Rodriguez, filled out the date and time. As she tabbed to the next line, though, a bright light of understanding circled in out of the cosmos and burst in her brain. She took one long deep breath, got up and walked back to Delaney's open door.

As soon as he saw her face, he knew what she'd come about. He nodded and said, 'Sit down.'

She sat. 'You thought it was me.'

'It was just a lousy coincidence.' He was holding a report of some kind and he began to fold it, precisely, into thirds. 'The problems started soon after you transferred over from Auto Theft, all the bitching about leaks. They'd set up a bust and all the stuff would be gone when they got there. We all defended our sections, told the Narcs they had their own leaker, or they weren't being careful enough. Then all the department heads got called on the carpet and told to look again at whoever was new about twelve months ago.'

'So you've been watching me ever since.' *Jesus. Almost a year.* 'I kept trying to get you to tell me what was wrong.'

'I know.' He creased and re-creased the paper in his hands. 'We should have thought to look for long-time employees with new problems. Jimmy's wife kept getting pregnant and two of the kids were sickly.' He opened the report and carefully re-folded it the opposite way. 'You'll see when you sit in this chair,' he said, watching his hands, 'that there are some things you have to do that are no fun at all.'

'When have I ever suggested—'

'It's all right.' He wasn't blinking now; he almost smiled. 'I always know which members of my staff are longing to replace me.'

'You make ambition sound like a bad thing.'

He rocked his hand. 'About half and half. The hard chargers are harder to take but they help me get the extra work out.' Again, he just missed smiling. 'You're going to do fine here,

Sarah. Just try to practice a little on the patience, will you?'

'All right.' She knew she should let it go now and get out of here while she was even with the game. But she still felt sore and it burst out of her, suddenly; against her better judgment she heard herself saying, 'I just wish I could figure out why everybody thinks it's OK to lie to me.'

Delaney began blinking again. Damn it! He had her in sharp focus now and was reconsidering his good will. 'Sarah, I never lied to you.'

'Maybe not exactly but you let me think I'd done something wrong. And everybody else – I mean you expect it from the bad guys but my husband, my sister, my partner ... even my darling little niece! Everybody I care about looks me right in the eye and tells me lies!' She meant Dietz. She was crazy from stress and anxiety and low blood sugar, and now she was losing it in front of her boss. *Damn.*

But Delaney didn't look disappointed or even puzzled. 'Well, I can't speak for your family members,' he said, 'but Jimmy Ibarra lied to all of us and so did Will Dietz. That's who else you're talking about, isn't it?'

'Well...'

'Dietz had no choice; they picked him out of the line-up to do their chores before he was ready, in my opinion. But he jumped at the chance because he was so anxious to show he could still hack it. You ought to cut him some slack, Sarah, that guy's been through hell.'

She stared at him, stupefied. *How did he know about... ?*

'Anyway, why take it so personally?' Delaney folded the report form one more time and it fell apart in his hands. 'People lie because they have things they need to cover up and a lot of times it's got nothing to do with you.'

Well, Jesus, now it's life lessons from Delaney. Maybe a fat lady is going to sing today. But she saw that it was the closest to an apology he would ever give her, and she gave him back as much gratitude as she could manage. She got up, said, 'Thanks for your time, boss,' and turned back toward the tapping keyboards and blinking screens of the workstations, toward the work she really had to get going on now.

She worked on at her desk as the light on Mount Lemmon turned to amber and then rose. Long after the mountain had purpled and gone dark, when 270 Stone was quiet and her arms ached from typing, she walked out of the building and went home. She had called her mother once to see if she was doing all right, but she got a busy signal, turned back to work and forgot to try again.

She was surprised to see the house dark; it was only nine thirty. Well, but they'd had a big day, it was good if they turned in early. She walked in quietly, turned the light on in the living room and found a note dangling from the light by the infamous Morris chair. In

Aggie's round inelegant handwriting it said: 'Sam called and wanted to play some cards, so I told him to come and get us. I'll see Denny gets to school in the morning. Rest up.' The last two words were underlined three times.

In a postscript crowded at the bottom of the page in tiny writing, she added, 'Janine called.' *My God, I forgot about her.* 'She said that she knows we want her to go back to detox, but she's not ready. She's got a chance to go to Denver and she needs the time alone. I didn't even argue, what's the use? Denny wants to stay with you anyway. Will you keep her? I'll help you all I can. M.' Underneath the signature, in even smaller letters, Aggie had written, 'I know it's asking too much but that's what families do.'

Sarah was still standing under the light, reading the note for the second time and thinking about calling her mother's house, when a car pulled in behind hers and Will Dietz got out of it with his hands full of roses and wine.

The elaborate gifts and something in his face as he walked up and rang her bell made her suddenly sure there had never been any call from Sam about card-playing. This troubled man with two parts in his hair was conniving with her mother. She would certainly have to put a stop to that, but not tonight.

'Sarah,' he said, when she opened her door, 'I want to explain—'

Sarah resurrected as much as she could remember of the barnburner smile and swung the door wider. 'Come in, Will,' she said. 'We're cool.'

'You, maybe,' Dietz said. 'Not me.'